THE PAGE TURNER

VIOLA SHIPMAN

GRAYDON
HOUSE

GRAYDON HOUSE®

Recycling programs
for this product may
not exist in your area.

ISBN-13: 978-1-525-80487-8

The Page Turner

Graydon House
22 Adelaide St. West, 41st Floor
Toronto, Ontario M5H 4E3, Canada
www.GraydonHouseBooks.com

Printed in U.S.A.

For Patty Edwards

&

*all the librarians and booksellers out there on the front lines
who continue to put books in hands, change minds,
save lives and fight the good fight.*

*Books saved my life growing up.
That will never change.*

*This story is a tribute to the power of literature
and how books connect us.*

The worst thing you could do in my family was need something from someone.

—Alison Bechdel

PROLOGUE

Third-Person Limited

"Let's start at the very beginning… A very good place to start."

I took a seat on the grass next to a young man dressed in a brown jumper and short, blond wig playing the guitar. This was the University of Michigan. Meaning this was just another normal Tuesday afternoon.

He was singing in perfect pitch—a vibrating soprano—to a group of acorns he had gathered from the university's famed, century-old Tappan Oak on its Central Campus.

When he realized he had a live audience, he stopped, turned to me and bowed.

"I'm Julie Andrews, and these seven acorns are the von Trapp children," he explained as simply as if ordering a Big Mac. "We're restaging *The Sound of Music* this year, and I got the lead."

"Congratulations," I said. "You sound just like her."

"Thank you." He beamed. "A lot of pressure. It's a classic. And people hate change. Especially when you change a classic." He stared at me and then said, his voice lowering about eight octaves, "Mostly people will just hate me for trying this. But it's what makes me happy. It's just sad that the world loves to destroy the unique when it's the only thing we have going that makes it so special."

My mind whirred to my family and the book I was writing.

"Please," I said. "Keep going."

I said this as much for him as for me.

"Where were we, children?" he asked the acorns, before beginning where he left off.

I joined him in song.

His eyes glowed with joy.

My parents taught me to appreciate poetry, to love lyrics and study short stories. They represented the pure essence of great literature, writing condensed to its finest form.

His phone trilled.

"Frauline Maria didn't have a cell, did she?" I asked.

He laughed.

"Can you imagine?" he asked. "She never would have sung to the children. Just sat them down to watch a movie or play a video game."

"Or Siri would have been their governess," I add.

"Why have we never met?" he asked. His phone trilled again. "We gotta go!" he said, patting his guitar. "My friend is over there. She's helping me rehearse. C'mon, kids! I need you for inspiration!"

He grabbed his acorn children, shoved them in the pocket of his jumper and began to run across campus, very much looking as if he was Maria skipping away on a mountaintop in Austria. As he took off, one wayward acorn escaped and bounced at my feet.

It was a perfect autumn day. I laid the book I was going to read on the grass next to me and picked up the acorn.

GiGi told me when I was a girl that an acorn was like a secret.

"Whether or not it ever grows to see the light depends on how deep you bury it."

I studied it, turning it round and round, and then placed it in my pocket.

I had a secret. And it was way bigger than any ol' acorn.

GiGi gave me my love of reading...

"A, B, C," I sang to myself.

...and she taught me to keep random mementos like these.

"Tangible time stamps," she called them, "to remind you of moments in your life when memories ultimately become cobwebs."

GiGi was like that, a Southern granny trapped in a Great Lakes grandma, warm and cold all at the same time, dispensing tough advice and homespun wisdom as easily as she did certain books to folks she believed needed to read them.

A flame red maple leaf scooted by in the wind, and I grabbed it on the fly.

It looked just like a leaf I picked up as a girl with GiGi not long after I found that acorn with her. I can still remember placing that leaf in the novel I was reading—a novel by GiGi's favorite author, S. I. Quaeris—as a bookmark.

I could even remember what GiGi was wearing that day—a gold turtleneck that matched the lake in the autumn sun and an L.L.Bean fleece jacket that was as white as her hair—just as clearly as I can recall the passage I was reading from her favorite author.

Family is often defined by many of us as some ethereal power, God if you will, a sort of otherworldly super-being that has control over our lives no matter how much time has passed. But which God is it? The one who loves us unconditionally and protects us from the world, or the one who seeks revenge?

I'd used that quote in many a lit class term paper about family.

I placed the leaf in the book I was currently reading, wondering if I would remember this particular moment and passage as well.

"Is it any good?"

Gin and Juice nodded at my book and flopped down beside me under the Tappan Oak, dappled sunlight making them look like the old paint-by-numbers portraits GiGi favored in her cottage.

"It certainly fails the Bechdel Test," I said. "How did Marcus Flare become the world's preeminent romance novelist? Listen to this." I grabbed the novel and read out loud. "'She needed me. Every woman needed a man. Otherwise, her puzzle would never be complete. I grabbed her, hard, kissed her even harder. Women were all emotion after all, raw, feral, but they kept it buried most of the time. Men were the only ones with the power—and equipment—to uncover it.'"

They threw their heads back and screamed in disgust.

"It's true, Angels!"

Niko Miller, a fraternity guy from class, stopped in front of us.

"And I'm the best plumber in town."

We all audibly gagged.

"Haven't you learned anything in class, Niko?" I asked.

"Yeah! I've learned this Flare dude is a great writer."

I shook my head, and he jogged off.

The four of us were in a class entitled Women in Literature and Popular Culture, and we had been pleasantly surprised (read: *shocked*) by the number of men taking it.

Many of our classmates referred to me, Jen and Lucy as "Charlie's Angels" because we were inseparable. Many, we also realized, called us that because we were two fair-haired white girls and Lucy was Asian American.

It was all vaguely racist and misogynist. Michigan was a highly diverse university, filled with students of every race, nationality, ethnicity and sexuality—but boys, especially frat boys, will always be boys.

Not to mention my friends were anything but angels. I called them "Gin and Juice," nicknames born after the pair partook of a few too many cocktails at the local bar the first week of freshman year and then got busted using misspelled fake IDs.

"Has anything changed in life or literature?" Juice asked. "I mean *really* changed? Look at what's popular today in fiction. Look at how guys still talk to women."

She shed her Michigan sweatshirt and sat on it like a blanket.

"But, despite that, *Charlie's Angels* would still pass the Bechdel Test even though you wouldn't think it would, right?" Gin asked.

I considered her question and nodded.

"Three women. Kicking Ass. Taking names. Having all the dialogue. Yep."

Our professor used the Bechdel Test to measure the representation of women in fiction and film as well as to analyze how women are depicted in any given work.

There are three main criteria for the Bechdel Test: two women must be featured, who talk to each other, about something other than a man.

Sounds simple, right?

However, a study of gender portrayals in the most successful US films over the past six decades showed that, on average, there were two male characters for every female. Moreover, a woman had the most dialogue in only about 20 percent of those films.

The same tends to hold true in literature.

I began to read a passage from our textbook. And, yes, I still carried textbooks. I was a unicorn on campus.

"Virginia Woolf mused on women's depiction in literature way back in the 1920s, writing, 'All these relationships between women…are too simple… I tried to remember any case in the course of my reading where two women are represented as friends…it was strange to think that all the great women of fiction were not only seen by the other sex, but seen only in relation to the other sex. And how small a part of a woman's life is that…'"

"And," Gin interrupted, "Virginia Woolf ironically had to use a pen name, E. V. Odle, to preserve her reputation as a 'serious' writer when she began to write science fiction. That gender neutral pseudonym not only allowed her to try her hand at something decidedly different but also profit within a male-dominated genre. Though we remember her for *Mrs. Dalloway*, it is her sci-fi serial *The Puppeteer God* that, decades later, influenced the megahit franchise *The Matrix* starring Keanu Reeves."

"God, we're smart," I said.

They laughed.

"Hi, Angels!"

Another fraternity boy, hat on backward, winked.

"Wanna study sometime?" he asked us.

We looked at one another.

"Really?" Gin asked.

He nodded.

We all remained silent, not fully trusting the situation. He suddenly smiled, mistaking our reticence for complicity.

"Cool. Three women in my room at the fraternity house. Now, there's a book Marcus Flare should write!"

"Do you think women need a man like you?" I asked.

He flexed a muscle and smiled. "I do."

"Well, I don't!"

"You do more than anyone, Emma," he said.

I gave him the finger and off he went.

"I'm so glad an English major and journalism major talked me into taking this class," Juice said. "It just reaffirms why I want to be a finance major. I want to control the money of the men who control the world. If women don't have their own money, they don't hold any power."

The three of us instantly positioned ourselves into the famous Charlie's Angels pose.

As we did, Juice glanced at her Apple Watch.

"Oh, hell, we gotta go, Gin," she said. "All the way across campus in twenty minutes."

"Meet in the commons at five?" Juice asked.

I nodded, and my friends took off in a run. I watched them until they faded into the fall light.

I stared up at the Michigan maples. They were still the same trees, the same red I saw as a girl every autumn with my grandma.

I looked down at the book in my lap, the edge of the leaf peeking from the pages. I opened the novel again with a sigh and began to read again until I came upon a passage that made me think I had lost my mind. I read it—again and again—not believing my eyes.

Whether or not it ever grows to see the light depends on how deep you bury it.

I immediately picked up my phone and called my grandmother.

It was a few weeks into the semester, and I'd been remiss to share with my biggest supporter what was going on in my life.

"Hi, GiGi!" I said when she answered.

"Emma!" she said. "Talk to me! Tell me everything."

I told her about my Women in Literature and Popular Culture and the Bechdel Test.

She began to laugh.

When she finally stopped, GiGi said, "I'm so glad you're enjoying school, but you don't need a class for that, Emma. It's called life. It's always been dominated by men. It always will be. We don't need a test to prove that. We need women who challenge those rules. And the best way for you to do that is to write the book *you* always wanted, a novel outside your parents' purview, a book that has the power to change a life. Isn't that why you're there? To write? To break the mold?"

She was right, but her tone irked me, mostly because her theory had already been proven correct today.

I mean, had anything really changed in life or literature over the years?

I read the passage in the Marcus Flare book to her. When I finished, I said, "GiGi, I believed you were a woman who tested the rules, not one who quoted misogynistic writers!"

She was silent.

She usually had a response at the ready, a story, a quip. After a moment, she said, "It must be nice to sit in college and critique books and the world at large. I never had that opportunity. I don't know much, Emma, but I do know this as a widow and a reader—there are difficult decisions to be made every single day in making art or just making it through another day. I think most people believe that creating art is either madness or salvation. One or the other. They're wrong. Art is both. And on the best days—for both authors and readers—art is salvation from the madness. Use *that* in one of your papers."

Her stern tone unnerved me. I didn't know what to say. I didn't know I would hit a nerve. We always debated everything.

GiGi took a ragged breath and continued.

"I want you to hear me on this, young lady. I do *not* plagiarize life. I am, and will always be, an original. You want an original GiGi quote? Well, here goes. A lot of people are like acorns—just plain nuts. And no matter how much you nurture them, they will never grow into a damn thing. Now, I suggest you grow into something that matters."

She hung up, and I sat there in stunned silence staring at the Tappan Oak.

I was so deep in thought that I didn't realize a guy I knew from my class—a fraternity pledge decked out in Greek letters— had stopped in front of me. He was carrying our textbook and the Marcus Flare novel.

"Hi, Emma."

"Hey, Carter," I said.

"You know they have to cut down this oak, right?" he asked. "It's old and diseased."

"I heard. It's sad." Carter's face was dappled in sunlight. I thought of GiGi and one of her favorite writers. "You know, 'a book is made from a tree,'" I said to him. Carter looked at me, his head angled. I continued. "Carl Sagan."

"You're the smartest one in class," he said with a smile. He looked at the tree. "I wonder what they'll find buried underneath this when they cut it down and dig up the roots."

"Probably a lot of secrets," I said, again thinking of GiGi.

"And beer cans," he laughed.

I nodded at the hardcover books he was carrying.

"You're an old-school reader like me, huh?" I asked.

"Yeah," he said. "I like to remove myself from technology when I'm reading. I love Kindle when I'm traveling, but there's nothing like holding a book."

I smiled. *Finally! One of the good guys*, I thought.

"Are you enjoying Women in Literature and Popular Culture?" I asked.

"I am," he said.

"I was surprised to see so many men in class," I said. "It makes me feel like things are changing."

I told him about what the other guys had said earlier.

He laughed as hard as GiGi had.

"You know why there are so many guys in class, right, Emma?"

"It's a popular elective," I said. "Great professor."

"Nope," Carter said. "Women in Literature and Popular Culture was named in an underground handbook as one of the most popular classes on campus to pick up women who, and I quote, 'need to learn what a real man is.'"

I swear I could hear GiGi laugh all the way from the other side of Michigan.

As if on cue, and with an impeccable sense of timing and irony, Julie Andrews began to sing again, lyrics carried across campus on the autumn breeze.

"Let's start at the very beginning... A very good place to start."

My parents always hated prologues in a book, especially my mother.

"Such a waste of time, don't you think, Emma?" she would ask in her inimitable way that forced you to agree. "Just start at the beginning."

I always disagreed as I believed—like the opening notes to a song—prologues built a sense of mystery and emotion.

So, let's start at the very, *very* beginning, shall we?

I know how much it would please my parents to think I actually listened to them for once.

PART ONE

First-Person Perfect

CHAPTER ONE

"Why are you wearing that dress, Emma?"

"The better question is, why is everyone here dressed like Wednesday Addams?"

Jess pinches the fabric of my colorful summer dress with her talons. Her nails are like beautiful, lethal weapons.

"People wear black because it's a serious literary event, not the Kentucky Derby!" Jess says. "You look like a rube."

"Rube?" I say, widening my eyes in amazement at her choice of words. "Someone's been reading Flannery O'Connor." I run my fingers up her bare arm like I did as a girl when I'd pretend they were a spider, and I wanted to annoy her. "Oh, I get it. Someone's trying to impress Daddy."

She doesn't wince. My family has grown up *Game of Thrones* literary-style. We just use words to wound. Our armor is Armani.

"No, I'm simply trying to act like a grown-up," she says. "Which you are now, remember? You're a shiny, new college graduate, Emma."

"But it's a beautiful summer day in Michigan. You're supposed to wear color."

As soon as the words leave my mouth, I know my sister has defeated me. I sound like a child. I don't mean to act like such a baby, it's just that my family's pretentiousness has a way of pushing every one of my buttons nonstop, like a kid at a vending machine that just ate his quarters.

"Just not today," Jess says. "It's a matter of respect."

Jess is wearing a little black summer dress that hits just below her knees. It has spaghetti straps, is formfitting on top with a touch of flounce at the hem. Her blond hair and makeup are perfect, and the gloss on her lips shimmers in the filtered summer light. She's one of those girls who looks like she hasn't even made an effort to look beautiful. I called her Peony when I was a girl because she was just so damn perfect, like GiGi's favorite flower.

"Well, you look like you're going to a funeral," I quip. "Which, I guess, we kind of are."

Jess shakes her head at me.

"Not *today*," she repeats.

I open my mouth to retaliate, but the screened door creaks and bangs shut, sounds that sing to me like the call of the gulls and the soft crash of waves on Lake Michigan. My family has always wanted to put a new front door on Eyebrow Cottage, but I refuse to let them. One summer when I was a girl, I positioned myself in the doorway all weekend, staging a screened door sit-in so that my parents couldn't change the historic red entrance, no matter how much it squawked and banged and disrupted their need for quiet and a "literary life."

"It's old, Emma," my father had tried to reason with me as the workers stood on the front porch, shaking their heads and laughing at my histrionics. "It's loud."

"It's supposed to be old and loud," I argued. "It's history. Do you know how many people have touched this handle? How many times you yelled, 'I'm home, Mom'? How many times I ran as fast as I could to open this door to see GiGi?"

My dad motioned for the men to come help move me. As they lifted me, I looked my father square in the eye and said, "This front door is like the perfect opening sentence to a book. You wouldn't change that if it was perfect, would you?"

My father shook his head, motioned for them to set me back down and sent them away. The opening sentence to our family cottage remained untouched.

But some things should never change no matter how much time has passed, right?

The screen door squawks and bangs again.

I watch well-heeled literati enter our shingled family cottage like a swarm of dragonflies, twittering and buzzing, as if they were carried from New York by the lake breeze and gently placed down at the crushed gravel pathway that winds past the white fence and lollipop-colored hydrangeas.

All of the men are in dark suits, hair slicked back, while the too thin women, like so many human X-rays, wear little black dresses similar to my sister's that dangle from protruding clavicles as if they're still on a hanger. Big diamonds glint in the sunlight.

These are my parents' literary friends, all of whom have descended from the city to the flyover state of Michigan for my father's latest book release.

Everyone must please my parents.

Their world is built on favors and compliments.

These city guests look so out of context away from their ivory towers, here in an old cottage on the beach. The guests remove their giant sunglasses, look around, waiting to be noticed. They move about as quietly as ghosts. Their heels don't even clack on the wooden floors.

"Old money doesn't make a sound," GiGi used to tell me. "New money screams."

Jess waves at those entering Eyebrow Cottage, the name my grandmother bestowed on this beach house a lifetime ago.

"Welcome to Michigan, Malcolm! Oh, Felice, you look stunning!"

Jess pokes me in the back with one of her talons, and I smile and parrot my sister.

"See?" Jess asks after the guests have moved on. "It's not so hard to act like an adult now, is it? Why don't you go change? Mom and Dad would be so pleased."

"You're right," I say. "I should wear black."

My sister is so surprised by my response that her body deflates and her shoulders soften.

"Thank you," Jess says.

"I mean, his book is already dead."

"I can't believe you."

"It's true," I say. "Haven't you seen the reviews?"

She continues to smile and wave at arriving guests.

"Did you read it?" I ask.

"Of course, I read it," she says in a dramatic whisper, shaking her head.

"And?"

"And I support his literary instincts."

I laugh. "Good answer, Switzerland." I wait until Jess looks me right in the eyes. "But what would The Swans say?"

My sister shakes her head at me. My whole family shakes its collective head at me. They don't understand why I can't just play along. Wear black. Act serious. Be "literary."

It's just that I don't like pretention. I can see through it. It's like my superpower. The more you try to be pretentious, the more I call you out.

And yet that seems to be the hardest thing to do in this world. *Especially* in the literary world, where too many want the next big thing that is exactly like the last big thing.

"The Swans are going to give it a rave," she whispers fiercely, "because it's literary fiction. It's high art. Effort and experimentation should be rewarded."

I nod my head dramatically. "Right," I say slowly. "How much is he paying you?"

Jess was one of the original BookTokers, hired by my parents in a stroke of genius to support their flailing independent press, The Mighty Pages, and its highbrow list of fiction. And now she's one of America's biggest book influencers.

Long before Truman Capote or his Swans—a collective of rich New York society wives—swam back into the public's attention, my sister, and parents, became fascinated with Manhattan's elite and their ability to make or break a person, business or book. Capote's "Swans" were the ultimate influencers of their time, and my sister's goal was to emulate that glamour and power.

Jess's Swans are a bevy of over two million strong now. The original purpose was for women to read and support women unequivocally, just like Truman's Swans. However, most of Jess's followers are teens and young women more enchanted with my sister's beauty and lifestyle than they are with my parents' books. My parents "list"—the list of books they publish each year—are not romances filled with angsty young lovers and fantasy realms so beloved by TikTok readers these days.

And I do give my parents credit for committing to what they believe in.

My eyes drift into the paneled library lined with bookshelves. It is filled with light, the lake sparkling beyond the wide, wood frame windows.

This was GiGi's sacred spot, the place she stored all her books, had tea with her boarders, talked about books with anyone who crossed her path, held book club meetings and handed beloved copies of her favorites to girls like me who she knew needed to read them.

GiGi loved summer novels with strong female characters— beach reads, as we now call them—and her library used to be as colorful as the umbrellas perched in the sand outside the expansive windows, a sea of aquamarine, yellow and pink spines, walls filled with bright paint-by-numbers paintings she completed with her boarders on winter weekends. Now her library houses my parents' published books, a dark collection that looks like it might belong to an evil magician. GiGi's collection—especially of her beloved S. I. Quaeris novels—has largely been relegated to her upstairs office or hauled off to Goodwill, but I keep a stack of her novels I've yet to read in my bedroom for whenever I return.

So I can remember her.

So I can remember why I'm writing *my* book.

So I can escape my parents' snobbish indifference to my chosen genre.

So I can guarantee a happy ending.

Publishing has changed greatly over the years, just not the judgment placed on what women generally prefer to read and write.

The incredible thing is there is more representation now than ever before—publishers like my parents are literally tripping over themselves to find books featuring characters—and written by authors—of all backgrounds, races, cultures, abilities, sexual identities, body types and neurodiversities.

I stare onto the lake sparkling outside.

There has been a sea change in the types of books I can access since I was a freshman in college. And yet we still judge what readers read.

"Earth to Emma," Jess says. "Did you even hear a word I was saying?"

I shake my head.

"Of course not," she continues. "I said, 'I'm paid in gratitude for the work I do.' Dad doesn't pay me. I only want his work and The Mighty Pages to return to its former glory."

"You should be the writer and not the promoter," I say.

"They're the same things today," Jess says.

Most readers do not understand that many influencers are paid for their adulation, either in cash or product. They say they loved a particular book, although they may never have read it. In essence, influencers piggyback on a title that a celebrity has already endorsed.

Pay for play.

Jess now gets lots of attention and lots of money for promoting every kind of book, save for the ones we grew up loving to read with GiGi. She believes, for profit's sake, that only one kind of book matters, just as my parents believe that only one type of book matters. The only catch is her influence isn't helping sales of our parents' books.

"Every book is important to someone," GiGi used to tell us.

The screen door bangs shut. A heavily made-up woman makes a beeline for Jess.

I recognize her as a heavyweight agent.

"Deborah! You look stunning as usual," Jess says, kissing the air.

"I have a book and author we need to discuss," she says to Jess.

"Of course!" Jess gushes. "Anything for you. Is that the new Birkin bag? Where did you find it?"

The way my sister speaks when she meets a rich or famous person would be amusing if it weren't so sad. Every word comes out in an up-speak lilt, every statement tossed into a Kardashian blender and remixed as banal blather. Jess is so smart, confident and pretty, and yet she becomes one of her followers when someone more influential enters her sphere.

"You don't have it?" the agent asks. Jess shakes her head. "Well, *I* have a client who could help you put a dent in the down payment."

"Really?" Jess asks, all doe-eyed.

She sounds as if she's questioning her own existence.

"Establish a relationship with my author and help her book

break out," the agent continues, "and I'll help you establish a relationship with my Hermès consultant." The agent smiles. "You scratch my back, and I'll scratch up a Birkin for you."

Jess nods her head so hard, I'm worried her long neck will snap.

I watch the agent depart onto the deck overlooking the lake.

I wonder if my parents' "dear, dear friends" came to support my father or schmooze my sister for their clients and future books.

Jess grabs a glass of champagne off the tray of a passing waiter and takes a long sip.

Her big eyes are still like saucers, her long lashes casting a butterfly shadow on her porcelain cheek. It's like my sister has never seen the sun.

"Is that the new Birkin bag? Where did you find it?" I finally say, mimicking her tone. "I'm still embarrassed for you. You're acting like Taylor Swift asked you to be her publicist."

"Such a grown-up," Jess says, shaking her head. "You will never understand publishing." She deigns to look at me. "And to think you want to be an author. Publishing is like chess. You have to know your next move way before anyone else. But you don't even know the next chapter of your life, even with that newly minted Michigan degree, do you? Now, please, go change. Have some respect."

I pluck a pretty pink peony from a small glass vase sitting on the black tablecloth and tuck it behind my ear.

I actually cut fresh peonies—big powder puffs of white and pink that smell like heaven—from GiGi's gardens and added them to all the bars and tables as a tribute to my family. I wanted to honor GiGi's love of summer as well as pay tribute to my sister, but she doesn't remember my childhood nickname for her.

My family chooses *not* to remember.

Ironic how our memories become so selective when we believe our tastes have become so discerning.

My mother, of course, will have the delicate blooms removed as soon as she sees them.

"My God, are we at high tea on *Bridgerton*?" she will likely scoff.

When I don't respond, my sister looks at me and says, "Gi-Gi's not here anymore. You can't love a ghost."

Jess's emerald eyes narrow, and I can tell she wants to take it back, but it's too late.

A family of writers, readers and influencers, I think, who can edit a single sentence countless times but has never learned how to edit one damn thing before it leaves their mouths.

"You all should be ashamed for trying to forget her so quickly," I say. "She's not even been gone that long."

My sister's face falls, and she opens her mouth to say something when I hear, "The party has arrived!"

I instantly recognize the face. I've seen it on the back of countless book covers, including the one I read in college.

"Marcus Flare!" Jess chirps.

They meet in front of the bar. Jess leans in for an air kiss, but Marcus grabs her, places a hand on the small of her back, kisses her cheek for much too long and then whispers something into her ear.

"Champagne, please," he barks when he pulls away.

"Yes, of course," Jess smiles awkwardly. "Welcome to Michigan."

"I didn't even know this was a state until now," he laughs.

I can't even with this jackass already.

Jess nearly trips over herself to get him a drink.

"How was your flight?" Jess asks.

"I didn't know there were airports here."

And now I'm done.

"Really," I deadpan. "Are you Kimmy Schmidt? Do you live in a bunker? Don't have a TV or cell phone? Didn't realize Michigan is the tenth largest state in the US or that the University of Michigan just won the national football championship, or is one of the best universities in the world, that Detroit is the hottest city in the country, or even, mind you, that the state is now one of *the* preeminent vacation spots in the US?"

"Who have we here?" he asks, bewildered but amused.

"This is my sister, Emma."

Jess gives me her "Behave!" look.

Marcus reaches in to grab me, but I step back, bumping into the bar.

"We've met before," I say. "Not in person, actually, but in class. I've read one of your books."

"Just one?" he asks. "So you're not one of my Solar Flares yet?"

"Solar Flare?" I ask.

"One of my devoted fans whose love for my work burns so brightly they scorch the earth to buy my books as soon as they're released."

I stare at him, eyes wide. "Are you serious?"

"Really? Are you serious, Kimmy Schmidt? Do *you* live in a bunker? Don't have a TV or cell phone?" He laughs in my face, mocking me. "You didn't realize I'm the world's bestselling romance novelist?"

Jess doesn't even try to hide a smile, payback for my earlier mocking of her.

"Funny," I say, "but I remember reading in class that you refuse to call yourself a *romance writer* and yet you just did. You've conducted countless interviews where you proudly pronounce that you don't write romance novels, only 'love stories.'" I shut my eyes. "I just want to get this right. Oh, yes." I open my eyes, clear my throat and continue in a tone close to Marcus's own voice. "'I would be rejected if I submitted any of my work as romance novels,' you once said. 'I do not verge into melodrama. I write drama.'"

"So you *are* a Solar Flare," he says. "Just in the closet."

His choice of words enrages me as he's not only been targeted as a homophobe in the past but also there are rumors of his sexually harassing women in publishing for years. I want to go there, but I look at my sister glaring at me and take a breath.

"When I was a student," I say tightly, "I studied your work in a lit class that focused on female writers."

"I'm flattered."

"You shouldn't be."

Jess glares at me to shut up. I can't.

"We studied your work in Women in Literature and Popular Culture. Your books failed The Bechdel Test every single time."

"The Bechdel Test?" he asks in a bemused tone.

"Yes, it's a famous cultural litmus test," I answer. "Yours failed every time because only a single female character was ever featured, and she was completely, utterly dependent on a man."

The light from the lake glints through the cottage windows and falls across Marcus's face.

He is ruggedly handsome in a manicured, bookish sort of way, like if you merged a character from *Yellowstone* with one of the Rockefellers: sandy hair, five-o'clock shadow, piercing grass green eyes, a crisp white shirt opened one button too far. I'm sure he became famous partly because of his good looks. Marcus is marketable.

He takes a step closer to me and stares into my eyes. I can feel my spine bend backward like a willow in the wind.

"The last thing I need is a lecture about my books from a woke lit major in a Forever 21 dress," he says. "Fifty novels and counting, 100 million books sold worldwide, all *New York Times* bestsellers. You get to that level, then we can talk."

I snap.

"Hashtag MeToo," I reply.

My sister grabs another glass of champagne from the bar and thrusts it into Marcus's hands as a diversion even though he's yet to touch his first glass. I think he's going to toss it in my face, but he sips it and says, "Ah, Moët not Veuve."

Snotty jerk.

I grab a glass of champagne and slam it back in one gulp.

"Tastes good to me," I say. "I just love that rich people are difficult simply to be difficult."

He clinks my empty glass, eyes me closely and says, "You are rich, sweetheart." Marcus waits a beat and then adds, "Hashtag NepoBaby."

Rage makes Marcus swim before my eyes. He has hit a nerve.

I never think of myself as well-off. It's my grandma's money. I'm just lucky. I did nothing to earn it. I feel I should protect it, use it to better the world. My parents believe it's their personal piggy bank, and they use all the pretty pennies to fund their publishing house and live a literary life in the city.

My whole life I've tried not to be defined by my parents. I've tried to swim in my own direction. And yet, here I am, just another swan.

"Cat got your tongue?" Marcus asks, before adding, "Something tells me we were meant to meet." He stops. "IRL."

Marcus sets down one glass of bubbly and walks away, saying to Jess, "You need to tame that filly. Find me later."

Jess lilts her goodbye until he disappears into the crowd.

"*Filly?*" I seethe. "He just said that out loud. Did you hear him?"

"You provoked him, Emma."

"No, he's a bully, and you just stood by and watched it happen." I glare at her. "You've turned out to be such a staunch supporter of women's rights, sis. Women deserve to be mistreated when they speak their minds or, God forbid—" I give her appearance and dress a long look "—wear something provocative."

"Don't lecture me," Jess says. "I've been bullied. I know what it's like."

I laugh out loud. "You've been bullied? What, did they used to call you, 'pretty girl'?"

Jess's face droops. Her cheeks quiver. I've hit a nerve. She closes her eyes for the longest time.

"You're only proving me right," she finally says, her voice steady. "Why can't you be nice?"

I think of Mom.

"Nice implies blandness," she's said so many times. "No one wants to look or be considered *nice*. It's like being invisible."

"Have some dignity, Jess. He's gross."

"He's misunderstood."

"Well, I'm sure you'll set him *straight*," I say, not attempting to hide my disgust at anti-LGBTQ comments he made a while back which he claimed were misrepresented. "Why can't you and The Swans do to Marcus what the original Swans did to Capote?"

Jess turns, grabs the glass from my hand and sets it on the bar.

"You don't bite the hand that feeds you, Emma."

I study her face. "Is there something going on I don't know about?"

"There is nothing you need to know right now except that if you're going to behave like an animal then have the dignity to act like the well-mannered purebred you are and not some mongrel fighting for scraps and barking to be heard," Jess says, her voice rising.

People turn, and she continues in a hush.

"Believe me, you wouldn't be acting like such a brat if all of this disappeared."

Applause explodes around me.

People swarm back inside from the deck. I watch Marcus inch his way through the crowd like a roach.

I glance at him and then Jess.

Why is he even here? I thought my parents only knew him in a cursory way. Maybe he's planning some big media endorsement for my father's latest novel, although it's a totally different genre. My father has always secretly dismissed Marcus's writing, and my mother has treated him as she has everyone in her life: an errant piece of trash she doesn't want to touch, but picks up with a smile—and gloved hand—because people may be watching.

Jess catches me staring, nods with her head and mouths, *Smile!*

I turn, my face a ray of sunshine.

My parents, Phillip and Piper Page, glide down the stairs, holding each other's hands. My father is wearing a vintage tux, shoes as shiny as the polished railing, my mother in an Oscar de la Renta black sleeveless cocktail dress that's a bit too short but shows off her stunning legs that she's drenched in baby oil.

Magazine writers and publishing editors have described them as a modern-day Jackie and JFK, old-fashioned elegance come to life.

But that's not an accurate reference. As a writer, I know who my parents really are.

Moira and Johnny from *Schitt's Creek*.

Rich, entitled, driven, obsessed with their lives, careers and personas. They believe in their hearts they are—as my grandma used to say—"salt of the earth," but the salt is pink Himalayan. They love Jess and me, they really do, it's just that if you asked our mother out of the blue what our middle names were, she would likely not be able to answer but blame it on the fact she hadn't gone to yoga or barre class that week.

In fact, my entire family is the Rose family from *Schitt's Creek*.

Jess is pretty Alexis, who loves the surface beauty of her life, and I am cynical, sarcastic David, who watches the spectacle with horror and bemusement but cannot keep my mouth shut to save my life.

I feel like I'm the only one in on the inside joke.

My parents wave as they descend. They stop on a landing

before a grand portrait they commissioned of us on the beach at sunset when we were not these people. I glance at their faces then and now. They are the same people, a bit older, a bit more work, but I don't recognize our family any longer.

"Speech!" someone yells.

"Soon," I hear Jess call. "Could everyone grab a cocktail and gather on the patio, please?"

My parents do not yell from landings. This is a choreographed dance. Their lives are a choreographed dance.

A swarm of people rush the table to nab a cocktail.

When the line clears, I make my way to the bar.

"I'm going to need something a bit stronger than champagne to make it through this night," I say. "Could I have a gin and tonic with extra lime and extra gin please."

The bartender laughs, and I realize he's about my age and looks like Michelangelo's *David* come to life.

"I like your dress," he says.

I smile. "Thank you."

"Your gin and tonic," he says, handing me the glass. "Extra lime. Extra gin."

"Thank you," I repeat.

I take a selfie of myself with the cocktail and text it to Gin and Juice.

In honor of you.

"Now that I know what you like, maybe we could get a drink sometime," he says.

He's good.

"I'm so sorry," I say. "You sure are pretty, but I don't have time for boys right now. Except in books."

His chiseled face softens, and I can see he's never been turned down.

"Rejection stinks, doesn't it?" I look at him. "I'm a writer, so it's going to be a big part of my life. As my parents have told a million writers about their manuscripts, 'I'm sorry, it's just not right for us at this time, but I'm sure it will be scooped up by someone who loves it.'"

"You're a writer?" the bartender asks. "Have you written anything I've read?"

"Ah, the question every writer hates at a party," I say. "I'm sorry to sound so dismissive," I continue, "but next time maybe just ask a writer what she writes."

He nods, his curly dark hair falling in his eyes.

Behind him, in the library, is a portrait of my grandparents with our family when we were all still babies.

Beyond, I see Marcus on the deck. He waves at me.

His nepo baby remark haunts me, partly because the creepy bastard is right and partly because the matriarch who started it all is hidden away, like her beloved books.

I look the bartender in the eyes.

"Can I ask you a question?"

His eyes light up. "Of course! Anything."

"Why is it so damn hard to talk about anything other than a man?"

He cocks his head at me, not understanding.

I grab my drink and start to turn. "Thanks for the extra lime. I may die tonight, but at least it won't be from scurvy."

He still doesn't understand me. Few do.

As I start to walk away, the bartender calls, "Hey!"

I turn.

"What do you write?"

I wink at his effort.

"I write happy endings," I say.

"But you don't seem happy," he says.

I smile.

"That's why I write."

CHAPTER TWO

I follow a flock of crackling grackles to the expansive deck offering breathtaking views of Lake Michigan. My grandmother had it updated and expanded before she passed, and now a sandy-colored Trex deck blends into the bluff and beach below it, arcing and edging out forever, making you feel as if you are floating in the air.

The guests murmur, stunned at the unobstructed views.

"It looks just like the ocean," a woman says to me.

"But better," I say. "No salt, no sharks."

Grey Grayling moves to the front of the deck and raises her glass of champagne. The crowd instantly quiets. I'm convinced Grey could part Lake Michigan right now if she simply lifted her hand.

Grey was my parents' first big literary find a decade ago.

Let me rephrase that: she was my parents' *only* literary find.

She *hit the list*, as they say in publishing circles, with her debut about postpartum depression following the birth of her first child. Grey was a child star and later a model, and the world believed her life was perfect, but she descended into unfathomable depression after the birth of her baby, and she wrote a compelling roman à clef that garnered interviews with every major media outlet.

Grey, not surprisingly, left The Mighty Pages with her second book to earn a few million dollars at a competitive publisher for an advance my parents couldn't match. I know they were crushed, but they never let it show, knowing they would need her influence in the future.

Like today.

"The world is an illusion," Grey begins, "of beauty, power, love—and there is only one writer today who can shatter that illusion with the power of his words... Phillip Page."

Grey—who, of course, went gray before it was in vogue, her perfect locks tossing in the wind—holds up a copy of my father's new book and continues.

"*The Boy and the Ball* is a masterpiece for the ages."

The crowd erupts in applause.

I smile and nod because I can feel Jess watching me.

Everything, it seems, is a masterpiece these days—Super Bowl commercials and halftime acts, the latest *Mission: Impossible* movie. Why can't something simply be quality entertainment?

"Ladies and gentlemen, *New York Times* bestselling author Phillip Page and his equally extraordinary publishing partner in crime, author and wife, Piper Page!"

The crowd lifts glasses of champagne.

"Hear! Hear!"

My mother and father are a gorgeous duo, no doubt about it. They look like those couples you see photographed at polo matches in *Town & Country* magazine, or at a Hamptons soiree in *Social Life*.

Ooops, they are.

"What a day!" My mother gestures dramatically behind her to the lake and then to my father. "I don't know which is more breathtaking!"

The crowd titters.

She holds up my father's book. The cover is of a baseball glove catching a ball that looks like the world on fire.

"You've hit another home run, my dear!"

The crowd applauds.

My father's latest novel is about a young boy who catches a home run ball in the bottom of the ninth inning of Game Seven of the World Series to give the New York Yankees the title. When the Yankees star slugger comes to retrieve the baseball, the boy hands it to him, and the crowd goes wild, thinking the child—as we think of all children—to be a saint. A TV replay later reveals that the boy was actually holding a regular old baseball in his hand when he caught the historic homer with his glove, and that simple ball was the one he returned to the player. As media attention spirals out of control, the boy demands a fortune to return it. He's both revered and reviled for his action, and becomes a cult hero. Angered, the team and slugger refuse to pay his price. As years pass, time turns him into a pariah and further deems him an outcast when the former slugger dies tragically. The team barred the boy—now a man—from attending games. He is chased on the street and forced to move from his beloved New York to a rural town in the Midwest. My father's book celebrated the boy's bravery at living life as an outcast.

A select few literary journals were hailing the book for its nihilism. The trouble is, no one outside of publishing circles actually reads these reviews from critics who tend to love anything that is cold and cruel, any literature that sees life and the world as dark and unrelenting.

But the masses, as usual, have not embraced it.

My father's Amazon and Barnes & Noble rankings are dismal, lodged between two books about raising goats.

I hated his novel.

It was depressing, not to mention the boy used words a boy wouldn't use. I mean, a nine-year-old kid with the vocabulary to say *metonymy* or *tautology* as easily as he would say *soda pop* or *bike*?

Dad, c'mon.

Moreover, my father knows nothing about baseball. He hates sports. When my grandma would listen to the Tigers or watch the Lions games, my dad would switch off the radio.

"Mindless entertainment," he would say.

"That's the whole point, son," GiGi would reply.

My father felt the same about movies and TV. His nose was always in a book—long before he founded The Mighty Pages or wrote his first novel—and he rarely let us watch television or go to the theater when he was present. But when he left the house, Jess and I would mainline TV just like we did popcorn and Milk Duds.

He knew it, though. He'd look at our viewing history, or see the movies we paid to watch.

So we played this game, my dad and I.

"Did you love *The Lord of the Rings*?" he might ask.

"Yes!" I'd gush.

He'd hand me the J. R. R. Tolkien book. "Read it."

And then my father would say, as he did every time—no matter what we'd watched, "The book, Emma. The book is always better."

The crowd claps again, and I am back in the present.

"My wife, business partner, literary muse and *New York Times* bestselling author…"

Again.

I love my mother, I really do, no matter how insane she can make me, but she has gone out of her way to erase her history because she's obsessed with what other people think of her. I'm *all* history. I am who I am because of all those who came before me, of all that happened to get me to this place, right here, right now.

Speaking of right here, my mother was a boarder at Eyebrow

Cottage, one of the endless stream of people who came and went through that screen door, a girl of meager means working summers at a bookstore in town to earn enough money for college. That's how she met my father. She was reading a book in a bikini. My father was intrigued by either her taste in literature or swimsuits, and they fell in love.

How's that stand up to the Bechdel Test?

But isn't hers an amazing story? A universal story of overcoming a horrible childhood, working her way through college and to make a better life, finding love? One that should be shared, written, shouted from the rooftops?

And yet it's the plot my family despises more than any other. So ashamed of their past for reasons I can never understand and which exacerbate my mouth and behavior.

Now my mother's entire existence is a carefully curated fifty-word bio that always includes the five most important words in the world to her: *New York Times bestselling author.*

No one can really confirm how she or my father achieved this status, and no one really asks anymore. It's a mystery as long and convoluted as *The Da Vinci Code.*

My mother has written three novels—quirky, dark, character-driven books about depressed women. Cumulatively, I think they sold a few hundred copies.

My father's novels have sold a few more, but not many.

I know this sounds like it may simply be a facetious remark, but I wonder in all seriousness: How did they achieve that bestseller status when their sales were so modest?

I don't think my parents would lie about this status. That would be certain death in the literary world, but I also don't know how it was achieved either, as I've heard my parents scream about titles that have been omitted from the list for years and know how the process works. Maybe it was easier back in the day, or perhaps my parents earned this bestseller status solely by writing the foreword for Grey's memoir, a combined five hundred words.

All I know is that they wear this single moniker like a royal crown, actually, a shield, and that deflects any questions or criticisms. My mother knows how to weave an image, though. She even learned, when asked where she went to university, a way to gloss over the word *Western* so that people only heard the word *Michigan*.

"Michigan?" they'd gasp. "Impressive."

Whatever happened to owning our own stories? We're now social media snippets and pretty pictures on Instagram that never tell the true tale.

We all give our lives a good copy edit these days, don't we?

My father finishes thanking my mother.

"And to our secret weapon, Jess and her Swans," he says, gesturing to my sister to take a bow. "And, of course, to our ethereal spirit, Emma, who just graduated from Michigan—"

My mother smiles and ducks her head.

"—who dreams of being a writer—"

"Yes! Of course!" the crowd murmurs.

I wave, face red, and sip my drink.

"This is a story as old as time," my father says, holding up his book.

I listen to him, rapt like the crowd. He is an amazing speaker, drawing you in, talking about the inspiration for the book, his writing process.

He worked on this novel for four years. I remember him telling me he stopped at page fifty for two years.

"Why did you continue if it didn't call to you?" I once asked.

He never answered.

"What makes a great book?" my father asks the crowd. "The protagonist. The hero. The antihero." He glances around the deck. For a brief second, we catch each other's eyes. He continues. "Sometimes they can be the same thing."

I smile at my father.

He looks away.

I'm by no means perfect. And the people surrounding me are not demons. If you're reading it that way, I need a rewrite. But somehow, in our own memoirs, we lose who we are, the person we wish to be, and we become an illusion of ourselves, a bloated pretense of the skeleton story we started long ago.

In the distance, a girl screams, her cry carried in staccato beats along the pulses of wind off the lake.

When I was ten, I got caught in a riptide.

One minute, my grandma GiGi was reading to me from *Jonathan Livingston Seagull* and I was splashing near the shore pretending I was a gull who could catch a fish and then fly to the lighthouse. The next, I was being pulled farther into Lake Michigan by the current.

I panicked and began to swim as hard as I could toward the beach, yet it only grew smaller.

I paddled and paddled, my arms flailing in the water, but quickly began to lose strength. My head bobbed. I was underwater, the next moment my face was in the sun.

Just a blink ago, I was safe.

My grandma GiGi always said there were times in life you should never take for granted.

Like the smell of a new book, puppy or baby.

The way you feel when you jump into the lake on the first summer day after a long winter.

The feeling of the sand on your legs when it trails from the pages of a really good book you're reading on the beach.

The breeze on the screened porch on a hot summer day.

The creak of the cottage in a thunderstorm.

Every day after you turn sixty.

When your family is together and happy.

A simple day at the beach.

As I went underwater, I knew, even as a girl, I was going to die.

I knew that life was shifting like the sand and as treacherous, deep and dark as the lake.

That's when I saw a gull circle above me.

"Jonathan?" I mumbled.

It caught my eye and squalled at me. It seemed more than a simple bird, more than—as my grandma had just been reading to me—"bone and feather, but a perfect idea of freedom and flight, limited by nothing at all."

This gull was an angel of white.

And then he was off, flying higher and higher, until he melted into the sun.

I mimicked this grand gull, spreading my arms out and rolling on my back. The lake rocked me, up and down, and I was no longer in my body, no longer a girl. I was a bird. I, too, was free and soaring toward heaven.

Suddenly, I felt GiGi's arms around me.

"I got you! It's okay."

"You can't fight the riptide," she yelled to me over the waves. "You'll just exhaust yourself. You have to swim parallel to shore until you're out of its pull and then the waves will carry you back. It's hard to realize when you're in the middle of a maelstrom, but patience is the answer. Always remember that."

I began to cry.

"It's okay, Emma," she soothed. "You're okay now. But you leave all those tears out here in the lake because when we get to shore, I'm going to tell everyone *you* saved *me*."

"Why?"

"It's a good story," GiGi said. "And the world always needs a good story whether it's true or not. That's the magic of fiction."

She kissed my wet head.

"That world needs to see how strong you are." She paused as we floated. "You need to believe in your own strength."

"I fought, GiGi."

"I know you did, sweetheart. That's why you're still here."

My grandma cried once, a horrible shudder of relief, and then it was over.

"And I saw Jonathan Livingston Seagull," I said to her as we neared the shore. "He helped save my life."

She didn't say another word, just stared toward the shore, where a crowd had gathered, their attention riveted on our return, cheering.

Just to their left, before GiGi's cottage on the lake, I saw my parents and sister sitting under umbrellas in their beach chairs, noses in their books, oblivious. For a split second, they lifted their heads in unison—as if all of this commotion were merely some summer annoyance like a squawking seagull—and then returned to their mighty pages, where the real drama and emotion of life should remain.

"Don't believe what your eyes are telling you," my grandmother said to me, a quote I wouldn't realize until later was from Richard Bach's book. "All they show is limitation. Look with your understanding. Find out what you already know, and you will see the way to fly."

As we neared the shore, GiGi said, "Remember, Emma, you're the hero in this story."

And, slowly, the waves carried us back home.

Another scream, a happy one, and I see two girls in the distance playing on the beach.

What do we remember of our pasts that is truly accurate? How much is filtered through our own sun-blinded lenses? Why do we bury our pain deep inside?

"I'm a plotter," I hear my father say. "I believe in knowing exactly where I'm going before I even start writing."

I think of the novel I'm finishing, the secret GiGi knew, the one my family does not.

I may act strong, but I am so, so weak. I worry I would crumble like a sandcastle beneath my family's judgment and disapproval.

I am different from my father in almost every way. As a writer, I'm known as a "pantser." As in, flying by the seat of my pants. I don't like to outline. It feels like work. I like the character to lead. I want her to surprise me with where she's going every single day. Otherwise, it feels a bit too much like forced finality.

And what fun is it knowing how it's all going to end, right?

That's what makes a great book.

I do agree with my father on one thing: you have to know where you're headed.

But you can only do that if you know where you've been.

On the golden shore, white gulls gather and squawk as my father speaks.

He doesn't acknowledge the drama, nor raise his voice. Instead, the crowd moves toward him.

CHAPTER THREE

"I finally found a bottle of Veuve."

I turn. Marcus Flare is walking toward me. I am standing on the edge of the lake, feet in the sand.

"I think your parents were hiding it," he continues. "Sneaky little bastards. I knew they had some taste."

"Did you microchip me?" I ask. "I *will* scream."

He raises his hands, still walking, holding two plastic flutes and a bottle of champagne.

"Truce," he says. "I'm just here to apologize and listen. I can come off as a bit brusque sometimes."

"A bit?"

"You're certainly no shrinking violet," he says. Marcus notices the flower in my hair. "More like a perfect peony."

Has he microchipped me?

"I think maybe I just need to shut up sometimes and hear the words of a younger reader," he continues. "Mine are certainly dying off in droves these days."

I don't say a word. He hands me the two glasses and holds up the bottle.

"Trick of the trade—you never twist the cork. You simply hold it tight and slowly turn the bottle."

Marcus pops the cork effortlessly. The champagne doesn't explode from the bottle, there is only a happy pop and a trail of steam, a small cloud that matches the one on the horizon.

"That plume of smoke from popping a champagne bottle is a kind of visible shock wave typically seen in supersonic exhaust streams from jets and rockets," Marcus explains, pouring the bubbly into the two plastic flutes. "These shock waves appear when the pressure of the exhaust outflow is more than about five times as high as the surrounding air. It's called a Mach disk." He takes a glass from me. "Research always makes a writer sound smarter than he actually is."

"Fancy," I remark. "And to think I was doing a keg stand just a few weeks ago."

"You're very clever, Emma."

I don't respond. I let the sounds of a clarinet and trumpet from the jazz band on the deck drift through the night air.

"Tell me about this place," Marcus says suddenly. "Michigan."

"Now you're interested? I thought you'd be back in Chicago tonight, on a red-eye out of this flyover state."

"Did you speak to your professors this way?" he asks, bending down to nestle the champagne bottle in the sand.

"Sometimes," I say.

"Feral," he whispers to the water.

My mind somersaults back to college, to the passage about women he wrote that incensed me.

Marcus scans the lake.

"Looks like the ocean," he says, inhaling deeply. "It's quite charming, as is your family cottage."

I glance at him. I don't know this man, but I know I don't trust him. I have that ability to suss out someone's essence.

I take a sip of the contraband Veuve and watch the water lap lazily at my feet.

I turn toward Eyebrow Cottage.

The small arched windows in the roof wink at me.

I wait for him to speak. He doesn't. The silence and his presence begin to unnerve me.

"My grandparents purchased Eyebrow Cottage decades go. GiGi—my grandmother—named it that because of the two dormer windows... See?"

Marcus nods.

"...which look exactly like two eyebrows that sit in the roofline. You probably know this already from research, but the windows are popular in shingled beach cottages like this, adding a curved facade that mimics the waves of a lake or ocean. But they are functional, too. They provide light and ventilation to a top-floor space." I point. "Those windows were where my grandmother's private office used to be. GiGi spent an inordinate amount of time in there, door locked. Eyebrow Cottage used to be a boardinghouse when my father was a boy."

"Do tell," Marcus says, interest piqued.

"I once heard my father say, after a few glasses of wine, how much he hated growing up with strangers in the house. He's always wanted to get away from this place I think."

I take another sip of champagne, mentally kicking myself for revealing too much information. Two drinks, and I'm an open safe. My parents would die.

"Go on," he prompts.

I consider what to say next.

I cannot tell him that GiGi had a lot of money, most of which she made all on her own.

I will not tell him that she used the money she earned from boarders over the years to invest in the stock market in the 1970s and 1980s, buying shares of unknown companies like Walmart or Apple for a few bucks. Over time, she used those dividends to buy undeveloped land on the lake, a parcel here, a tract there. Like those stocks, she bought land for a pittance, sold it for a mountain of gold, knowing she was sitting along the edge of heaven and people would want that paradise one day and pay a pretty penny to get it.

"You have to be in control of your story," she used to tell me. "No one else can write your happy ending."

I stare into the eyes of her office.

No one was ever allowed entrance into her private retreat. On occasion, I'd get a glimpse inside. A few times I was playing with my sister, chasing one another up and down the giant staircase, and GiGi opened the office door as I was racing by.

Inside was a big wooden desk—as big as a ship to me as a girl—a lone typewriter sitting in the middle of it. The desk was covered with pens, lined notebooks and color-coded folders. File cabinets stood like sentinels below the sloping ceiling.

"Go!" GiGi would yell at us, and we'd scamper away, hearts in our throats.

She had a skeleton key to her office, which she wore around her neck like jewelry, and she never took it off, even when she swam in the lake.

That office was the one place—in a cottage filled with people—where she could finally be alone, pay bills, track her stocks and read.

A sacred spot.

I still can't get into that office. It's been locked since the day GiGi died. When I asked my parents once about the key, my mother said, "Your grandmother wished to be buried with it."

I never believed my mother. I don't believe most of what she tells me because the words she utters are only meant to improve her own standing. They are not used to aid or comfort another. She is a writer after all.

I watch people dancing on the deck before an orange sherbet sunset.

Jazz echoes along the shore.

"This all feels very Gatsby, doesn't it?" I finally say.

I see my father spin my mother.

The Great Gatsby is, of course, my mother's favorite book.

"Your GiGi sounds like quite a character," Marcus says with a wink. "Perfect for one of my novels."

"She's too good for one of your novels!" I snap. I know I sound like a child, but I can't stop. My mouth is a runaway train. "She was too smart. She was too independent. She didn't need a man after her husband died. She did it all on her own. You write books for women, but they center on men."

Marcus doesn't say a word for a moment.

"And we're back to square one," he finally says with a sigh. "We were making such good progress."

Marcus sips his champagne and looks for far too long into my eyes.

"You realize you cannot walk through this world blurting out anything that crosses your mind, especially in publishing. It's a small world. Word gets around. You have a wonderful life ahead of you, Emma. Don't spoil it by acting so...*spoiled*."

"Why are you here?" I ask. "Not just at this party, but here on the beach? Why did you seek me out?"

"I'm here because your parents invited me," Marcus says. "And I'm *here* because you are unlike any woman I've ever met. Most women would put on an act and be nice to me for the sake of their parents. Too many women your age don't even know how to talk much less speak their minds. Their entire worth is summed up by the number of likes on an Instagram post. I also can tell you don't like me, and I don't actually meet too many people these days who are this..."

He laughs and waves his hands, searching for the right word.

"...I was going to say openly hostile toward me, but I'll choose the word *honest* instead."

"You do realize that you *are* a romance writer?"

"But I'm not."

"But you are."

His chest inflates. I continue.

"I think you're just too much of a macho, pompous ass to

admit it. You should be a proponent for romance, rom-coms, women's fiction—whatever it's called—and not a late-to-the-game, oops-now-that-I'm-successful-I'll-reject-it apologist. You should champion other writers. I mean, you're not Shakespeare. And you couldn't even stand in Emily Giffin's heels." I pause. "Which, by the way, are *way* cuter than your shoes."

"Are you done?"

"No. You asked why I don't like you, and I'm telling you. Your verbal sludge is the crap female authors—really, any author who writes books with strong female characters who just happen to want unconditional love and a life of their own choosing—fight against."

Marcus stands straight as a board. I think he is going to turn and walk away, but he stares me down until I stand straight as well.

"Oh, my God! I've already figured it out!" he says. "You're a wannabe writer, aren't you?"

He spits his words.

"Those quick comebacks and the snappy dialogue. The heroine who has it all but is so self-aware that she doesn't want to be a nepo baby and wants to make it on her own. The protagonist whose grandmother instilled in her the value of hard work although she was rich. The author who wants to write a novel that her parents would never publish just to prove a point. *Please!* Your character arc is just as clichéd as you are, Emma Page. You're already your own down-on-her-luck, angry-at-the-world character. Your family did everything wrong by giving you everything. You've never had any real struggles, so you create your own. Am I getting warm?"

I feel as if I've been slapped in the face.

"No!" I shake my head at him. "Because I know people. I know you want something. Or my parents do. I just know it. And I will find out and put an end to it."

"Oh, you will?" he asks, again mocking me. "Our little literary Hannah Montana is all grown-up and a big girl writer cum detective?" Marcus laughs. "I'm actually one of the world's most successful writers, Emma, so I'm a few chapters—and a few million dollars—ahead of you already." He stops, retrieves the bottle from the sand and refills his champagne glass. He again studies me closely. "Shall I go on since you've psychoanalyzed me already and made your own snap judgment?"

I lodge my feet into the sand.

"You started writing a novel in college," he continues, "because you were better than any ol' Hemingway and Steinbeck. You were so much more *woke* than stupid ol' Marcus Flare. You wanted to be Emily Giffin! Jen Weiner! Ann Patchett! So you pulled out your laptop, which was covered with stickers of classic book covers from *Little Women* to *Pride and Prejudice*, and you wrote and wrote your little book while wearing your favorite Taylor Swift T-shirt. Am I getting warmer?"

I have to hold myself from pushing him into the lake, but dammit, if he isn't as good at pushing every one of my buttons as my family is.

But I am pretty good at that, too. I was taught by the best.

"You want to know why I write, *Mr.* Flare? It's because I don't see myself represented in your love stories. I don't see strong women, like me or my grandmother. I don't see real women. I see a man's idea of what a woman should be, someone who needs a man's love to save her rather than a woman who only wants to be loved as equally as she loves herself. Even your sex scenes are horrible. No woman wants her private parts described as 'pleasure caves,' or a man's described as a 'hungry boa constrictor.' Not all women want to be thrown down on a bed, we don't like to be passive while you amaze us with your prowess. We are equals, in sex and love. And someone needs to write about that!"

Marcus Flare applauds.

"So you have read and remembered me it seems," he says. "You are such an idealist. Lord knows I love a young dreamer, but most dreamers never actually do much to make those dreams come true. It's all just talk."

"Why are you really here?" I ask. "Just tell me."

"Let's just say it's an opportunity to build my legacy and improve my literary credibility, especially with readers like you," he says. "Oh, who am I kidding? It's a way for Marcus Flare to get even richer."

He clinks my glass.

"And it's a way for Marcus Flare to get even," he continues. "With the publishing industry, that is. You know, you're not the only one who has lost someone you love, Emma."

From out of nowhere, a curious gull lands on the beach, tilting its head this way and that, scanning for a piece of food we may have dropped.

Marcus shoos it away.

"Nasty birds," he says.

My mind flies to a moment not so long ago in this exact same spot.

GiGi got married on her eightieth birthday.

She threw a simple wedding for one—herself—at sunset on the beach in front of Eyebrow Cottage. She didn't wear a wedding gown, or shoes, only shorts and a T-shirt with a Nora Ephron quote: *Be the heroine of your life, not the victim.*

An electric blue hydrangea was pinned into the bun of her long, silver hair, and she sported the veil she wore when she married my grandfather. She carried a bouquet of her own peonies.

Only a few people attended. There were more curious onlookers strolling the beach who stopped to watch than those who were actually invited.

Such is the result of a long, quirky life.

My parents and sister didn't attend, much less RSVP.

I always thought my mom and dad believed GiGi had early dementia. Jess thought old age had exaggerated all of GiGi's eccentricities into "old coot kookiness." Mostly, they were just embarrassed.

But they weren't there to see the incredible love on display.

I served as minister. I wasn't ordained, but that didn't matter to GiGi.

I could read the vows she had written, and that was enough.

"Do you, Pauline 'GiGi' Haskins Page, take yourself to love, honor, comfort, and keep in sickness and health, forsaking all others, for as long you shall live?"

"I do."

The moment she took herself in marriage, the wind off Lake Michigan blew the veil off her face. She shut her eyes and let the lake breeze kiss her lips.

I wept.

And then I read a passage from *Jonathan Livingston Seagull*.

GiGi had wanted my father to read it for some reason, and I think she still believed her son might show up at the last minute to do so. In the days leading up to the ceremony, GiGi would hurry into the entryway every time the screened door creaked in the wind, or banged shut when I'd head outside.

"'Instead of being enfeebled by age,'" I read, "'the Elder had been empowered by it. He could outfly any gull in the Flock, and he had learned skills that the others were only gradually coming to know.'"

I looked up. GiGi smiled.

"'Jonathan's one sorrow was not solitude, it was that the other gulls refused to believe the glory of flight that awaited them; they refused to open their eyes and see.'"

When the ceremony was over, we danced on the beach to "Single Ladies" and the Beatles' "Paperback Writer."

"Listen to the lyrics, Emma," GiGi said. "An entire story in just a few lines."

After it was all over, GiGi and I walked the shoreline together.

Not far from the lighthouse, we stopped to watch the sun slink and bid farewell to another day.

"I found the love of my life with your grandfather," GiGi said, her voice soft. "But I've spent the majority of my life alone, and I've had to learn to love just me to survive this long. That's not an easy thing to do, Emma. We're taught to hide our dreams, polish the edges off our uniqueness until our square peg becomes round. We're told to fit in, be like everyone else, but that just robs the world of our power. You must love yourself unconditionally and completely or you cannot truly love another in the same way. You will not ever be able to become who you were meant to be. But when you do, when you take your own hand in life, you can change the world. Some will admire you for that, others' hate will be just as strong."

GiGi took my hand and shook it hard.

"The greatest romance you will ever experience is a love of self, and the greatest love story takes place right here."

She touched my heart.

"Look!" GiGi said, nodding at the sunset. "The final wink!"

Just as she said that, a white gull took flight from the beach and soared over the lake until it melted into the orange sunset.

"'Jonathan's one sorrow was not solitude, it was that the other gulls refused to believe the glory of flight that awaited them; they refused to open their eyes and see.'"

"Excuse me?" Marcus asks, confused.

"Emma?" Jess's call pierces the air.

"I'm going to get into trouble for disappearing," I say, now wanting only to extricate myself from Marcus. "My family hates it when I go all Houdini on them during a literary event."

I begin to turn away but stare into the horizon one last time.

"Emma," Marcus says. "I hope we can put this behind us. We're going to need to get along in the future."

His words make my heart race anew. *Why?*

I stare at him and then toward the approaching sunset to calm me.

"That's the future calling," Marcus continues.

"No, that is the final wink," I say.

"The what?" he asks.

"That's what my grandma called it," I say, pointing to the horizon, half of the sun still peeking over the lake. "It's the time when the most magical moments occur." I gaze upon the sunset and the day's final light. "You just have to be present to witness them."

The sun disappears.

"Here's to a lifetime of magical moments," Marcus says. "Truce." I turn.

"Scout's honor," he continues, holding up his fingers.

I stare at him unconvinced.

GiGi once told me that when people said "Scout's honor" to convince you they are telling the truth, they are most likely lying. It's the equivalent of someone looking away when you ask for the truth.

Play nice, Emma. My gut is telling me that I need him to like me right now.

He refills my champagne glass.

"Truce," I say.

"Marcus?"

My mother's voice. I turn. She folds her arms.

"Can you come say a word or two?" she calls. "Please! For me!"

"Now I'm in trouble," he says. "Canoodling with the hosts' daughter." He winks. "The final wink."

Ugh. Truce already over.

I watch Marcus head back to the party as my mother watches me on the beach.

She shakes her head at me, a silent, long-distance retribution.

No, I'm the one in trouble. I'm always in trouble.

Another figure moves toward the railing. Jess, watching. She sees me, turns and walks away. I track her silhouette heading up the stairs.

CHAPTER FOUR

GiGi used to tell me she always heard a profound silence at the end of a great sentence.

"That period is almost like the final note a symphony plays. It hangs in the air for the longest time, slowly fading away, and yet you can still feel that reverberation even in the silence," she said. "That period is not just perfunctory punctuation. It serves as a visual stopping point to consider what has come before and what is yet to come. We need such stopping moments in both life and writing, and yet we treat a simple period as if it's nothing special at all."

I open my eyes.

It is dawn, and the waking world's orchestra echoes.

The locusts in the trees buzz, the tree frogs groan, cicadas moan, the dune grass whispers and the cottage creaks in the breeze.

These are sounds of a South Haven summer.

The sounds of a stopping moment that don't come often enough in life.

My parents love great writing. They admire the perfect setting. But I have a feeling—as clear and concise as the perfect ending to a book—that they are more and more willing to close this particular chapter on their lives.

They have been spending more and more time in the Hamptons. I overheard a guest say last night that my father's event was a "goodbye party" to Michigan. I thought he was speaking to my father's busy schedule, or being overtly literal in reference to my father's novel, but my gut tells me otherwise.

I think of Marcus.

My gut is rarely wrong.

Between Marcus, Jess and my growing uncertainty about the stability of The Mighty Pages, I tossed and turned all night long even after a few drinks.

I sit up in bed.

The silence is very, very loud now that the guests have gone and the cottage can speak again and be heard.

It needs to be heard.

I glance at the clock: *6:17 a.m.*

The old stereotype that college kids stay up all night drinking and then sleep until noon is largely a myth. Yes, we have our fun, yes, I have a bit of a hangover, but there is great pressure of going to a great school and, well, doing great in life. There is great pressure in trying to make a mark in a family that expects greatness.

In reality, I—like so many of my peers—am used to staying up late only to cram and study, waking at dawn for classes or internships and using my hours wisely so that I can land the best possible job out of college.

Please our parents. Impress the world. Make tons of money. Pay off those student loans.

Life is filled with—to pardon the obvious pun—many chapters and many periods. Some chapters are short, some are long, but there is always a period.

I am in the middle of a profound silence right now, caught between college and real life, the family I have and the one I created in college, my present and my future which sits before me like the horizon, so close and yet so far away.

I reach my hand out to touch the air.

I have job interviews lined up, including one with my parents.

But I don't know yet if I want any of them. I realize that I am blessed, spoiled, entitled—#NepoBaby—whatever you wish to call it, but I simply want to make the right decision with the next step in my life. I feel as if my entire life, like so many of my peers, has been plotted out for me until now: the right private school, the right college, the right graduate school, the right internships, the right job, the right husband, the right house. Some were predetermined to be an attorney or a doctor before they even learned to jump rope.

Whatever happened to the right fit?

Gin's parents are both doctors. Juice's father works on Wall Street.

Gin infuriated her family when she majored in journalism.

"We didn't spend a fortune on your education so you could grow up to be poor!" I heard her father yell over her cell one night.

But she wants to better the world.

Juice followed in her father's footsteps, no questions asked. Is she happy? I don't truly think so, but she believes money is power in America, and she wants to live her life on her own terms, even outside of her father's influence.

This is why I never shared with my parents that I am writing a book. I still marvel at the power it took Mamie Gummer, Meryl Streep's daughter, to say, "Hey, Mom, I want to act, too."

I know my parents wouldn't just hate the type of book I'm writing, they would utterly dismiss it as if it didn't exist.

And I don't know if I have the strength to endure that type of silence.

I reach over and grab my cell. Although it's early, I know

Gin and Juice are not only awake but also likely headed to or at work.

How's the real world?

Gin is the first to respond.

Like college. But with money. And Southern men. Who have money. And act like fraternity boys. It's like living in the reality show Southern Charm.

LOL! I respond.
Juice chimes in.

Like college. But with money. And New York men who act like Roman emperors who just got out of a fraternity. It's like living in a movie version of Wall Street and Caligula.

I lower my head into my hands and laugh like I haven't since we said goodbye.
How's life in Michigan? Juice asks.
How was your father's book launch? Gin follows.

Let me sum it up this way: I think Marcus Flare—the famous author—was either trying to hit on me or take possession of my soul. Both options were super creepy.

A string of laughing emojis fills my phone.
When they stop, Gin texts: The world is a never-ending college exam. A constant Bechdel Test.
Remember why you're there, Juice adds. You are a writer. Shut out all the noise! WRITE!
I send a row of hearts and final note: MISS YOU! LOVE YOU!
They thumbs-up my text, and my cell goes quiet.

I grab my laptop from the designer nightstand. I joke that my mother should have renamed me and Jess *Serena & Lily* because she loves the store so much.

I power on my computer and open the Word doc titled "The Summer of Seagulls."

I stare at the words "A Novel by Emma Page."

This is why I'm here. This is my passion.

But can it be my career, too?

Can I finish the dream GiGi and my parents set in motion by pushing books into my hands at the earliest of ages?

My parents are publishers and authors. I know countless full-time writers. You would think the answer would be easy, but it's not.

I glance out the window at the lake.

Growing up, I was fascinated by books. My grandma used to walk me to the local library, and I'd walk out with my arms full. As I got older, GiGi would walk me into the local IGA and beeline toward the spinning racks filled with romance novels. I'd exit with my arms full, much to my parents' chagrin.

"If she's reading, that's all that matters," she would say.

As I got even older, and learned more of what my parents did, I became fascinated with authors.

Who are these creatures that create these make-believe worlds?

How do they do it?

Could I?

When I would visit my parents in their offices in the city, I would sit in the lobby and watch authors walk into The Mighty Pages—my stomach in knots, totally fangirling—as if writers were movie stars. And they were to me. When I'd meet an author, I'd read all of their books, even if they were "too old" for me.

As a girl, I attended a fancy literary luncheon in Manhattan, where—upon the publication of my father's first novel and a solid year for The Mighty Pages—I saw him receive a key to the city from the mayor.

For the longest time after that, I believed there was a "golden key" in publishing and that it was granted to only certain anointed writers in fancy clubs, late at night, over expensive drinks. When an author was handed that golden key, it unlocked every door in publishing, and the world opened before them.

I told my father this a few years later, and he laughed hard, but in a kind way.

"There is a golden key that is granted, sweetheart," he said. "But there is a golden key that lives inside you, and all you need to do is overcome all your fears and self-doubt to discover where it's hidden. When you do, it will unlock any door. The only magic that exists in publishing is the power of writers to believe in their own words and voice."

I trusted him until I began to see all the relentless rejection that authors experienced, the good books—and people—my parents turned down because the timing wasn't right, the book wasn't the right fit, or they didn't believe, despite a book's excellence, that it could sell well enough to buy it.

I began to watch authors leave The Mighty Pages in tears, many of whom had published numerous books with my parents. Their careers were over. Their dream was no longer a manuscript covered in red ink to make it the best it could be; now their dream had been reduced to a profit-and-loss statement drenched in red.

And that's when I began to doubt that I had a golden key inside of me.

My entire life I've seen the rejection that authors experience. It is a battering tide. And publishing is undergoing a sea change: shrinking sales for most authors, domination by a few, booksellers holding less inventory, publicity coverage shrinking.

Moreover, I've been told my entire life by friends and teachers that, while writing is a nice hobby, a career it does not make.

"Get a real job, make real money," my college classmates told me.

But what if that real job doesn't make you happy?

Won't you end up with a very unhappy ending at some point in the not-too-distant future?

And let's be honest: Where would my parents be right now without having used and leveraged my grandmother's money? Unpublished authors living in an apartment somewhere? Working odd jobs to finish that next manuscript?

I don't want success handed to me as a gift from my parents. I don't want to be a nepo baby. I want my accomplishments to be my own. I want my book to make its way in the world on its own merits. Otherwise, how will I ever know if I'm any good? I want to earn it. I've spent the last four years writing it.

And now?

I'm pushing commas and periods around.

I read the opening to my novel, "The Summer of Seagulls," for the millionth time.

The first word I said as a child was not Ma or Da, but Sis.

My sister had been my best friend since I opened my eyes and saw her beaming upon me.

"I finally have a sister."

You might not believe me, but I can still hear Mia's voice saying that to me when I was but a few days old. It's the first moment that Mia—hovering above me like the mobile of books my parents placed over my crib—became my entire world.

But that's the thing about memories and sisters: we distort and rewrite them until they become what we need them to be in order to survive.

I shut my eyes after the final period.

I hear...

Profound silence.

I hear...

The judgment of my parents.

We gave our daughter every academic advantage to write a silly novel? A book filled with sentimentality and a happy ending? Hell has certainly frozen over.

I open my eyes. The light from the lake glints into the bedroom. It moves and shape-shifts on the comforter, walls and ceiling. I think of GiGi dancing by the lake.

Guide me, Grandma.

I shut the laptop, ease out of bed in and into a pair of shorts and a Michigan sweatshirt. I slip on my Vionic terry cloth slippers that feel like a cloud, hit the bathroom, and then search through the piles of books stacked on the shelves and floor of my room. I need a distraction from my own work. And there is only one place to turn: my grandma's favorite author, S. I. Quaeris.

I've squirreled away hundreds of books in my room, nearly all summer novels with pretty beach covers, romance novels, so my parents wouldn't have a truck come and haul the rest of them away to the local Goodwill.

"Romance novels," my parents always say in that tone they also use to utter "Hallmark movie" or "What do you mean you're all out of the sea bass?"

I grab a book I haven't read titled *Summer's Promise* and tiptoe out of my room and down the stairs, navigating them in a snaking pattern to avoid the ones that shudder and moan if I step on them.

The kitchen is at the back of the cottage, with wide windows above the sink and counters overlooking the lake. It's a hearth room kitchen with an old fireplace made of lake stones, blackened from years of roaring fires on cold days. Shelves filled with cookbooks flank the fireplace. Pots and pans hang from a large rack above the island. GiGi's beloved blue Spode plates—mimicking the color of the lake—are displayed on the walls. My parents have updated the counters and island with a beautiful granite, new appliances and lighting, but the original kitchen remains largely intact. I didn't have to stage a sit-in here. My parents love this kitchen as much as I do.

How do you perfect perfection?

I start the coffee and lean against the counter.

My grandma made breakfasts in this exact spot for her family and her boarders every day for decades: pancakes, French toast, muffins, casseroles, coffee cakes, fresh Michigan fruit.

Mornings were my grandmother's special time. She rose before dawn and slipped away to her office usually by 4 a.m. to work for hours before the sun even thought of waking. She loved the dawn of a new day. GiGi used to tell me, "A new day is an unwritten book, filled with promise and possibility."

I pull a mug from the cabinet and fill it with coffee. I take a sip, and I can feel my eyes widen. I make it too strong, like my grandma and my dad.

I head toward the deck.

The house is pristine, as if no one was here just a few hours ago.

I take a seat on a blue-and-white-striped outdoor sofa overlooking the lake. The cushion is still damp from the dew, and I jump up quickly—nearly spilling my coffee—and wipe the moisture off in quick strokes with my bare hand.

The view from Eyebrow Cottage is breathtaking. A long, sandy stretch of beach that leads in the distance to the South Haven Pier, a postcard-perfect, bright red lighthouse with a long pier that has gathered tourists and beachgoers for nearly 125 years. The area, as I was taught by GiGi, was first developed by Native American tribes who named the land Ni-No-Kong or "beautiful sunsets."

They, too, loved the final wink.

GiGi loved to read out here in the morning after she left her office and made breakfast. I am a chip off the old library card.

I pick up the novel.

The cover is a throwback, the title and author's name—S. I. Quaeris—are designed in a vintage typeface where the *r*'s are stretched like bird wings, the dots on the *i*'s are big suns, and the ends of all the letters look like Aladdin's shoes. The image is of a sunset over a red lighthouse. I glance down the beach.

This red lighthouse.

In the foreground, a woman scans the horizon. From behind, I can't help but think that she looks like me.

I try to remember how GiGi pronounced the author's last name. I whisper it to the wind.

"Kware-dis," I whisper. "Kware-dis."

I open the cover to read.

I start with the Acknowledgments.

I first must thank my readers. Without you, I would not be able to live my dream. Writing is what keeps me sane, how I make sense of an often senseless world. Books are the great connector. They bring us closer, bridge the gap, remind us that we have more in common than what divides us. My novels are about family, friends, the wisdom of our elders, the overlooked women in our lives, the overlooked soul within you, and I write them to remind you that you matter, and that it is the little things in life that mean the most: A sunrise. A sunset. Love. Happy endings. Each other. My little novels are meant as threads of hope and beacons of light for those who are drowning in the world. Know there will be a better day. And that can start right now by escaping into a better one.

I look up and stare at the lake, the lighthouse down the beach.

Her words are beautiful and heartfelt. And this is just the acknowledgments page. No wonder my grandma loved this author so much.

A big thank-you as well to my team: Harlequin (and now Silhouette), you are the best publisher an author could dream of having. You give a voice to women, their issues and their hearts, and I could not be more proud to call you my home away from home and my literary soul sister.

I turn the book and look at the publisher's logo on the spine. So much has changed in publishing over the years. I've seen it firsthand. Mergers. Disbanded imprints. Layoffs. Fewer options for writers to have their work discovered and published. How wonderful for this author to feel so loved for so long.

"Men know best about everything, except what women know better." That's a quote from George Eliot (aka Mary Ann Evans, the author of Middlemarch*) and a favorite of mine. I keep that in mind with every book I write.*

I laugh out loud. "Atta'girl," I say. I look at the author's name again. "Or boy."

I flip to the author bio, which simply reads, *S. I. Quaeris is the author of over forty novels and one of America's most beloved romance writers. The author lives and writes in a remote and beautiful setting which inspires their novels. They do not make appearances. "I prefer that my work do all the speaking for me."*

I flip back to the Acknowledgments.

Gratitude! This is the motto by which I live. I am grateful for each sunrise and sunset. I am grateful for each day I get to watch my family grow and laugh. I am grateful, despite all that life has thrown my way. Mostly, I'm grateful that my simple stories will, hopefully, live forever, something none of us can do.

I am eternally grateful for my friends and family, who inspire me daily and support my dream. I'm also grateful they continue to speak to me even after I've written about them (names were changed!).

I laugh again.

Grateful for all of you! Every single one of you. Your letters that the publisher forwards to me are hugs, constant reaffirmation that my novels are touching you, helping you, changing you. As a result, they save and change me, too.

I must also thank my "invisible team," who helps me write two books a year. They plot while I "pants." They edit as I write. They are the foundation of this big, beautiful dream.

Page by page, word by word, sentence by sentence...that is how each and every one of my glorious days are filled (oh, and with some coffee and wine, too!). I race out of bed every morning, excited and humbled to begin my days. I get lost in my stories. I become my characters. I pour out my heart and my secrets. And, oh, what a glorious way to live!

A final nod to home, a place I love (and never leave) more than any. This place inspires me, fills my soul, and when I sink my toes in the sand, or dive into the crystal water, I know I am part of this place, and it is a part of me, and we will forever be one.

Go now and read! Anything and everything! Hug your librarian! Support your local bookseller! And go to places you never imagined, be people you never dreamed, walk in shoes to places you thought you'd never travel, experience the world, and be changed. It is a privilege to evolve and change. We should never be the same people we were. Books help us on that journey.

Eliot again writes, "It is a narrow mind which cannot look at

*a subject from various points of view." Books saved my life. And
I believe they just might save the world. XOXO!*

I have tears in my eyes. My heart is in my throat.

I grab my cell to google S. I. Quaeris. I did in college, but
I shoved the author to the back of my memory banks after my
fight with GiGi that day on campus. There is no author website. There is a generic author page on the publisher website,
and a Wikipedia page devoted to the author's books.

*Prolific romance author… Secretive…not much known about their
personal life…*

There is a list of all the novels the author has written. I
begin to count, trying to keep my eyes from blurring. I stop
at eighty-two.

Eighty! Two!

"I still have a long way to go, S. I.," I say. "Impressive."

I cannot wait to start the novel.

I turn to the first page.

The patio door slides open.

My parents emerge, holding matching coffee cups, looking
like literary Ken and Barbie.

I subtly tuck the book I am reading underneath my legs.

"You both look nice," I say to cover, realizing too late that
nice is an adjective my mother despises more than a Target run.

"Dapper," I suddenly add. "Dapper and beautiful."

"*Nice* save," my mother says with a chuckle. "You remember."

This memory seems to touch her, and her face softens.

"Thank you anyway," she adds.

Mother-daughter moment over.

My father is wearing a lovely linen suit. On anyone else,
the outfit would be a wrinkled disaster by the time he reached
Chicago, but I know my father will emerge from the town car
looking as if it were just ironed.

Meanwhile, my mother is sporting a crisp white pantsuit that is one coffee drop away from being a thousand-dollar donation.

But my mother even sips her coffee elegantly. Her every move is as beautiful, deft and choreographed as *The Nutcracker* ballet.

"Anderson's Bookshop today, right?" I ask.

"Yes," my mother says. "We were able to wrangle Gillian Flynn to do an in-conversation."

My sister actually wrangled it, but my mother would never admit that out loud.

"So you know our schedule," my father says. "Chicago today, Cuyahoga Public Library in Cleveland tomorrow, then the book tour swings through the Northeast: Browseabout and Bethany Beach Books in Rehoboth Beach, Thunder Road Books in Spring Lake, New Jersey, then back to New York for a few events and parties."

"Your sister is leaving later today, so you're on your own," my mom reminds me. "Be a good girl."

I smile. I know that is code for *Jess told us what you said to Marcus Flare last night and then I saw you talking with him and have no idea what happened so don't fuck anything else up, okay?*

"Jess has a big mouth," I say. "Guess it's what made her famous."

"Emma," my mother scolds. "She's just concerned about you. Navigating the world is not like navigating a college campus. You have to learn to play the game."

"I actually don't think the two worlds are all that different," I say. "Believe me, I had to learn to play a game or two. But I was always honest about the game I was playing."

My parents exchange a look.

"Well, good. It's the way the world works," my mother says with a sigh, focusing on any positivity she can take from my inference.

"Well, the world needs a solid rewrite," I say. "And—just

to ease your minds—I didn't *do* anything wrong. I just don't understand why you would invite Marcus Flare. He's a lech."

"Obviously, our money was well spent on that English degree from Michigan," my mother says archly, shaking her head, completely over this turn in the conversation.

"Okay, creep, then. Or, how about predator? Pompous ass? Any of those better?" I ask. "I know not to use the verb *get*, as it's so lazy, but I'm having trouble describing Marcus. Perhaps you, as a writer and editor, can help me?"

My mother's eyes actually rotate in her pretty head.

"That attitude is exactly why your sister is concerned," my mother says. She brushes off an invisible piece of lint from her jacket. "You expect to get a job just saying whatever comes into that dark trap of a mind of yours? You want to be a success in publishing? You have to learn to edit not only what's on the page but what leaves your mouth."

"Really, Mother?" I blurt. "Perhaps you should take your own advice. Everything that shoots from your mouth leaves shrapnel."

My mother inhales all of the air in Michigan and releases it very slowly to calm herself.

"Okay, you two," my father says in a diplomatic tone. "You both love using words. Often—too often—as weapons. Some are well chosen, some are not. Let's restart, shall we?"

He looks at my mother. She nods to make peace.

"We just want the best for you, Emma," she says.

"I know," I concede. "And I want the same for you." I look at my dad. "So, in keeping with that sentiment, why *was* Marcus here? I feel like you're keeping a secret from me. You know I hate secrets."

"Oh, my God, Emma," my mother says, "you are like a dog with a bone."

"Woof woof," I say.

"He was here as a favor to me," my father says. "He's going

to post about my novel. He has a few million followers, Emma. He does the summer book picks for the *Today* show. I need as many eyes on this book as possible. The Mighty Pages needs the eyes, too. He can provide that."

I nod, though I don't truly believe what my father is telling me.

"Marcus did tell me last night after he spoke that you were… Oh, hold on, I want to make sure I get this right—" my mother pauses as she thinks "—'a very clever girl.' He said you had a deeply personal conversation on the beach. What did you discuss with him, Emma?"

"What does it matter?"

"Tell me," she presses.

"See? There is something going on. I knew it."

My mother stares me down while picking more invisible lint off her body.

"I told him I read his work in one of my classes," I say innocently. "I told him how much I admired his work."

My mother gives me her I-don't-believe-you-young-lady look.

"I told him how much I loved reading on the beach," I add. "He liked that. He said he met his wife on the beach in the Hamptons." I smile at my innocent lie. "Didn't you two meet on the beach?"

I'm good at changing the plot line.

My dad hates that about me as much as my mother hates to discuss that part of her history.

My mom and dad glance at one another again. They look so young all of a sudden just standing here before the lake on a beautiful summer morning. They've gotten a little color on their faces, and urbanites look so much more alive when they get a little sun-kissed.

"You know the story," my mother says dismissively.

"Tell me again," I say. "Please."

"Why?" she asks. She lifts the glasses dangling from a chain around her neck onto her nose to study my intent, then pushes them to the top of her head, a literary headband.

"So I can lock it in my memory, right here, in this moment, forever."

"You're such a romantic," my father says to me.

"Weren't you?" I ask.

They look at each other even longer this time, and, for a flash, I see it.

A spark!

My dad places his hand on my mother's lower back, and my heart melts.

My parents are not demonstrative with their affection like my grandmother was. She could be stern, but she hugged everyone, told everybody she met that she loved them. She wanted them to walk away feeling it, so that even when she was no longer there, they still felt the love.

My mother has always hated what she calls PDAs, admonishing my sister and I for kissing high school boyfriends in public, or hanging on to them at restaurants.

My handsome father tilts his head at my mom, and the distance that separates them defined by the comma of light from the lake between their bodies closes just a touch as my mom leans into him.

"We met on a perfect summer day, just like this," my father says.

"Phillip," my mother interrupts. Her voice is higher than normal.

"Your mother was so…" my father continues, eyes on her.

Suddenly, his phone trills. He looks down at the screen. "I've got to take this."

Moment over.

He steps away to the other side of the deck, and I watch my

mother watching him go, mouth wide-open, a figure in a relief painting staring into nothing, waiting for the unsaid word.

Beautiful?

Magical?

Breathtaking?

Intelligent?

Now forever an incomplete sentence.

She finally closes her mouth, clears her throat and smiles. "Well, we'll see you in two weeks. I've left some cash in your account. This will give you a little alone time to think seriously about what you want to do. I know you have interviews set up already, including the ones with the big five publishers that we helped arrange. But you know we'd love to have you on our team, and I can't wait for you to meet everyone and talk. The decision is yours and yours alone."

Is it ever?

"I know."

"It's okay to let us help you," my mother says. "You're so full of pride."

I smile at my mom. "That actually means *full of crap*, right, Mom?"

"No, Emma, it doesn't. That mouth of yours is going to get you in trouble," she admonishes. "I just know you want to do things your way. You're just like your grandmother. Let us help pave the way for you."

My father returns to find my mother and me staring at one another in a silent standoff. "I obviously missed something," he says.

"My prideful ways," I say. "And my mouth."

"Same old story," he says with a laugh and wink.

"Story as old as time, right, Dad?"

He looks at me curiously, takes a breath and asks, "You didn't like my new book, did you?"

I'm going to kill Jess. But I will give my father points for bravery and honesty.

"I'm so sorry," I say, "but I didn't love it, Dad."

"That's okay. Books affect each of us differently. May I ask why?"

I look at him and my sudden nervousness at being so direct with my own father causes me to shift uncomfortably. My contraband book pops free.

It's too late.

My parents look down at the cover, then at each other before gazing upon me again, waiting for me to answer.

"A little boy wouldn't talk like that," I start. "And there was no one to root for in the book. Every character was icky."

"Icky?" my mother asks. "Again. Money well spent."

"No," I say. "Icky seems fitting." I have to force myself to look at my dad. "I don't want to upset you, but it just didn't work for me. And I don't think you truly love it either."

Silence. For the longest time. But on my father's face, I can see his eyes lift, then drift, and then return to me. He knows I'm right.

"That's hard to hear from my own daughter," he begins. "It always hurts from those you love most. You know how much I trust your opinion."

His voice is quiet, and my heart cracks right down the middle, a fragile vase forever damaged.

My mother is right. My mouth will get me into trouble.

My dad begins to open his mouth to say something else.

"But you can read a book like that?" my mother interjects angrily, her hand gesturing at the novel in my lap.

"I haven't started this one yet," I say, "but I can tell you that I do love this author. Remember how much GiGi loved all of these books? I did, too, growing up, and then I just set them aside. I have to tell you, the acknowledgment and author's note are works of art all on their own. They almost brought me to tears. I just needed to read a book where I could escape for a little while."

"Escape from what?" my mother asks, astonished. "The indignity of spending the summer after graduating college on the beach? Deciding *when* you want to go to work?"

"Piper," my father says. "Don't punish her for speaking her mind."

"And you're grown-up now," my mother carries on anyway. "There are actually grown-up books for grown-up people that your parents publish. *That* book is not a work of art, Emma."

My mother glares at me, glasses now back on her nose, her eyes magnified, blue microscopes trained on my soul.

Would it be wrong for me to push my mother off the deck and into the sand just to shut her up?

She's angry at me for reading a book like this?

I can imagine how angry she'd be to read "The Summer of Seagulls," how ashamed she'd be that her daughter wrote a romance novel.

She would probably require a face transplant if she were pictured in the press holding my novel.

Piper Page! Romance Reader!

The horror!

I think back to college and Virginia Woolf. Part of me would like to send my manuscript to my parents under the pen name E. V. Odle just to see if they would take it—and me—seriously.

Part of me would love to see The Mighty Pages deign to publish my pages. "Who decides what's a work of art, Mom?" I finally answer, trying to keep my voice unemotional. I can hear it rise. I fail every time. "A few chosen critics who despise happy endings? Reviewers who pick apart books because they would have written them differently? Why can't a work of art simply be something that touches your heart?"

"Because *nice* is not extraordinary, Emma," my mother says.

"You sound like a snobbish high-brow elitist," I say.

"Thank you," she says.

I refuse to let her trump me.

"But you're just out of touch with the real world. You know, those people who do their own laundry, push a cart around the grocery store, worry about the price of gas."

"I don't believe our electric car uses gas."

"You're just proving my point, Mother. You've become part of the 'intellectual elite' many people despise in the world today. You have deemed that in order for a writer to be 'literary' she must reflect not the world she sees or dreams, but the world *you* see."

"That's my right as a publisher and editor."

I take a breath. "But you, Mother, believe that world is full of pain, loneliness, hopelessness, awfulness and despair. As a result, only books that mirror your point of view receive the hot fudge sundae with the cherry on top: the *New York Times* reviews and bestseller lists, the Pulitzer Prizes, the National Book Awards, as well as a contract to publish with The Mighty Pages. But those aren't always the books people like to read."

I wait a beat to finish for drama's sake.

"And you're learning that a bit too late, aren't you?"

"*Please,*" my mother says even more dramatically. "Go on. Enlighten us with all the wisdom you've gained the past twenty-two years of life."

My eyes flash.

"I shall, Mother," I say. "When—and more importantly, why—did sentimentality and emotion become curse words in critical review and critical respect, considering some of our greatest books and movies are steeped in sentimentality? Why is saying 'I love you' or a happy ending seen as a literary weakness because you and elite reviewers see it as a cop-out? I personally think that life has beaten the crap out of most of us and made us scared to open our hearts again, which, in turn, has made too many of us unsentimental and believers that arm's length is better than a hug."

My mother crosses her arms. I've hit a nerve. I continue.

"That's why intellectuals often act so unfeeling, isn't it? It's not because they're superior, it's because they're afraid, and so they use their supposed intellect to keep emotion at a distance. But if intellectual distance and posturing is not the best way for humans to navigate life, why is it seen as a strength in the narrative that parallels our existence?"

I pick up the paperback and shake it at my mom.

"Sometimes, we just need a hug instead of a lesson, Mom," I forge on. "Sometimes, we just need to escape. Sometimes, we just need to be reminded that the life and the world will be okay."

My mom reaches down and nabs the book off my lap.

"You're a Michigan grad. This is not what Michigan grads read."

My nostrils flare. "You know, I told my lit professors that they need to add a few more women to their syllabus," I say. "It's 2024, and we're still reading about old men writing about death and war. I suggested they add a little Joan Didion, Nora Ephron and Erma Bombeck."

"And that's why you got your only B minus, isn't it?" she asks. "We've given you every advantage in the world. You can't live your life like it's some Hallmark movie. *This*," my mother says, shaking the book, "is for the masses. We write and publish works of great erudition and originality for bibliophiles. Can you imagine if one of The Swans took a photo of you reading this and posted it online? 'Daughter of The Mighty Pages reads…*fluff*'?"

Bingo! I knew it.

My mother looks at the cover of the novel and shakes her head. "I thought we'd seen the last of these trashy novels. And yet you pluck them from the heap every summer."

I can feel my cheeks flush.

"It's not a requirement for readers to have a PhD, Mother! A bibliophile, by the way, is any person—*any person!*—who has a great love of books, no matter what they read, or where they buy them!" I take a quick breath and continue. "GiGi didn't even finish high school, and she loved to read. That common woman, as you would call her, pushed books in my hands. She read with me. She read with you! She started our love of reading, she started my love of writing. That common woman earned all of this on her own—" I gesture all around me, from Eyebrow Cottage to the swath of lakeshore before us "—that woman of the masses, who never asked for a damn thing her entire life, who never judged a soul, gave you the money to be an elitist snob, so I'd be as careful with the words you use as much as the ones you're so proud to publish."

I grab the book back.

My mother pushes her glasses back onto her head. She smooths the front of her pantsuit and smiles. "Such a beautiful morning, isn't it?"

My mother can only handle extreme conflict in a novel.

"I think I heard the bell ending the first round," my father says, joking to break the tension. He takes a seat and reaches to jostle one of my feet in a gesture of reconciliation.

"You're such a smart young woman, Emma. I worry that you're going to get hurt wearing your heart on your sleeve. You have to bury that emotion just a little to survive today. It's a tough world." He sighs. "You need to plot it out, Emma. Life just can't happen."

Plot it out.

I see myself reflected in my mother's glasses. She's trying so hard not to shake her head at me.

"Why not?" I ask. "Why can't you listen to your heart? Why can't that guide you? It worked for GiGi. After Grampa died, she had nothing, no plan, no education, no job and yet she refused to lose this cottage. She took in boarders, she bought stocks, she purchased lakefront property from those earnings, she made her own way." I stop. "She never had a plan, and she was able to write her own happy ending. She did it by listening to her gut and her heart and that voice that said, 'Don't give up, GiGi.'"

"Your mother and I know you are still grieving her loss," my dad says. "It hasn't been that long. We know how much you loved her, and how much she loved you. She helped raise you. You spent your summers with her while we were working in the city. We get that. But we're your parents, and we only want the best for you. That will never change. If we're hard on you it's only because we love you so, so much."

My father is so adept at emotional CliffsNotes.

I look at my parents look at each other. *Emotional Emma*, they silently say to each other. *Let her get it all out. She'll come back eventually.*

Ironically, my parents were actually once grunge kids. Nirvana fans. They wore baggy cardigans over vintage T-shirts, flannel shirts, baggy jeans, floppy hair. GiGi showed me all the pictures. They were a very literary, post–*Daisy Jones & the Six* couple. They penned poetry. They started The Mighty Pages to publish unconventional work.

GiGi once quoted Linda Ellis—when writing her obituary long before she passed to save us the pain of doing so, a true sign of inner strength and self-awareness if there ever was one—that it is not the date you were born or died that matters, it's the dash in between.

At some point, my parents' dash changed to a dollar sign.

"You're right. I'll get my act together," I finally say to appease them. "I promise to be a *nice* girl."

My mother smiles at my word choice and then lowers her glasses to inspect me. *Is my little girl telling the truth?*

I blink out a tear. It's not a real one. I've been staring into the sun waiting for this moment. "I miss her so much. It still seems like yesterday she was here."

"Oh, honey," my mother coos. She reaches out to caress the air between us with her perfect manicure, a substitute for actually touching me. My dad jostles my foot again.

"That's my Emma," he says.

He stands, pleased at how this scene has ended.

"We'll see you in two weeks," my mother says again. "I'll have Carrie send you some books from our fall list to read. I think you'll quite enjoy them. They'll challenge you."

I nod. "Thanks, Mom."

She heads inside. My father stands and follows her. He stops by the patio door.

"Give my novel another read," he urges. "Great books often require a second read."

"I will," I say with a smile. "I'm sorry. I didn't mean to sound so harsh. I didn't mean it. You're an extraordinary writer." I stop. "And father."

They exit, a trail of Tom Ford cologne and Maison Francis Kurkdjian perfume dissipating in the lake breeze.

I wait for their footsteps to grow quieter, then—when they're gone—pick up the novel to continue reading.

"You're an even better bullshitter than I am," my sister calls from an upstairs window. "You should write a novel."

CHAPTER FIVE

TWO weeks!

I scribble these words in the notebook on my lap.

I look up and think of GiGi.

What is time? What is its value? It must hold more for some-one at eighty than it does at twenty-two? Some of my favor-ite days in college were ones that I could simply waste, going to the Big House for a football game, drinking beer with my friends, ordering pizza at midnight to talk when there was a dating emergency.

Right now, I feel as if time is against me, as if it's against my whole family.

I want to use it as wisely as I can, and part of me just wants to wile it away.

Fourteen days!

Three hundred and thirty-six hours!

I constantly write down any random thought that runs through my head in case I might use them one day in a book.

I have a laptop filled with file folders and dozens of such notebooks, saved since childhood, filled with words, phrases, quotes, memories, scenes, themes, questions I seek to answer.

They are often indecipherable scribbles at midnight. Sometimes, they are nonsense, arrows that point to other arrows that point me to another page where I have simply jotted a question mark.

And yet they are my guide to where I've been and where I'm going.

I jot the following in my notebook.

Obviously, our money was well spent on that English degree from Michigan.

It's a damn good line, delivered by a well-known author, and I'd probably laugh if it weren't directed at me and said by my mother.

Fine line between truth and pain, I add below the quote. *Fine line between life and literature.*

My journals have grown up like I have over the years, from diaries filled with girlish confessions to lined journals filled with things people have said over the years—observations, turns of phrase, colloquialisms…

Painful truths.

…that I have collected for use.

When I told my father as a girl that I wanted to be a writer, he looked me in the eye and said, "Writers are the unicorns of this world."

He told me the world is fascinated by such creatures, and their goal is to capture them—not whole—but a piece of them, their spirit, magic, muse.

"Everyone wants a piece of a writer to take root in them," he said, "just as everyone wants a writer at their parties, until they see themselves—even just a single unflattering glimpse—depicted in one of their books. Then writers are persona non grata."

I can hear my sister on the phone in the cottage.

"The Swans," she is saying, "would love to consider your client's book for promotion."

I glance at my notebook and think of my novel, my sister and family thinly veiled behind fictionalized characters.

Truman Capote once quipped of his infamous feud with the real-life Swans of Fifth Avenue when he aired their dirty laundry, "What did they expect from me? I'm a writer."

Is that really why I've kept my book a secret from my parents and Jess?

Is it a fear they will know I've written about them, even though I'm not shy about hiding how I feel?

Am I scared of losing the rest of my family like I lost GiGi?

Or is it that I know I will be judged yet again, dismissed for my uneducated use of words, held to an invisible standard that shouldn't even exist?

The gull takes flight and sails down the arc of golden sand.

I put down my notebook, pull on my socks and running shoes, and head to the beach.

Often, the only way I can deal with my emotions, past and guilt is to—quite literally—run from them.

There is a perfect stretch of beach that I run nearly every summer afternoon when I'm in South Haven. It stretches from GiGi's cottage to the South Haven Lighthouse.

I have traveled the world with my parents, and there is nothing more beautiful than a South Haven summer. Cottages peek from the dunes, verdant dunes grass framing each scene. South Haven is set on the shores of grand Lake Michigan—our unsalted ocean—at the mouth of beautiful Black River.

South Haven is known as The Catskills of the Midwest for its abundance of natural wonders: water, boating, hiking in stunning state parks, maritime museums, charters, fishing, wineries and fresh fruit.

As I run, I see a family seated on the beach having a picnic lunch. The faces of a little boy and girl are Willy Wonka blue, and they are stuffing fresh blueberries into their mouths.

I wave.

South Haven is famous for its National Blueberry Festival. The festival has been celebrated annually in August for over sixty years. Michigan produces over one hundred million pounds of blueberries each year, and Van Buren County, where South Haven is located on the shores of southwestern Michigan, produces more highbush blueberries than any other county in the nation.

The little boy and girl wave a blue hand back at me.

My grandmother signed our entire family up for the National Blueberry Festival's Pie Eating Contest one year, unbeknownst to my parents. When we arrived in the tent and were seated before blueberry pies, GiGi and I shoved our faces right into our pies.

When I came up for air, my parents and sister were watching us in horror—pies untouched. GiGi—wanting to win—refused to stop, and didn't lift her head until the Blueberry Queen yelled, "We have a winner!"

A strapping farm boy in overalls seated on GiGi's other side—who looked as though a pie might just be an appetizer for him—had his arms raised in victory.

"You were so close, GiGi," I said, pointing at the last bits of crust and filling sitting in the aluminum pan.

"So close," she said, pie falling from her blue face, before belching loudly to the delight of the crowd.

"Why would you embarrass us like this?" my mother, in a crisp white shirt, asked.

"This has nothing to do with you," GiGi said, glancing at me and Jess. "It's a pie-eating contest, not the National Book Award, Piper. Why would you spoil a summer memory for everyone?"

My father handed GiGi a stack of napkins.

"Clean yourself up, Mother."

In one sweeping motion, GiGi took my father's uneaten pie and smashed it into her own face.

"You both used to be so much fun," she added, with great emphasis. "Remember that time?"

My parents stormed out of the tent. I remember watching my sister stand frozen, torn, not knowing which way to run, until my mother yelled, "Jess!"

I felt as if I'd done something wrong, chosen one side over another in a war that would never end.

"What do we do now?" I asked GiGi.

"We get ice cream." She shrugged.

I know I am at fault in our family war. I feel as if I chose GiGi. I feel as if I always chose GiGi.

And now my alliance is down to one.

Me.

My parents don't see the beauty I see here, the beauty GiGi saw. They run as fast from their memories as quickly as I am running the shoreline right now.

How did time damage my parents? I wonder. What is their war?

I look up. A flock of gulls, heads tucked into their sides, are before me.

"Fly!" I yell, waving my arms.

And they do, mini white masts sailing onto the lake.

I do not stop when I reach the lighthouse, which sits at the west end of the south pier at the mouth of Black River. I race onto the long pier, zigging and zagging between walkers and pylons, not stopping until I reach the end.

I bend over at the end of the pier, catching my breath, and turn, stretching high into the air, facing the South Pierhead Light.

The lighthouse was built in 1872. It's a huge tourist attraction. If you googled "quintessential lighthouse," South Haven's would undoubtedly pop up. It's painted bright red and reaches some thirty-seven feet, and it features one of only four boardwalks built to connect the shore to the lighthouse that's still standing.

And it is spectacular.

The elevation provides a 360-degree view of the entire area, water lapping into infinity one direction, beach arcing forever in another.

It looks so similar to the one on the cover of the book I took from GiGi's collection.

I've stared at this lighthouse my whole life.

Whenever I've returned home, it has greeted me like an old friend.

Today, however, it seems more like a stranger, and that makes my heart ache.

How much time do I have left with this old friend?

A gust of wind scoots across the lake, and I steady my body against it on the pier. Gulls ride the current down the beach.

I turn and fly home.

CHAPTER SIX

I come down the stairs after showering, hair wet, and can see a glow of light—as bright as the afternoon sun—emanating from the library.

I round the corner and stop.

It's not the summer sunshine.

It looks as if Greta Gerwig has shown up to shoot an alternative ending for the *Barbie* movie.

Jess is wearing a pink wig, lips and nails the same color, standing before a pink backdrop with lights and electrical cords snaking everywhere. There is only a single object positioned on a stool covered in gold fabric before the backdrop: *Pink Sand Beach*, the brand-new novel from Summer Sparks, the beloved, bestselling beach read author.

Summer Sparks owns summer. Every bookstore in America—be it an independent bookseller, Barnes & Noble, Costco, Walmart, Target, Meijer grocery store—has their own table, if not window, devoted entirely to—of course—Summer.

Summer Starts with Summer!

Put a Spark in Your Summer!

You get it.

The cover features a woman in a wide-brimmed hat, turned away from the reader, of course, which is all the rage these days among book covers—sitting on a beach gazing into a Dreamsicle sunset.

Jess points and directs her assistant, Babe, to move a light.

Although we're the same age, Babe conducts her every move with the drama of one of Capote's real-life Swans.

Jess hired Babe as an intern a few years ago after they met in college at New York University, when Babe still went by her given name, Karen. Karen was a girl prone to wearing hoodies and ball caps, a book always in her hands. She dresses like a fashionista now.

Karen was branded "Babe" when The Swans took flight. Jess thought it would be a cute play on words for marketing, but Karen literally transformed into a junior Babe Paley, calling all the shots for my sister behind the scenes.

And the ultimate irony is that I feel like Karen cum Babe has driven an even bigger wedge between me and Jess, turning our sisterly rivalry into a cold war.

Now the two are inseparable, almost like twins, speaking a language only they understand.

Babe was here for my father's party, but she stayed in the shadows, orchestrating clandestine meetings between authors and agents in GiGi's library. The two even shared a room.

"Hi, Babe!"

She waves.

Olivia Rodrigo music plays in the background, pop rock with angsty lyrics about boys who've done girls wrong. The lyrics are smart, razor-sharp, clever.

I pick up the novel. "What did you think of Summer's latest?" I ask.

"Please don't touch the props," Babe says, grabbing the book from my hands and placing it on a masking tape X that has been marked on the fabric. "We've carefully positioned everything already for the shoot."

Death stare from Jess.

"Why are you doing this today?" she huffs. "Didn't you get it out of your system with Marcus and Mom? Can't we just pretend to get along like we used to?"

"We used to get along?" I deadpan.

"See what I mean?" Jess says. "I'm overwhelmed. One day you'll understand when you have a job. If I were you, I'd actually be paying attention. You might learn something."

Babe trains a light on Jess.

"Such as?" I ask.

Jess turns and folds her arms.

"What it's like to run your own business. What it's like to be responsible. What it's like to build something out of nothing, just like Mom and Dad did."

"You mean like GiGi did," I say.

Jess plows through my interruption. "What it's like to know that you wouldn't make a dime if you didn't do every single thing yourself."

"And how many dimes are you making off of this book you didn't even read?"

Jess unfolds her arms and takes a big step toward me, moving out of the lights.

"That's none of your business."

"You're too ashamed to say, aren't you? But I already know. I heard you on the phone."

"I deserve every dollar I earn."

Jess doesn't raise her voice, but her eyes flash even in the shadows.

"You *deserve* ten thousand dollars to promote a book you haven't even read, from a writer who doesn't even need your help to become a bestseller?" I ask. "Or do you deserve that money because Mom and Dad's authors don't pay you that many dimes and your social media following is shrinking because they don't read the books you're forced to recommend? You do realize readers out there blindly believe you're doing this for free just because you love a book."

"I do love books, Emma!"

"Not more than followers and money."

Jess takes another step closer. Babe watches.

"Wasn't it nice to be in college and sit in an ivy-covered tower where you could discuss a book's themes, an author's intent and the ethics of publishing with a group of like-minded Pollyannas who've never worked a day in their lives and believe they know more—and better—than anyone else?" Jess takes one more step toward me until we're face-to-face. "But the real world is a different place. You have to make decisions. Tough decisions. Decisions you don't like. Publishing is a big business that's evolving every day. Staying on top is like running across quicksand. I'm an influencer. When I help authors, I deserve to be paid well for my expertise and reach just as much as authors deserve to be paid for their talent. And they deserve credit for trying to stay on top or trying to get there. You can create the best widget in the world or build the biggest outlet mall in the country, but no one will buy it or visit if they don't know it exists. I make people know it exists."

"But what about all the other authors who can't pay enough, have enough followers or are seen as competition to the ones on top? Why don't they deserve a chance for their books to be seen and read?"

"You don't even realize how the world works, Emma," Jess says dismissively. "America is a capitalist society. How did GiGi make her money? Land and stocks. I mean, she was John Dutton on *Yellowstone* decades ago. I'm sorry, Emma, but you don't understand a thing about publishing. But you will one day, and then you will see me in a totally different light."

Babe moves a ring light, and its beam hits me right in the eyes.

★ ★ ★

I lift my head, shut my eyes and feel the sun on my face. I open my eyes, and little "floaties"—as round as the inner tubes on which I'm floating with my grandmother—spin before my eyes.

"Book that good?" GiGi asks. "Need a break to consider what the author wrote?"

I use my free hand to spin my tube toward her.

I nod. "My head hurts."

GiGi laughs, a ricochet booming over the flat lake.

One end of a long bungee cord is tied to our inner tubes while the other is anchored to a heavy cooler filled with ice, lunch and drinks. We are floating a few feet into the lake, spinning round and round, reading mass-market paperbacks, our feet bumping into each other's every few minutes. Every so often, I will wrap my foot around my grandmother's to steady myself.

My parents and sister sit with their hardcover books under umbrellas on the beach.

I try to remember the last time they've actually stepped foot into Lake Michigan.

"Got a question?" GiGi asks.

I nod again. "What's free will?"

"Oh, my goodness," she says. "That's a biggie."

My grandma closes the book she is reading, holding it on the edge of her tube.

"Free will is the ability to choose between different possible courses and actions in life undeterred by past events and influences in your life," GiGi says. "Many believe that is possible, others believe that free will is simply an illusion."

"Why?"

"Well, are our wills of our own making, or is every thought, action, decision and intention we have a result of our pasts, those moments in our lives that make us who we are?" GiGi asks. "Do we even have control over the decisions we make, or are they unconsciously already decided for us? Do we have the freedom we think we have, or do we have no control over our destiny?"

I study GiGi's deeply tanned face. When she widens her eyes, white lines show—like the veins on the lake rocks we find after a storm—as if to show me her history.

"Can't you overcome your past to make your own decisions?" I ask. "Like sometimes when you have to put your hands over your ears when the music's too loud to think?"

GiGi glances at the S. I. Quaeris novel I'm reading. Her face explodes into a smile.

"Now, I think you're really considering what the author is asking," she says. "You are so smart, Emma. Such an empath. You feel things more than other people, and that's a blessing and a curse in this life. But you can't study everything in life. Sometimes, you just have to feel your way through it. You have to be a student of life. Being book smart only gets you so far."

GiGi releases my foot and gives my inner tube a little kick with hers. I begin to spin. When I come to a stop, my sister is laughing, tugging on the bungee cord, trying to pull me to shore.

"That's free will, Emma," GiGi remarks, "spinning alone in the world and trying to decide which direction you want to go even when family wants to pull you in a direction you may not want."

I blink, and the floaties slowly become one image: my sister's face.

She is a few inches from my face, lips pink, cheeks red, her breath smelling like the peppermint Altoids she mainlines all day long to hide the smell of the coffee she drinks all day long instead of eating.

Her mouth is still moving. She's still telling me everything I don't know about the world.

I hold a finger to my mouth, silently shushing her like a stereotypical librarian. Her eyes flash in anger.

"America is actually a mixed economy, Jess," I say. "We have the freedom to choose."

"I can't do this right now," she says, turning. "Because I just learned that I have the freedom to ignore you."

"What's your favorite book, Jess?" I ask, taking her by surprise.

"Excuse me?"

"What's your favorite book? It's a simple question."

"Oh, my God," she says. "This game again, Emma? You know my answer."

"Then just tell me."

"*Crime and Punishment* by Fyodor Dostoevsky," she says finally, clearly exasperated.

"Right," I say. "What's your favorite line from the book?"

"It's been so long since I read it," Jess says. "I'm a few years older than you." She smiles at me. "Not that anyone would realize that."

"Surely you remember something from the book that resonated with you. I mean, it's your favorite book ever."

"The themes resonated with me, Emma. Why do you always pick these meaningless squabbles? You're not eight."

"'To go wrong in one's own way is better than to go right in someone else's.'"

"What?"

"That's my favorite line from *Crime and Punishment*," I say. "I remember something from it, and I absolutely despised that book. It's the novel every pseudo intellectual says is their favorite just to impress people because no one has really ever read the whole damn thing because it's torture." I hesitate. "You're just parroting Dad."

"Now look who's judging books."

"No, Jess, I actually read the novel, so I get to have some opinion! I just personally didn't love it. And yet, despite that, I took something important from it. It's actually one of my favorite lines from any novel."

"I don't have time for this anymore," Jess says, turning.

"C'mon, Jess. You never answered my question. What's your favorite novel *really*? Be honest."

"What do you want me to say, Emma?"

"The truth, Jess! It's not shameful to love a book that's never won the National Book Award."

"I have work to do."

"Say it, Jess!"

"*Hollywood Wives* by Jackie Collins!" Her voice booms across the library, the title echoing off the covers of my parents' esteemed collection of books. "There! Are you happy now?"

Her lips are trembling, the wings of a pink butterfly in motion.

"I am," I say.

"Stop it!" Babe looks at both of us, shaking her head.

"Do you know I always dreamed of having a sister growing up?" she says in our stunned silence. "I always hated being an only child. I just wanted someone to talk to, someone who would always have my back, someone who would always be my friend. You two are pathetic. One day, you'll realize that you need one another, and it will be too late. I hope to God it's not, or else—despite having a sister—you'll end up exactly like me—an only child for the rest of your lives."

Babe glares at me until I meet her gaze.

I cannot look at Jess. Babe grabs her cell. "I'm ready whenever you are, Jess," she says.

For the first time, I can detect the slightest waver in her voice.

Jess moves in front of the lights and places her hands around Summer's novel.

"It looks like you're choking the book," Babe says.

Jess glances at me and slowly loosens her grip.

"Three, two, one..." Babe whispers, pointing at Jess to signal she's recording.

The Swans go live, and I glide from the library in silence.

CHAPTER SEVEN

The Mighty Pages office is housed in a renovated triplex in SoHo.

I stand on the sidewalk and look up at the etched door.

The building is a beautiful old brownstone that has been tuck-pointed and renovated with new windows. You'd think Carrie Bradshaw might come bounding down the stairs in Gucci, a latte in her hands, late for an appointment.

My parents wouldn't publish Candace Bushnell novels, though.

Perhaps that is why—in a world where romance and feel-good books have come storming back—The Mighty Pages is not as mighty.

But they do have a knack for spending money like Carrie.

My parents scored this place in a cool neighborhood long ago, just as it was becoming gentrified, when funky art galleries and restaurants lined the narrow cobblestone streets. And they got it for a steal—I mean, relatively speaking as nothing in New York is a bargain—just like they did their prewar apartment on the Upper East Side. A woman had died in it. That didn't scare my parents off the way it did other potential buyers.

I think a terrible thought: *my parents have always seen someone's death as opportunity.*

GiGi made a lot of money in her life, but she was not ostentatious. She never showed her wealth. A perfect summer day for her was reading on the beach, burgers on the grill and a glass of wine at sunset. She didn't need a second home to go to in the winter months, though she could have afforded it. She didn't wear designer labels. She preferred to make dinner at home in jeans than reservations at a fancy restaurant.

Her difficult childhood, early loss and bringing in boarders kept her grounded.

My parents do not talk money with me. I wonder if they even talk about it with each other.

"It's gauche to discuss numbers," my mother is fond of saying. "We have people for that."

However, they sure like to spend it, and I'm starting to wonder if their "people" know how to count. I don't know how they convinced GiGi to spend a big chunk of their inheritance to fund this life in the city, and I will never know why she agreed to it. The taxes and overhead on this building as well as the taxes and monthly association fees for their apartment must be eating a big hole in the remaining trust.

Does that worry me for selfish reasons? Of course.

Does it bother me that they have treated GiGi's legacy with such disregard? Yes.

I've seen the articles in the trades. The Mighty Pages is struggling. Sales are down. Profits are down. Costs and expenses are up. The big publishers have gotten even bigger, gobbling up rivals and smaller presses like Pac-Man.

But all publishers are facing challenges. All have had downturns in sales post-Covid. But publishing also loves to wring its collective hands. I mean, it wasn't too long ago that publishers believed the success of ebooks meant the certain death of print books.

But everything comes full circle.

I suddenly remember the call I inadvertently received from the Student Accounts department my junior year after GiGi passed away, stating I was not a student "in good standing" as my fall tuition payment was delinquent.

Alarmed, I gave them my parents' number, and my mother assured me it was just an oversight due to the stress and magnitude of dealing with GiGi's trust.

I believed her, but then I overheard my parents—after a few glasses of wine that summer—discuss selling the cottage.

I again attributed it to grief and stress, to their growing love of the Hamptons and desire to leave Michigan behind.

But now it's hard not to wonder if my perfect parents' publishing house is really just a house of cards right now, and one strong gust is going to crush the King and Queen of Diamonds.

I move out of the way of a swarm of shoppers.

Although most tried-and-true New Yorkers tend to avoid this packed neighborhood and its luxury designer boutiques on most summer days, my parents' building would sell for twice what they paid.

But they could never do that. They will always try to save face. Image is everything.

They started their publishing house in SoHo long before Gen Z associated SoHo with the cool kid SoHo Houses that have popped up all over the US.

I head up the stairs, stop to look at my reflection in the glass of the front door.

I smooth the wrinkles out of my blouse. I am wearing nice slacks, flared at the bottom, a sensible shoe for walking in New York, and a pretty pink blouse with some of GiGi's vintage jewelry.

I feel as if I look very "literary" just for my mom. Yes, I am understated, but for my New York interviews, I want my résumé and answers to serve as my style guide.

I open the doors, a whoosh of cool air, classical music and the scent of lemons washes over me.

My mother is near.

I head to the front desk. It's a massive, old wooden desk—like one that Mr. Potter sat behind in my grandma's favorite Christmas movie, *It's a Wonderful Life*—polished until it gleamed like a Chris-Craft boat. This is Herman Wouk's writing desk. You can still see his words etched in the wood from his handwriting.

He was the Pulitzer Prize–winning author of *The Caine Mutiny* who became known as the king of television miniseries in the 1980s with his monumental war novels, *The Winds of War* and *War and Remembrance*. My father was a huge fan of his—an author he deemed the perfect mix of literary and commercial—and he paid a pretty penny to buy the desk and have it shipped to New York.

"May I help you?"

A young woman who is as glammed up as a Kardashian at the Met Ball greets me.

"Hi, I'm Emma. I have an appointment to see Piper Page."

She doesn't acknowledge me as much as she looks through me. I'm human glass. I look at the name plaque sitting on the desk.

"Elizabeth?" I ask sweetly to get her attention. "I'm here for an interview."

She taps on her computer screen with a very ornate nail.

I suddenly think of my sister's nails and the New Age GiGi advice she gave me long ago about women, money and manicures.

"Old money—even young women with old money—doesn't deign to do anything crazy with their nails. No extensions, no color, maybe a beigey-pink color," Jess told me. "That's because your nails equate to your money. You don't have to scream to be noticed."

I look at my nails. They are beigey pink.

"New money," Jess said, "will go for a little more attention, perhaps an Aprés extension on her nails with a chrome dusting to mimic the sparkle of the sand on a summer day. They don't have the history of their great-great-grandmothers whispering in their ears to tone it down."

She concluded: "For women seeking attention—read, a man—nail art is life. She lives for color in order to be noticed, and her nails would be, let's say, a DayGlo yellow with painted white daisies on the tips."

I glance at Elizabeth's nails as she pecks away.

Yellow with daisies.

I'm shocked my mother isn't aghast at this, but Elizabeth would stop a man—or angry bill collector—in his tracks.

The irony is that Jess is newer money pretending to be old money in order to appeal to a group of want-money women who aspire to be her.

I wait for Elizabeth to tell me that my mother will be coming, and ask if I would like something to drink while I take a seat. But my generation is not the best at interpersonal communication. She is still focused on her screen, then the ringing phone and then her cell.

Finally, she looks at me, a long once-over, and I feel like I want to disappear into thin air, become ether. She nods toward the reception area.

I turn.

The first floor of The Mighty Pages is more Louis Vuitton showroom in Paris than "reception area."

It is artful.

Illuminated shelves are filled with books, covers out. These are The Mighty Pages' current books and biggest sellers.

I take a seat on a luxurious leather couch that rests atop a Persian rug that covers the gleaming wood floor. Little side tables with beautiful reading lights and the newest releases are placed just so.

French doors lead to a generous—by New York standards, anyway—patio. At night, this space is transformed into an ethereal literary hot spot, the trees wrapped in lights, tuxedoed waiters serving champagne, hushed talk about the book business. Sunlight shines through the trees, glints into the office and the book covers look burnished in gold.

"Emma!"

I turn, and my mother glides toward me.

She is wearing a short sun-yellow capped-sleeve dress that's so formfitting it looks as if she stepped into a can of curb paint. Her hair is tousled perfectly. The sun glints off her ears.

My mother is wearing GiGi's favorite diamond stud earrings.

She looks so happy and confident.

This is my mother's world, my mother's home, my mother's city, far away from Michigan, where she's always seemed so uncomfortable, her past a relentless deer fly that tracks her no matter how far or fast she runs.

Small-town Piper Brown wanted to turn the page on her life.

And she did.

Deep inside, I'm so proud of her for that. Everyone deserves to be the heroine in their own story, and my mother certainly wrote herself a grand tale.

I only wish she would tell *that* tale to the world.

"You look gorgeous as usual, Mother," I say.

"Thank you," she says, holding out her arms to hug the space between us and kiss the air.

Elizabeth stands and rushes over.

"I see you've met my daughter Emma," my mother says. "Elizabeth is a rising senior at Columbia."

Elizabeth's heavily made-up face droops as she puts the pieces of the Page puzzle together.

My...daughter... Emma.

"Would you care for anything to drink?" she now asks me.

I shake my head.

"Elizabeth has taken very good care of me," I say.

Her eyes widen.

I smile as if to say, *I have your back. Women should always have each other's back.*

My mother beams and claps her hands together, pleased. When she does, it's as if she is actually squeezing fresh lemons.

"You smell as amazing as you look, too," I add, turning to my mother.

This pleases her even more. She cocks her head, taken aback by my compliments.

"Well, thank you, sweetheart. I'm wearing Acqua di Parma, one of my summer signatures. I think it's the ideal summer perfume. Rich in Sicilian citrus."

"Oh, so lemony with the hidden power of preventing scurvy," I say, recalling the joke I told to the bartender that now seems so long ago. "That should be their new advertising slogan, don't you think?"

Elizabeth blinks.

"My daughter has a very unusual and self-deprecating sense of humor," my mother says. "You'll never quite get used to it, no matter how long you're around her." My mother winks at me to soften her insult.

"Especially if she decides to work with us," my mother adds.

"Do you want to be a writer?" Elizabeth asks me.

I open my mouth to answer, but my mother cuts me off at the pass. "Elizabeth is a very gifted writer, Emma," she says. "She hopes to be published soon after she graduates." My mother beams. "I'd love for us to be her home."

If this were *Yellowstone*, Beth Dutton just stuck a knife into her unsuspecting victim's heart.

"Oh?" I manage to say. "What are you working on?"

"I'm doing a modern take on *Lord of the Flies* but with women," Elizabeth says.

"I think that's called high school," I joke.

She looks at me, bewildered.

"There's her odd sense of humor again, Elizabeth. It's like liver pâté. It's deliciously rich and unusual, but it takes a while to accustom your palate to it."

My mother smiles at me.

"You keep working on that new classic," my mother says to Elizabeth, "after hours, of course."

She takes me by the elbow—almost as if I were a shopping cart—and guides me through the office.

I notice Elizabeth and the staff at The Mighty Pages watch my mother. Here, she is what people see, a beautiful blur of yellow.

A perfect paragraph in motion.

The ultimate book cover.

"Let's take the stairs," my mother says, glancing down at my stomach. "We can always use the exercise."

A beautiful staircase—original to the triplex—leads to the second floor, where sales, marketing and publicity have their offices. Up we go to the third floor, which is home to the editorial staff and my parents, who decide which books will be published.

My mother escorts me to her office, which is, again, generous by New York standards. She takes a seat behind her desk.

"I'm amazed you can sit in that dress, Mom. How did you even get to work?"

"Fashion is pain," she says. "Just like great art." My mother pulls a pair of dramatic cat-eye glasses off her desk and peers at me. "Speaking of which… You look…" She stops. "Professional."

"Thank you, I think."

"Did Lucy dress you?" she asks.

I stayed with Juice last night instead of my parents, who had an event.

"Those Wall Streeters don't know how to dress," she continues. "Boring suits. They could afford anything but still look like wallpaper."

"No," I say. "I barely saw her. She works 24/7."

"Well, Lucy has always had an incredible work ethic," she says. "What happened to all those outfits I sent you for these interviews? You brought those, right? I think you will have time to change after this, don't you?" My mother smiles. My mom has a magical way of not only saying something positive that is a really a putdown but also a way of posing a question that is really a command. I term it the *question-command*. My mother never asks a server, *Does a house salad come with the entrée?* She says, "A house salad comes with the entrée, correct? I couldn't imagine it any other way!" She never gives the listener a chance to respond. Never gives an option.

"I did bring them," I say. "They just seemed a bit impractical for getting around the city."

"A first impression is everything," she says. "And it's our reputation on the line here, Emma. We're recommending you. A sommelier doesn't recommend Cupcake wine. Right?"

I nod.

"If you just made a bit more of an effort." She stares at my ponytail. She won't give it up. I think of what she said to me just a couple of weeks ago: *She's like a dog with a bone.* "And do something with your hair. This isn't your sixth grade class photo."

Thanks, Mom. Now I feel completely motivated for my interviews after this mother-daughter pep talk.

She lowers her glasses and peers at me.

"So?" she asks. "I trust the last two weeks in Michigan gave you time to reflect after our last conversation?"

I hear the muffled sounds of the city outside, and thoughts of the last two weeks run through my head: the sound of my sister's luggage being dragged through crushed gravel followed by the rev of a car engine. She left without saying goodbye after our fight.

I then spent the rest of my time fine-tuning my novel and reading S. I. Quaeris novels.

There is a photo of our family on my mother's desk, turned away from her so that she doesn't actually look at the image all day but instead gives the impression to the world that she loves family.

A passage from the most recent novel I read swirls in my mind as I stare at our family:

I didn't read much until my husband died.

I found him in his favorite chair on the patio, overlooking the lake, his coffee still hot. I thought he was asleep at first. He did that a lot when he read. Just nodded off. I hated to bother him as he got so little time to relax. I wonder now if that time I wasted thinking he was dozing might have saved his life.

Perhaps, in all irony, it saved mine.

Believe it or not, I wasn't much of a reader until he died. In fact, I didn't pay much attention to what he read until that day. I knew he was gone, so I pulled the book from his hands, pulled up a chair next to him and read to him, like I often did in bed.

Yes, I was in shock, but also shocked by what he was reading: a summer romance, filled with hope and happy endings.

A man reading romance.

But that's what he needed, right?

Hope.

That's what we had, right?

The world's greatest romance.

Until death do us part.

At the age of thirty-five.

This book was now what I needed.

It was a thread of hope.

A belief there would be better days. That I, too, might again have a happy ending.

And so I read the chapter he was reading just so he would know how it ended.

And then the next so I would have a reason to stand up again.

Then I kissed his cheek—whispered, "I will love you forever"—and called 911.

No wonder GiGi loved this author so much. It's like they were writing our family story.

"Emma?"

I snap out of my memory. My mother is glaring at me, her head tilted dramatically. She lowers her glasses to inspect my sanity.

"Your father and I are elated you are doing all of these interviews," she says. "Especially with us! But you must remain focused, do you hear me? It's like you went into a catatonic state just now."

"Yes," I say, nodding. "I will be focused. I promise. I'm just a little nervous."

She seems skeptical but produces what one might call a smile. "That's natural, but you're a mighty Page! Remember that. You come highly recommended by me and your father. That's like receiving a golden key."

"I know."

A door closes down the hall.

I remember what I used to believe as a girl about a golden key and what my father told me.

I look at my mother.

Do I have what it takes to unlock my own success?

"Emma!" my mother snaps. "Do you need some coffee to wake up?"

I shake my head.

She continues.

"I know I've prepped you on all of this, but you're going to be speaking with Diane, who's head of publicity, and her team.

Then at eleven, you're meeting with Ingrid at Penguin Random House, then with HarperCollins at three." My mother glances down at her calendar. "Oh, and dinner with Vivian Vandeventer at eight." She looks up. "That one's all your own doing, God help you." She laughs. "Then Friday night your father's special event in the Hamptons."

"What?" I ask.

I give her a questioning look.

"I didn't have that on my calendar," I continue. "I was going to enjoy the weekend with Juice and then head back to Michigan. Isn't his book tour over?"

"It is. Let's just say this is a rather important moment for your father and The Mighty Pages. A large group of esteemed authors and publishing insiders and influencers will be in attendance." My mother smiles that smile, which seems to imply, *And we'll need you on your best behavior. No more Marcus Flare flare-ups.* "But we're getting ahead of ourselves. Mostly, we're thrilled you're speaking with us today. You know how much we would love to have you on our team. You would be a tremendous asset, just like Jess."

Her voice trails off, the word *was* left unspoken at the end of the sentence.

My parents are still miffed at Jess, although they would never say that to *me*, for taking their idea and then growing The Swans into her own business. They cannot say a word, however, as it would jeopardize their own list. My parents need Jess's influence. It is now the influencers who influence what we buy, and we follow along like sheep.

"I know," I say. "And I'm excited to speak with everyone. I certainly feel like—after the last two weeks of consideration—publishing is where I should be."

I should actually say, *Trying to get my book published is where I should be spending my time*, but instead I nod my head with conviction.

"I agree, Emma. Your love of books is the number one thing needed in our business." My mother smiles at me and pretends to fix a hair on her head that is not out of place.

"But a love of books isn't everything."

I turn at the sound of my father's calm voice. He is standing at the door.

"Hi, Dad."

"Hi, honey. It's good to see you." He leans down and kisses me on the cheek. "As I was saying, a love of books must be merged with a mind for books."

"Publishing is BART," we say in unison. "Business meets art."

"Exactly," my father says with a laugh. "Heard that before?"

"Only about a million times."

"In this business, your heart will want to publish every amazing book you come across, but that's not possible. There's a business model for what works and what will sell. You have to follow your gut *and* your spreadsheet. That's the key."

Again with the key.

A soft knock on the door.

"We're ready for Emma whenever you are."

Diane has been a book publicist forever and head of publicity for The Mighty Pages the last couple of years. My parents hired her away from Hachette hoping some of her magic and influence might rub off on their titles. Diane has worked with every author of note for the last two decades, and the trades are saying my parents not only paid a small fortune to hire Diane but also need their fall and winter titles to be big successes to right the ship.

"Emma's ready, aren't you?" my mother asks, standing.

The question-command.

I nod.

"Right this way," Diane says.

CHAPTER EIGHT

"Thanks for taking time to meet me for lunch."

"We could have gone somewhere a little nicer."

Juice and I are seated by the window at a tiny table in a claustrophobic pizza joint.

"You know I gotta get my fix when I come to New York."

I fold my slice and inhale it.

"You got a little grease right here," Juice says, taking a napkin and dabbing my chin. "There you go."

"Thanks, Mom."

"Speaking of mom…" Juice starts. "How is Piper?"

"Piper's Piper," I say. "As usual. She would have preferred to have you as her daughter. She said you had an incredible work ethic this morning."

"I need time to process that," Juice says with a laugh. "I'm sure there was a dig in there, too."

"You could dress better," I say.

She looks down at her navy suit and shrugs.

"I'll give her that. So? How are your interviews going?"

I shake my head.

"Remember when we went to Vegas on spring break that

one year and saw Cirque du Soleil?" I ask. "There was that one woman who spun plates at the top of ten-foot poles not just in her hands but balanced on her chin, forehead and nose."

"Yeah?" Juice scrunches her face, not understanding.

"That's what book publicity is like."

She laughs.

"Every publicist I've talked to has to juggle so many books," I continue. "At the bigger houses, they might be working on four books a month."

"A month?"

I nod.

"You have to read the books, develop the press materials, pitch the media, help build an author's brand if they have yet to establish one, set up their book tours, oversee a budget, all in a world with shrinking book coverage," I say. "The saddest thing is it's really all a self-perpetuating circle, like a literary Shark Week."

Juice laughs. "Meaning?"

"Nearly every penny of a publicity budget—not to mention all the publisher's power—goes to celebrities or famous authors whose books are already going to be bestsellers, simply because they have been paid a lot of money for their books and contracts. Those celebrities and authors are going to be the ones who get those huge media interviews, like on *Good Morning America* or *Today*, or reviews in the *New York Times* or *People*."

"Because their names will bring ratings or sell copies," she says. "Money begets money."

"Exactly!" I say. "Which will then sell tons of copies of their books. It's not fair. When do the little guys get their shot?"

"Emma, it's just the way American business and consumerism works, you know that. How many great small businesses out there work their tails off every day just to break even, and then there are the few celebrity companies and IPOs—from Goop to tequila—that use their brand power to make millions off something that's probably no better than the others. It's not fair, but it's the way it is. You either play the game or you break the cycle and become your own brand."

"I hear you," I say. "And publishers say the money that big authors and celebrities make allows them to publish books that might not otherwise have a chance, but it's just so difficult to listen to these publicists talk about all these incredible new books they're publishing that will never break out, and yet every debut author believes their book will be a bestseller. They expect *you* to make it a bestseller. And the saddest thing is all the incredible books these publishers have to turn down because they either have something similar on their list or because they run it through a model and see that it likely won't make a dime for them, even if it's an incredible book."

I shove the rest of the slice into my mouth and continue.

"I just don't know. I feel like it might consume my soul, just like I'm doing to this pizza."

"Spare me the sob story, Emma."

I nearly choke.

"Excuse me?"

"It's life after college." Juice shrugs. "I hate to say that your sister and parents are a little bit right, but they are. We're done sitting in classrooms and dorms theorizing about life. We're *doing* life now, and it kinda sucks and yet it's super exciting. I mean, I don't *have* a life at the moment. I work anywhere from eighty to a 120 hours a week as an investment banker, Emma. I don't sleep. I barely eat. And yet it's everything I ever wanted. This is why I worked so hard in college."

"Why do I feel so lost, then?"

"Because you're scared of your dream. It's natural to worry about whether you're good enough or if you'll make it. Sometime, the dream is easier than the reality. You want my advice?"

"No."

Juice laughs, reaches out and takes my hand. "You just talked about the importance of becoming your own brand, Emma. Become your own brand!"

She looks at my baffled expression.

"Get your damn book into the world. It's good. Really good. I think so, and I don't even read books. Gin thinks so, and she does read, and we wouldn't BS you. If your book sucked, we'd tell you to go ahead and be a book publicist, or go into corporate communications, or do what your sister is doing and just make a shit ton of money and be happy with that. But that's not you. The Emma I know and love always puts it on the line for the world to see, so put it all on the line. Get it out there. That's why *you* worked so hard in college. Your dream can't breathe unless it has oxygen." She squeezes my hand. "Neither can you."

"But my parents," I say. "They'll *hate* it. They'll hate me even more. I mean, what if you told your parents you wanted to become an actress right now."

"My Asian American parents would kill me," she says with a laugh. "But that's not my dream." Lucy lets go of my hand and wipes her mouth with a napkin. "And your parents don't hate you."

"They will hate my book."

"No, it just might be the thing that challenges their very calculated little world, just like you do. And just like GiGi did. And don't you ever stop doing that or I won't be your friend anymore."

"My sister hates me, too," I say. "I can't lose you."

"Aww," she says.

"And I might need a place to stay after my family disowns me."

Or loses everything.

Juice laughs. "You *are* my sister."

"What if I fail?"

"You will. We all fail," she says. "But that's the wrong way to approach life. I always prefer to think of making your dreams come true as 'What would you do if you could not fail?' You have to look at life in a new way."

"I'm beginning to realize that the way we view the world and our family is very different than when we were little," I say.

"And isn't that nice?" she says. "You can't blame your parents for creating a facade that makes you feel safe and protected. And you can't blame your parents for only wanting the best for you and challenging you to achieve that either. I'm glad mine did. I feel sorry for those kids whose parents didn't give a damn, or let them opt out of life and just stare at their phones. Parents are supposed to care."

"I hear you," I say. "But what if it is all a facade?"

Juice cocks her head at me and takes a swig of Diet Coke. "Meaning?"

"Meaning…" I stop, searching for just the right words. "What's the difference between a facade and a lie?"

"Are you writing a mystery now?" Juice asks.

"I don't know yet," I say. "Just saying what I'm feeling out loud. I know it doesn't make any sense. This pantser is trying to figure out a lot of plot holes."

"Well, if you need me for anything—ever!—know I'm here. I love you."

"I love you, too."

I stand, and we hug in the middle of the pizza parlor.

"You know, we just passed the Bechdel Test, like in college," I say. "Two women talking about something other than men."

"You know why?" she asks.

"Why?"

"We're not drunk."

She laughs and hugs me again.

"PS, you smell like garlic," Juice says into my ear. "Get some mints at Duane Reade before your next interview, which, by the way, you're going to nail. You can do anything you dream."

"My mother smelled like Italian citrus, I smell like garlic," I say. "Such is my life."

"Good luck," she says. "You'll probably be home after I'm in bed, so don't wake me up unless it's really good news or you've brushed your teeth and gargled."

She hugs me tight again and kisses my cheek

A construction guy ordering lunch yells, "That's hot, ladies! Do it again!"

At the same time, Juice and I flip him off.

CHAPTER NINE

This ain't no pizza joint.

Liber is as wondrous, mysterious and powerful as my dinner companion.

"Right this way, ma'am."

An impeccably dressed front-of-house staffer escorts me to a table in the dimly lit, historic restaurant whose name means "Book" in Latin. It's the place where every literary star of note eats, where agents take authors to celebrate a new deal. Publishers wine and dine novelists whose books just hit the *New York Times* bestseller list. Industry insiders gather to share the latest dirt over forty-dollar martinis and old-school wedge salads.

I take a seat at the table, which is covered with a white tablecloth. A candle flickers in the center. Delicate china gleams.

A tuxedoed maître d' appears from the shadows to retrieve the napkin off the table and place it gently across my lap just as another server materializes to fill my water glass.

The maître d' clasps his hands behind his back and says, "Your server will be with you immediately. But may I let him know if you'd care for a drink to start?"

He gestures to the wine list on the table.

"Yes, thank you," I start. "I mean, no, I can't. I'll wait for my guest."

The maître d' bends at the waist and whispers into the cool, hushed air, "Ms. Vandeventer will most certainly have a drink." He pauses. "Or two."

He stands and gives me the slightest hint of a smile.

"I think I should wait," I say. "Proper etiquette. I'd hate to be dismissed before I'm even interviewed. I mean, you can't show up drunk to an interview, can you?"

"With Ms. Vandeventer? Yes!" He winks. "Good luck, ma'am."

"Thank you."

He is gone like a whisper.

I fidget with my napkin and nervously sip my water. I've grown up in atmospheres like this and yet have never felt entirely comfortable in them. Everyone has such an air of confidence. They believe that they belong here. I always felt a bit like the rescue puppy who got tossed in with a bunch of pure-bred dogs.

In prep school, I was not as popular as the pretty girls. I was newspaper editor, the girl the other girls begged to let them make over, the girl in every teenage romance movie who simply needed to take off her glasses and let her hair down and then—*boom!*—she was every guy's fantasy.

In college, I was not *that* girl—the stereotypical one who was rushed by every sorority on campus—despite my mother's urging to do so. She pulled strings to get me invited to the best parties, even accompanying me and wearing the appropriate sorority letters—but after she left, I didn't rush any of them.

"Fine, don't have the quintessential college experience," she told me, the same words she said about my time at prep school. "Be an *independent.*"

She said the word as though she were tasting bad milk. *An independent.* Alone in the world. I know she simply wanted me to have the experience she wanted and never had, but she could never say that to me.

And now?

She wraps herself in the cloak of independence—I mean, isn't that what she is? The leader of an indie publisher that claims to think and do things differently—or is that merely a front? Has my mom always just wanted to sport sorority letters?

I feel a tap on my shoulder.

"Ms. Vandeventer?"

I turn and begin to stand.

"Jess? What are you doing here?"

It's my sister standing behind my chair.

"I have a meeting," she says. "I take it you kept your meeting with that monster VV?"

"You want to talk about monsters?" I ask. "I'm not the one who left Michigan without saying goodbye. Your departure was more shocking than Brexit."

She ignores me and looks around the restaurant. "Welcome to Liber," she says. "This is sort of my second home."

I try not to roll my eyes. I want to be a bigger, better person. I'm just not there yet. When they return to their rightful place, I notice Marcus Flare sitting in a booth across the restaurant.

"You're not...?" I start. "And I'm the one meeting with a monster?"

"He needs to stay on top," Jess says. "I'm willing to help."

"Have some dignity, Jess. He's gross. He's like Godzilla but with more bluster."

"He's misunderstood."

"Climate change is misunderstood," I say. "Marcus Flare is not misunderstood."

"I almost didn't recognize you," Jess says, changing the subject. She looks me up and down. "You actually look nice."

"Gee, thanks," I say. "You sound like Mom."

"No ponytail. Nice makeup." She eyes me up and down. "Speaking of Mom, did she dress you?"

I nod. Jess laughs.

"She's good," Jess continues. "You should keep this going. It's nice to see you looking and acting so professionally." She stops. "At least to everyone but me."

"Ah, women supporting women, as Babe said. Just look pretty, ladies! That will get you the job instead of your talent."

"God, you're so *sensitive*. I was just trying to compliment you. And it's true. It may be a double standard, but it's a standard for a reason." Jess looks around the dark restaurant. "I'd wish you good luck, but I don't want you working in a coven with that witch."

"And I'd wish you luck, too, but I don't want you working with publishing's version of Harvey Weinstein."

"You're making all of that up in your head," Jess says. "He's never been called out publicly."

"No, he's never been caught because he has all the power and money." I glance over at him. He waves sweetly. "And something is going on between Mom and Dad and that troll. I don't trust him, Jess. And you know I have good instincts."

"You have a vendetta, Emma. Let it go. Business is business. I mean, you're the one dining with a snake."

"Better than dining with a snake pretending to be a dove," I say. "I prefer people who are as they appear."

Jess glances around the restaurant nervously. "Well, I better go before…"

"*I* arrive?"

Vivian Vandeventer—legendary head of her eponymous literary agency, VV Lit—appears out of nowhere. Her look has never changed over the years. She is Katharine Hepburn come to life as a lit agent, wearing her trademark black pantsuit, Valentino belt wrapped around her shockingly tiny waist—a gold V buckle letting you know who she is lest you ever forget—

plus a diamond ring the size of Saturn that she received as a gift from Liza Minnelli for taking her on as a client and making her memoir a monstrous bestseller.

And, speaking of planets, her hair is flame red. In dimly lit Liber, VV's head resembles Mars. She is wearing Iris Apfel frames that engulf her face, and a kooky collection of necklaces that makes you wonder if it's her age that is making her bend slightly at the waist or the sheer weight of her jewelry.

"Vivian," Jess says, voice chilly. "I'm shocked I didn't hear you coming."

She leans out to air-kiss her.

"Still kissing oxygen, are we?" VV says. She grabs Jess by the shoulders and plants a kiss on her cheek.

Jess's eyes grow into saucers, and she starts to wipe her cheek but stops.

"What can I say?" VV says. "I'm like cilantro. Some people love me, some people hate me." VV looks at me. "Your sister and parents have never had a taste for me."

Jess places her hand on my shoulder.

"Don't get in bed with the devil, Emma."

"Ditto," I say.

Jess looks at VV. "Vivian."

She turns and struts across the restaurant like a lioness on the prowl who happens to be wearing an impossibly high heel. When she's seated, VV blows a kiss to her and Marcus Flare.

"Well, that had all the warm fuzziness of a slow dance with Dracula," she says. VV glances over at my sister's table again. "I bet they're having red meat tonight. Extra bloody."

Our server appears.

"Oh, hello, Lionel. My usual please. What will you be having, Emma?"

"Oh, water's fine."

"Water is *not* fine," VV says. "You're not a fish. Although we do drink like them in publishing. And you're a new college

graduate, so don't play all innocent with me. I may have graduated when prohibition was law, but I still drank."

"I'll have what she's having," I say.

"Very *When Harry Met Sally*," VV says with a laugh. "If you
have two of what I'm having and can still hold a conversation,
you're hired!"

I laugh. "Thank you for doing this. I really appreciate it."

"So let's get real," she says as the waiter scurries away. VV
puts her elbows on the table, places her head in her hands and
stares at me through her glasses, her eyes enormous as if she's
using a TikTok filter to magnify them. "Are you here as a fuck-
you to your parents, or are you serious about working with me?"

I choke on a mouthful of water.

"I would never do that."

"Sure you would."

She raises an artificially dark brow over the rim of her glasses.

"Yes, I would," I say, "but I'm serious, which is why I reached
out to you against their wishes. Look, I don't know exactly what
I'm doing right now, or where I'm going, but I love books. I've
loved books my whole life, thanks to my grandmother. I love
the books and authors you represent. And I feel like, despite
your history with my parents and The Mighty Pages, it's perhaps what I should be doing."

She eyes me closely and then sits back in her chair.

"I didn't know your grandmother personally, but I feel like
I did," VV says out of the blue.

I look at her, not understanding.

"You didn't know?" she asks, looking pensive. "Were you
even born yet? Time flies. Well, your parents trotted out her
hard-luck history when they started The Mighty Pages—grew
up poor, lost her husband at an early age, ran a boardinghouse,
opened her home to those in need and those wanting to read.
It was quite the story in the entertainment rags." VV lifts her
hands and her voice.

I think of what I shared with Marcus Flare on the beach.

Why did he act like he didn't know any of this?

"A new publisher that really cares about books," VV continues, releasing a throaty laugh. "Your parents left out the part that she was richer than Croesus, of course, but they raised a ton of money and got top-notch clients. I still have no idea why your grandmother would give Phillip and Piper so much money on what I always considered to be a vanity project, other than she really did love books and perhaps saw this as her legacy. But she was never involved with it. They never wanted her involved, it seemed to me. Now methinks that your parents' literary baby is all grown-up but still having trouble walking. Your parents present quite the image, as you know. Your mother could break her leg, but she'd still wear Manolos and strut about town without so much as a limp." She glances over at Jess and Marcus. "And I wouldn't be surprised if those two were cooking something up to keep The Mighty Pages relevant. I'm just worried your parents are going to get desperate and toss out the baby with the bathwater." VV laughs again. "That's an idiom much older than you are, my dear, considering you're still a baby."

My heart races. VV senses my anxiety.

"Don't worry," she continues. "I don't know anything at all. People think that publishing is all about books, but it's really one-third gut, one-third gossip and two-thirds booze."

Our server arrives with our drinks.

"Your martinis," he says. "And, by the way, your math doesn't add up."

"Neither will my tip, Lionel, if you keep eavesdropping and taking so long with my drinks," VV says. "My God, is the bartender now squeezing his own potatoes to make the vodka? Is that the new trend these days? I can hardly keep up with the fancy ice cubes and cocktails that smoke."

"No, Ms. Vandeventer," Lionel says. "He had to wait for the truck to bring more vodka. You drank it all last night."

VV tilts her head back and roars like a dragon.

"God, this is why I love Liber. Now, you go to restaurants and pay two hundred dollars for a chopped salad and glass of shitty rosé, or the martinis are in two-ounce Dixie cups, and the server never returns to your table but expects a 30 percent tip." VV looks at Lionel. "I want the sea bass, and Emma will have the same. And tell the chef you have my permission to break his arm if he cranks that saltshaker more than twice, got it?"

"Yes, ma'am. Thank you."

VV lifts her glass.

"To women who do it all on our own!" she says. "Men talk about pulling up their bootstraps, but we still do it wearing SPANX, hose, bad bras, high heels…" VV glances over at Marcus "…and outwitting men who stand in our way and never give us credit. Cheers!"

"Cheers!" I say.

I take a sip of my martini. VV laughs.

"Your eyes are as big as mine now," she says.

"Strong," I cough.

"Well, I like strong drinks and strong women. No time in this life for anything less. And I like to know the people I work with. I want them to be genuine and honest. I mean, I ask the same of publishers who are merging, how will that impact my authors, their books and lives? I ask every editor and publisher I consider working with if they're committed for the long term. Your parents have always been a bit like portraits behind museum glass."

I nod in agreement. VV continues.

"I want the editors and publishers with whom I work to love not simply the books I send them—with all their heart and soul—but also my authors. I think your parents never liked me because they felt I was crass, but I'm just direct, probably like your grandmother was. No secrets. I tried to send them some submissions that were both literary and commercial in the beginning, but they were always very coy with their plans and budget, and very modest with their advances. I understood that. They were just starting out, you don't want to overpay, and I was willing to support that vision. But then I saw the way your parents lived, their offices, and I didn't like the dichotomy. I remember a lunch I had right here with your mother, and I asked her directly about that, and she looked at me as if I had two heads and told me that business was much different than personal life. She told me VV must stand for 'very vicious.' But all I wanted was complete transparency. They stopped responding to my calls and emails, so I returned the favor. I refused to send any of my clients to them. I mean, *everyone* knows your parents are a bit snobbish in life and literature. They enjoy being elitist. The parties, the authors, the hobnobbing. But I think they've forgotten why they got into this in the first place: A chance to make a difference."

VV glances over at my sister and Marcus.

"And I worry eventually they're going to have to get in bed with someone who will promise to keep their lights on, but it will actually be a dark day of reckoning for them. So, my dear, why are you here? Against all their wishes?"

"I'm not the cover of a Mighty Pages novel," I say.

"What are you, then?" she asks.

"The insides," I say. "All the words and feelings. Art is pure. Isn't that the state which we should always seek to exist?"

Vivian shakes her head, smiles and lifts her glass.

"In theory," she says, "but life is like the East River. We may fall into it all clean and shiny, but we get dirty fast. Do you want to know what's pure in life, Emma? Good liquor, great books and Ivory soap. That's it. Oh, and love, if you can swim through all the pollution to reach it."

She takes a big sip of her drink and continues.

"Now, let me get down to brass tacks. You'd be an agency assistant, Emma, a job that doesn't pay shit, but it does pay big in feels. And I know you're loaded, so you don't really need the cash right now, and that's a win–win for VV." She laughs. "Seriously, I pay well when you earn your stripes. You have to work your way up, Emma. Essentially, I'm a gatekeeper for the publishing industry. And you'd serve as *my* gatekeeper. Agents seek to find the best books they can and rep the best authors they can. My career has been built on finding those books and authors before anyone else, or taking on great books other agents have rejected. You'd be a first read for authors who are querying VV Lit. Are their query letters professional? Do the initial pages of their manuscripts capture your interest? Are they right for whom we represent? Do their manuscripts have potential? If so, you forward to me or one of the agents on my team."

"Wow, I didn't realize all of that," I say.

"Wow is right. It's a lot of not-so-glam grunt work. You'd follow up on contracts and royalty payments, serve as a liaison with our foreign rights agents, work closely with the publishers and editors to make sure they have what they need." VV peers at me through her glasses. "But you'd get to read. A lot. And possibly discover the next big thing. You'd learn the business from the ground up. You would work your way up eventually to become an agent like me. You'd get to publish the books you love. And I think that's exactly what you want. You received a great education, you already know the business, and I respect anyone who bucks their family and follows their dream. You're like a unicorn."

Her choice of words fills my stomach with both butterflies and rocks.

"I've always been fascinated by this side of the business," I admit. "It's sort of the magical part readers don't know exists."

"It is magical. To read a book before anyone else and see its potential. Oh, Emma, I still get goose bumps when a first page calls to me." VV leans across the table, her necklaces landing loudly atop her bread plate. "So how did your interviews go? What do you think of the world of book publicity?"

"They were…" I stop, searching for just the right word. "Enlightening."

"Meaning?"

"It just feels frustrating that a certain few books and authors get all the attention and money, and the vast majority of wonderful books do not," I say. "They just disappear into the ether."

"No, they don't, Emma. Bestseller lists and public notoriety are certainly wonderful for branding and sales, but they don't define the worth of a book." VV smiles as if a distant memory has returned. "That book was still written from the heart of a writer who had a story that called to her, a story she had to write to make sense of the world. That book was still published with great love. It will remain forever, long after we're all gone. And if it touched even one reader somewhere, if it changed her world in some way, isn't that enough? I wish the world were equitable, but it's not."

"I feel being a book publicist today is kind of like going to battle with a pencil as your sword and one shiny nickel as your shield."

"Another great analogy," she says. "Maybe you should be a writer."

I duck my head.

"Oh, God," VV says loudly, causing tables of diners to turn and look. "You do, don't you? You actually want to be a writer. That's why you're here!"

VV lifts her arm and snaps her fingers, shockingly and surprisingly loudly. Lionel looks over, and she points at her glass.

He nods.

VV looks at me, so intensely I feel as if I'm going to disintegrate under her fun house–eyeball gaze.

"Just please tell me you're not that daughter of a famous singer who goes on *American Idol* and is tone-deaf," she finally says.

"I don't know."

"You do know!" she says. VV points at her head and her heart. "You know it here, and you know it here."

She wags a finger at me and polishes off her drink. I look at mine. I've barely started.

"I've already written a novel. I think it's good."

"Would your grandmother love it?"

I nod. "I think she would," I say. "It's about family, and sisters, and romance. It's really an ode to her and the books we used to read together. Good ol' summer beach reads. I've read fiction my whole life, and I've never read characters like I'm writing. Characters like my grandma. Kind, hardworking women who get knocked down by life and get up and soldier on with as much faith, grace and dignity as they can muster."

VV stares at me. "Then I think I need to read it."

"Oh, no. I didn't ask you here to run an endgame."

"I know that," she says. "But I still think that's ultimately why you're here. Call it irony, or call it fate. In the end, we all forget the origin story." VV lowers her glasses and gives me a close once-over. "Speaking of origin stories… I have to ask you the same question again. Are you here as a fuck-you to your parents, or are you serious about working with me? Either as an assistant or writer?"

"I already told you…"

"No, be honest. Do you want me to try and sell your debut so you have your full-circle gotcha moment? I mean, it's a great story." VV alters her voice to sound like an ominous narrator. "Author's parents own a snooty publisher, but it's a book her parents wouldn't publish because they look down on its genre, so author approaches enemy agent to sell debut, agent—being the world's best agent—performs Hail Mary, and author screams in family's face, 'Told ya so!'"

"No, no," I stammer. "I promise."

"I think I struck a nerve," VV says. "So, aren't you the least bit curious about what your parents think about your novel? I mean, they're writers. They're publishers. They're…"

"I don't think I could survive that criticism."

VV reaches out and takes my hand.

"Emma, this world is filled with judgment, especially for writers, from those we love and those we will never meet," VV says, still holding my hand. "Philip Roth once told a young Ian McEwan, 'Write as if your parents are dead.' You cannot authentically share your soul and story when you are always looking over your shoulder." VV glances over her shoulder. "And, by the way, Philip Roth could make Marcus Flare look like the Pope in real life and fiction. His female characters never interacted with one another. They always needed a man around to give their scenes intellectual heft."

"The Bechdel Test," I say. She looks at me. I explain.

"Another reason I should read your book."

"I just don't think it's the right time."

"Emma, sweetheart, you're young, but Bret Easton Ellis and Mary Shelley were only twenty-one when they published their first books, which I think did just fine, don't you? Margaret Atwood and James Joyce were twenty-two. Capote and Hemingway were twenty-four, and Joyce Carol Oates was twenty-five. Shakespeare and Alice Walker were twenty-six. Emily Brontë was twenty-nine. On the other hand, Laura Ingalls Wilder was sixty-five and Frank McCourt was sixty. What I'm trying to tell you via this literary history lesson is that you need to realize there is *never* a right time," VV says. "There's no right time to fall in love, there's no right time to die, there's no right time to write a book, there's no right time to let your baby bird test its wings and fly into this very scary world. That book should just explode from your soul, and it will at the exact right time." She takes a breath. "But, Emma, there is always a wrong time."

"How do you know the difference?"

"You'll know," she says. "You'll know when to hit Send *if* you have the courage. But just know most never do. And just know those two times—the right time and the wrong time— will blur the longer you wait. One night, you will walk into your kitchen decades from now, bone-tired, and glance at your microwave clock. It will be 10 p.m., and then it will finally hit you."

"What will hit me?"

"That it's too late."

VV's second martini arrives, and she dives into it as if it were a pool filled with vodka.

"How would you describe your novel, Emma?"

"It's women's fiction," I say. "Heartfelt family fiction." I look over at Jess and Marcus Flare. They are in a serious conversation. "But I hate to categorize it."

"Readers really don't care about genre and things like that," VV says. "Our business does. Publishers need a way to market and sell books in this oversaturated world. Readers do have favorites—genres, authors, themes, characters—and we need a way to hang our hat on those hooks. It's a catch-22."

"But why are books written by men typically classified as fiction or literature, and when women write a book it's called women's fiction, chick lit or romance?"

"Because this is a patriarchy!" VV yells. "Didn't you learn that in college? In one of your classes? From your grandmother?"

VV nods over at my sister's table and continues.

"Look, Marcus Flare is the patriarch of feminism, a wolf dressed in sheep's clothing. Take it from me. I've been around long enough to see it all, and I can sniff a wolf a mile away. He is someone who thinks he's too macho to write romance or women's fiction. It's a story older than Greek mythology. Although I'm sure ol' Marcus there would likely claim he invented that genre, too." VV winks at me. "So what are you going to do to change all that? This world doesn't need another shy, demure woman. It needs someone who believes in herself, stands up for herself, just like your GiGi. It needs someone who speaks and writes her truth and changes the way we think about books that are written by, about and for women." She takes another sip. "So, Emma Page, what are you going to do to change all that? Talk is talk. Action is action. I'm a woman of action. Do you want to be an agent who finds those writers, or do you want to be one of those writers?"

I stare at her, then at my sister and Marcus Flare.

VV begins to hum the music they play during Final Jeopardy.

"I want to be one of those writers."

"Cheers, then!" she says. "If it's in your blood, like vodka is in mine, there's nothing you can do about it. You're cursed." She lifts her glass. "And blessed."

I lift my glass and take a huge sip. And then another until my martini is mostly gone.

"Well, you certainly drink like a writer," VV says with a laugh, motioning for Lionel to bring me another. "Now, let's go write your happy ending, shall we?"

CHAPTER TEN

I am stopped at the velvet rope at Le Pompeux in Sag Harbor by a single, very tan finger sporting a clear nail polish. The young woman to whom the finger belongs has her head down, analyzing a list on a screen set on the hostess stand. She is wearing a simple black dress.

There is a long line of people behind me that seems to stretch from Sag Harbor to Montauk. They are all waiting to be granted entrance into my parents' favorite Hamptons haunt, a French restaurant famed for its food and service.

It is the place to be seen.

And my parents like to be seen.

In fact, they have rented out the main restaurant for my father's book event—a mystery wrapped in an enigma—and this line will likely only grow more restless when they realize they will have to wait hours just to get into the bar.

But they will.

Everyone wants inside.

My generation is no longer patient for things that take time— a garden, a homemade meal, a long book, love—we want Instacart, Uber Eats, a clickbait headline and Tinder.

But, ironically, we will gleefully give hours of our precious time on this earth for a few seconds of acceptance and attention. We will give our souls for the perfect picture.

And, ironically, *I* want inside.

My conversation with VV bounces in my head like the lights on the water.

Is my book actually good enough to get published? Is it good enough to secure VV as an agent?

Moreover, do I really, really want my dream at the expense of my entire family?

As my father told me so long ago, fear is the one thing that holds a writer back from achieving her dreams.

A voice knocks me from my thoughts.

"Emma Page?"

The hostess looks up, and she's instantly familiar.

"Gretchen?" I ask. "Gretchen Wright? What are you doing here?"

"Hey, Emma! I'm working here this summer," she replies, grinning. "My family lives in New Jersey. My grandparents have a home on Long Island. *Not* the Hamptons." Gretchen looks at me. "Which is why I'm working here."

I smile. "What a small world. From the University of Michigan to here. You have one year left right?"

She nods. "How are things in the real world?"

Gretchen says "real world" with a deep voice and ominous tone as if she's playing with a Ouija board.

I laugh. "Very, very real."

I tell her about my recent interviews.

"Weren't you writing a book in college?" she asks. "You discussed it in our Women's Lit class. It sounded amazing. About sisters, women, and why we don't stand up for and empower one another, right?"

I'm flattered. "You have a great memory."

"I think I remember because two guys hit on me after class that day," she says. "And two the next class."

I laugh.

"We need that book in the world," she continues. "Like, now."

"Thank you," I say. "It's finished, I'm just trying to figure out that fine line between life and literature."

Gretchen scans the snaking line that seems even longer now. A man with silver hair appears behind Gretchen. I recognize him instantly as Chaz Billari, the billionaire owner of the restaurant. He does not recognize me. He leans close to Gretchen and says, "Keep the line moving, sweetheart." He is so close that I can see her hair move with his breath.

I feel an arm around my waist.

"Marcus Flare," Gretchen mutters.

The velvet rope separating the real world from the one inside rises as if it's made of helium, and Marcus steps inside.

He turns to me.

"We don't wait in lines, Emma," he says. "Haven't you learned that by now?"

Before I can corral my shock at his appearance, he is gone.

"You *know* him?" Gretchen asks quietly.

I can see the pieces click together in Gretchen's mind.

"Why didn't you say something," she says, shaking her head. "Phillip and Piper Page. This is your parents' party, isn't it? I'm so embarrassed."

"No, I'm the one who's embarrassed," I mumble.

Gretchen turns and scans the restaurant. Mr. Billari is handing Marcus a glass of champagne.

"This is why we need your book in the world," Gretchen whispers with a wink.

"You're late."

My mother appears from inside the restaurant, looking absolutely luminescent in a monochromatic pantsuit with shiny lapels and white square toe mules. She is wearing only the jacket, no blouse underneath, her long neck and collarbones gleaming. Her pants are trendily high-waisted and flared.

Her comment, as usual, is also a question-command: *Why are you late?*

She's mad at me for not arriving even earlier to endure this pain.

"That's why I didn't say anything," I say to Gretchen with a smile. "Mom, this is Gretchen Wright. I went to school with her at Michigan. She's going to be a senior next year, and she wants to be a writer."

"It's nice to meet you," my mother says, extending her hand.

"You, too, Mrs. Page. Your daughter is quite talented."

My mother's face actually registers surprise despite—from what I can tell—a round of Botox and filler earlier today.

"Thank you," she says. "We're quite proud of her."

Her statement comes out more a question than statement.

"Good luck, Gretchen."

My mother ushers me inside as if she's trying to shoo a hummingbird that accidentally flew inside the house. I move inside as Gretchen says, "Next? Name?"

"You're late, young lady," my mother scolds.

"Planes, trains and automobiles," I say to her with a laugh.

She stares through me, not realizing that I watched that movie every Christmas with GiGi.

"We offered you a car," my mother says.

"I know," I say. "I'd rather do it on my own."

She shakes her head.

"Hi, sis."

Jess sashays past Gretchen and the velvet rope and into the restaurant, resplendent in a gold jumpsuit that shows off every curve.

"You're Emma's sister?" Gretchen calls as she struts by, quickly scanning the list to check off her name.

"Unfortunately," my sister says, pivoting on impossibly high

heels. She turns and winks at me. She looks like a golden Greek goddess. Her face sparkles. Gold is literally woven into her hair.

She air-kisses Mom and disappears inside.

But she's not late. I am.

My mother pulls me through the plush reception area and into the ladies' room. She does a quick scan to make sure we're alone and then begins to brush wrinkles out of my dress.

"You took the Jitney, didn't you? In a five-hundred-dollar dress that I bought you?"

I don't answer. She shakes her head again.

"The Jitney," she says again, spitting the word. "Good Lord, Emma. It's a *bus*. You might as well have taken a Greyhound here. Actually, it looks like you rode a horse." My mother looks at me. "Why didn't you just ride out here with us?"

"And spend the day here?" I ask.

My mother laughs. "Oh, right, it's so horrible here in the Hamptons. The indignity. How awful for you."

My mother drops her hands.

"I know you think the Hamptons are pretentious, Emma, but it's really you that is. You can no longer behave as if you're above everything. You're no longer in college. The real world is filled with hard work and compromises. Take a hand when it's offered." My mother's voice echoes off the richly wallpapered walls. She shakes her head, reaches into her bag and pulls out a tube of expensive concealer. She dabs it under my eyes. My mother studies my face closely. "You're hungover, aren't you?"

"I told you that woman is nothing but trouble," she continues, her dabbing now more of a jab as she mutters, "VV. Very vicious. Ugh."

"I actually had a wonderful dinner and meaningful conversation about my life and career."

"And you can remember it? Well, that *is* an accomplishment." My mother drops the concealer back in her bag and pulls out a tube of lipstick. She puffs her lips into an O as instruction for me to do the same and says, "Jess saw you at Liber. Said the drinks were flowing the entire night."

"Did she happen to mention that she was dining with Marcus Flare?" I ask. "If you want to take issue with your children's dinner companions, I think you should start with her. And why is he here again tonight, Mother? He's like a roach."

"Marcus is a legend."

"Marcus is a pompous ass. And Jess is a sellout."

My mother grabs my chin a bit too tightly. "Hold still please."

She finishes the lipstick and then retrieves a brush and a tiny can of hairspray from her purse.

"You could go to war with everything in your handbag," I say.

"I am," my mother says, brushing and spraying, my hair going from flat to voluminous in the mirror before me.

"Well, Jess did say you looked lovely last night," she says.

This is my mother's olive branch.

"Have you come to any career decision?" she continues.

I know not to say anything yet.

I shake my head. "But getting closer."

"Well, maybe hearing your father this evening will seal the deal. Our publicity team was very impressed with your intelligence and your love of books. I think we'd make a great team. And you could learn our business from the ground up."

"Thank you, Mom," I say, the throb of a headache beginning to return.

"I'd also love to get you back in the city," she says. "I know how much you're missing college. I know how much you miss GiGi. It would be wonderful to have you near us again and, of course, you'd get to see Lucy all the time here."

"Thanks, Mom," I offer as my own olive branch. "Those have been big life transitions."

My mother rubs the air around my shoulder.

"I know, sweetheart." She flicks at my hair, holding the tiny can of hairspray before her. "I'd love to be able to tell everyone tonight that you've joined our team. The optics would be ideal as this is such a big night for us."

I begin to ask why, but my mother continues.

"We have so many incredible families here tonight to support The Mighty Pages. It's been a tough year in publishing as you know. We need a shot in the arm."

I again open my mouth to ask what is going on tonight, but my mother fogs the room with a final spray.

"There," she says.

As the air in the bathroom clears, my mother is smiling. Her unsaid words—*There...now you look presentable!*—dissipate with the fumes.

"Let's go charm the wallets right out of their Birkins, shall we?"

It is a dreamily *Gatsby* evening on Sag Harbor.

The doors to Le Pompeux patio are open, and the lights of the yachts blink on the water beyond. People spill from the restaurant to the patio. The plush banquettes are filled with those who not only need to be seen but also yearn to be noticed. They only look up—and occasionally stand—to greet those who meet or exceed their imagined criteria.

There seem to be four waitstaff for every guest, and no glass goes unfilled after more than a few sips of champagne, rosé or red wine. People nibble on caviar, seared sea scallops, crab and avocado, and Le Tartare de Thon, yellowfin tuna with a sesame dressing on a wonton crisp.

This is *not* my grandmother's idea of an appetizer. She would be serving ham and pickle pinwheels.

How much did this shindig cost? I wonder. And what is the reason for this Met Ball-esque occasion?

I watch a hedge fund manager who could be Jess's great-grandfather chat her up. He owns a $150-million estate on the ocean in Southampton. His hand moves steadily and stealthily down her back, and she giggles as it does. Her voice lilts, and her words sound like a question—an invitation. My stomach lurches.

The hedge fund manager's wife is watching all of this. She has had so much work done that she resembles a trout. Her face is frozen, her eyelids barely able to close, her mouth cavernous, and only her jaw moves up and down. She has published a string of self-help books over the years, ironically promoting good nutrition and yoga over plastic surgery to stay young—and, now, she is trying her hand at a novel.

She needs Jess's help so, of course, she will turn a reworked eye.

"Champagne?"

I turn, and a young server is standing before me with a bottle wrapped in a white cloth.

"I'm just having water tonight," I say. "Thank you."

A glass chimes, and Chaz Billari walks to the back of the restaurant—framed by the patio, boats and water behind him—and welcomes everyone.

"You're all very lucky to be here tonight," he says in an accent that I can't quite place. "You know this is the hardest reservation to get all summer!"

People laugh and applaud.

"But instead of being surrounded by Real Housewives and movie stars, this evening we're blessed to be in the presence of literary heavyweights. Phillip Page is here to discuss his latest novel, and a new vision for his esteemed publishing house, The Mighty Pages."

I turn and look at my sister and mother, but they have their backs to me, watching Chaz.

"Phillip will be in conversation with none other than the world's number one bestselling author, Marcus Flare!"

I am taking a drink as Chaz finishes the last part of the sentence, and I aspirate water.

A few people glare at me as if I should be removed from the premises.

I see Jess out of the corner of my eye. She finally looks at me. *What the hell?* I mouth.

She smiles.

I sear a hole into the back of my mother's skull until she actually turns. I raise my brows, silently asking, *Why didn't you tell me earlier?*

She ignores me.

Marcus Flare slithers in front of the crowd and raises his glass of champagne.

"To books!"

"To books!" the crowd responds.

Without any semblance of embarrassment or humility, he launches into his usual schtick about inventing his own genre and how he is single-handedly saving publishing.

I roll my eyes so many times I think that they might get stuck in the back of my head, and—despite my residual hangover—I cannot deal with this, and grab a glass of champagne from a passing server and slam half of it to calm my escalating nerves.

"And now," Marcus says with his usual flare, "the man of the hour, Phillip Page!"

My father takes a seat next to Marcus, and they discuss their writing processes, tropes they don't like and their favorite authors.

"Your greatest influence?" my father asks Marcus.

"Let's answer at the same time!" Marcus offers. "Three, two, one, go!"

"Dostoevsky!" they both say.

The crowd laughs and applauds.

The internal gag I intended manifests itself into a booming sarcastic "HA!"

My mother does not look, but she shifts her body just so, an intended move to let me know how gravely disappointed she is with me and my childish, brutish behavior.

I finish my champagne as their conversation swings to the state of publishing.

"I'm trying to keep the entire industry afloat, but my back hurts," Marcus jokes. "Where are we headed, Phillip? What does the future of your esteemed house look like?"

"As many of you are aware, this has been a hard couple of years for the publishing industry," my father says. "Retailers are taking fewer books overall. Costco has nearly eliminated its once grand book section." He stops. "For those of you who don't know, Costco is a place where you can buy things in bulk or purchase a hundred-ounce box of cereal."

Many in the crowd gasp, I kid you not.

"Can you even imagine?" Marcus asks.

I still can't with this jackass.

My dad continues after the attendees stop laughing.

"It's becoming more and more expensive to produce books, and as costs rise, we try to do the same work with fewer people to save money." My dad takes a dramatic pause, looking into the eyes of every person in Le Pompeux. "We are a small but mighty publisher. We require the voices of independent booksellers and independent publishers more than ever these days to bring new voices and important books to the forefront.

"But the landscape has changed," he continues. "The Big Five continue to dominate publishing. It's hard for us little fish to compete for big authors. We cannot afford to pay what they do, and our promise of personal attention doesn't seem to sway today's writers as it did in the past. But that doesn't mean we give up, or refuse to compete. No, we think outside of the box."

My father nods at Marcus.

"As a result, I'm excited to announce a brand-new venture with The Mighty Pages," Marcus says. "I will continue to publish my books with PRH, but I am thrilled to launch a new imprint, Books with Flare, with The Mighty Pages next year."

The crowd bursts into applause.

The world around me ceases to move. Voices sound as if they have been slowed.

"I will be publishing books like mine," Marcus continues. "I will be looking for brand-new writers—authors like myself—who are inventing, or redefining, genres. And we need your support! We are seeking investors who want to keep independent publishing alive and well!"

As the crowd breaks into applause, I beeline through Balmain dresses and Louboutin heels to make my way onto the patio. I lean against the railing of the deck and gasp for air.

"Dramatic much?"

Jess is standing a few feet away, arms crossed.

"You knew about this, didn't you?"

"They can trust me," she says.

"This makes me sick. *He* makes me sick. Why?"

"It's business, Emma. We need a shock to the system to stay relevant. To stay afloat."

I look at Jess, my eyes imploring her for more of an explanation.

"Things aren't great," she says. "They're actually worse than what Mom and Dad are saying or the trades are reporting. We need Marcus. This is actually fortuitous."

"But we're in bed with the devil."

"A very rich, powerful devil," Jess says. "He is capable of saving us, Emma."

Jess takes a deep breath and seems to calm herself. She is as gold and shimmering as the glass of champagne she's holding. "At some point in your life," she says, "you are going to find yourself in an extremely difficult position that not only impacts your future but also the future of your family." Jess pivots and looks into the harbor. "You will have to make a choice."

"No, I won't, Jess, because the decision will already have been made."

She turns.

"I will always choose my family," I continue. "Do you ever wonder why I'm so outspoken, why I act like such a brat sometimes? It's because every decision this family has made since GiGi died has taken us one step further from who we are. The Pages are not an image or a logo, we're not simply socialites like The Swans who glide effortlessly through life. We are a family. And though we hurt each other, we should trust one another and love each other more than anyone else in this world."

"Do you trust me, Emma?"

"Do you trust *me*, Jess?"

The hull of a boat moans in the harbor.

Neither of us answers.

Jess heads back inside to the throng.

I stand alone outside for the longest time. I shut my eyes and listen to the cacophony of old and new money blend with songs from French singers Édith Piaf and Charles Aznavour.

"I take it you didn't care for the big announcement?"

I open my eyes. Marcus Flare is leaning on the railing beside me.

"Why do you keep seeking me out?" I ask. "You're either taunting me or you desire my approval. You're like that kid on the playground who pushes everyone down and then cries because no one will play with him. What do you want?"

"I don't play games," he protests, "and I don't need your approval, but your family does. You should be grateful to me. You should be genuflecting in my direction. I'm literally saving your ass, young lady. Why don't you show me more respect?"

I think of VV. "People either love or hate cilantro," I say. "Different tastes."

He laughs.

"Well, I'm saving your family's business with my good name

and taste. I'm saving your family's future with my influence and money." He waits for me to meet his gaze. "I'm saving *your* future if you'd just open your eyes—and mind—and see that."

"My eyes are wide-open," I say. "And my future doesn't need saving."

"You do realize The Mighty Pages is drowning in a sea of red, right? Let me be clear with you since it's obvious your parents have not. They have a couple of years left before someone sweeps in and buys them before they go belly-up, a year if they publish another of your fatuous father's novels."

I start to speak, but Marcus holds up a finger to silence me.

"I know your family has money, but how much is left? Do you even know? Do you even realize how close your parents are to losing everything, and yet they glide along as if their facade will protect them from doom. You do not strike me as the type of girl who would be happy, say, living in a studio apartment and writing press releases for an ambulance-chasing law firm."

"Why would that be my future when I have a degree from the University of Michigan?" I ask.

"An *English* degree."

"English majors can do anything," I say. "Do you know what's ironic?"

"What?"

"You actually do seem like the type of man who would call a grown woman a girl and expect her to do worse than you simply because of her gender." He actually snickers. "Can we just cut to the chase since I'm so out of the loop? What do you want with my family? Why would you want to be a part of a small publisher that seems like such an antithesis to your entire being?"

"Antithesis? Big word," he says, lifting a dark brow. "That's an easy answer." He looks around. When the coast clears, he whispers, "I want to destroy your family."

His tone is casual as if he's ordering an iced coffee.

My heart stops. I look at him to make sure I heard him clearly.

"You heard me," he says, nodding. "But this little secret is just between us for now." He smiles and then says in a sad, little voice, "Now I am that kid on the playground you just described, and it's all your fault."

He takes a step toward me. I square my shoulders.

"Why us, though? Who are we to you?"

"We," he says, pointing at each of us, "are more alike than you know."

"Enlighten me, then, please," I say. "Right now, you just sound like a villain from those old movies who twists his handlebar moustache while tying the heroine to the train tracks. Why would you want to hurt my family? You don't even know us."

"That's quite an old movie reference for such a young..." he catches himself "...*woman*."

"Old soul," I say. "Thanks to my grandmother. You would have hated her, too. I'm a lot like her."

"So, I take it I'm the villain, and you're the heroine?" he asks. "Perhaps you have the characters backward."

"I don't," I say. This time, I take a step toward Marcus. "But you haven't answered my question. Why us?"

"Because your family is a bunch of hypocrites," he says.

"I totally agree," I say.

Marcus's eyes widen in surprise.

"You make a fortune already," I continue. "I'm sure your current publisher would even consider launching an eponymous imprint for you. Why do you need The Mighty Pages? It makes zero sense."

"A great author never gives away the surprise ending so early in the book, don't you know that?" Marcus says. "Let's just say I not only know a good business opportunity when I see one, but I also know a secret about your family that they would never want revealed for, well, vanity's sake. Because of that, I want the Pages to be like the Joads in *The Grapes of Wrath*. You read that book in your fancy college, didn't you? I want you all dirt poor and living in a hovel in the middle of nowhere, totally depleted of resources and ego. And if you ever say a word about our little talk with your parents or sister, I will have you in that motel sooner rather than later, and—believe me—it won't be a comedy to any of you. I think this whole experience will be good for all of you. Who knows? Maybe one day you'll write a memoir about it. You can call it *The Page Turner*," he cackles. "I won't publish it, of course, because you are—and will always be—an ungrateful little bitch."

I can't believe I'm hearing this.

Marcus crosses his arms in satisfaction.

"Go ahead and cry. I love to see women cry."

I can smell his musky cologne.

Of course, he would need a scent that made him smell more like a man.

"You don't know me very well at all, or my family. The Joads were strong and proud. I may be able to call my parents hypocrites, but no one else has that right. And that's why the female characters you write are such failures. You don't understand women at all. We don't cry. We get even." One step closer. "You've poked the wrong hornet's nest, Mr. Flare. For every ounce of hurt and pain you intentionally inflict upon my family, I will return to you a thousandfold."

"There actually might be a writer in there somewhere," he says, jabbing his finger into my shoulder. "An unpublished writer, of course. Now be a good little girl and fetch me a drink."

As if on cue, a server passes by. I nab a glass of champagne from his tray and toss the contents into Marcus's face.

I hear the crowd gasp. I didn't realize until this moment that a large group was watching our interaction.

Marcus licks his lips.

"At least your parents had the good sense to serve Veuve this time," he says with a smile. He leans in and whispers, "They'll be drinking Budweiser out of a can this time next year."

Marcus grabs a napkin, dabs his shirt and jacket.

"She can't handle her liquor," Marcus announces loudly as he rejoins the party. "Why do young women think they can hit on me. I'm a happily married man!"

The crowd titters. Someone takes a photo of me.

"What have you done, Emma?"

My mother is at the front of the gathered crowd. She remains composed, so much so that even the glass of champagne in her hands does not tremble. And yet I see a sea of rage in her pupils.

"Mom, I can explain."

"Please, Emma," she hisses. "You always want to explain after it's too late. I can't tolerate one more lie that leaves your mouth. You insist on meeting with VV, who hates our family, and then confront Marcus Flare, who only wants the best for us."

Marcus stands behind my mother, absolutely beaming.

"He's not what you think, Mom."

"Stop!"

My mother's voice echoes across the harbor. She takes a breath.

"Only you make me like this," she says. "You were drunk last night, according to your sister, and you're inebriated again. This isn't college, Emma. It's real life. I think it's best if you just leave. Now."

"I'll head back to the city tonight, stay with Juice and fly home tomorrow."

My father comes out to the patio and slides his arm around my mother's waist.

"No," my mother says to me with a definitive tone. "We're staying at the Cutlers' mansion on the ocean in East Hampton. They're out of town, and it's breathtaking. I think a good night's sleep is just what the doctor ordered."

"I agree," my father says in a hushed voice. "You've been under a lot of pressure with these interviews. We should talk in the morning after you've had some rest."

"This was supposed to be a celebration, Emma, a huge night and a new start for our family and The Mighty Pages," my mom says. "What is *wrong* with you?"

Her eyes implore me for an answer. Marcus hovers behind her. *Well?* he mouths.

I keep my mouth shut.

Good girl, he mouths, walking back inside.

"We have a surprise for you tomorrow that just might change your mood and perspective," my father says.

"I don't know if I can handle another surprise."

"Emma," my mother warns.

"Go get some rest, sweetheart," my father says.

He leans toward me to give me a hug and a kiss, but my mother touches his arm, and he stops.

"Please, Emma." My father's voice is raspy.

"Fine," I finally say.

"This is all good news, Emma, I promise," my father says as I leave. "It's a new chapter."

I walk back into the restaurant. As I pass by Marcus Flare, now sequestered in a VIP area cordoned off by a velvet rope, he covers his face with a napkin and yells at me, "We're all out of champagne!" People laugh.

I move past Jess, who shakes her head, and Babe, who looks at me sadly, and out the front door of Le Pompeux.

"You're leaving already?" Gretchen calls when she sees me.

I slow my pace and turn.

"I think I'm on the wrong side of the rope," I say.

"There's always a rope keeping someone out of a place they want to be," Gretchen says.

A security guard lifts the velvet rope for me to pass.

"But," Gretchen continues, "sometimes it's not the place they really should be."

Her words hit me harder than the martinis I shared with VV last night, and I stumble sideways stepping off the curb. The guard catches me by the arm as if I'm made of nothing more than the cottonwood that used to float in the summer sky in Michigan. He pulls me upright just before I fall headfirst into a planter box filled with flowers.

"Are you okay?" he asks.

I look at him, bewildered, feeling like a child who has misbehaved and has been sent home scolded.

But I have done nothing wrong.

"I don't know," I say.

I stare at the flowers. A bee—even in the midst of this chaos—floats from bloom to bloom, doing his job, unnoticed.

You can catch more flies with honey than you can with vinegar.

GiGi used to say this to us all the time. Though she was tough as nails, she learned to play nice when she had to.

Because she had to in order to survive in this world.

"There is nothing better than keeping your head down and your mouth shut for a while," she also told me.

I think of how Marcus's silence unnerved me on the beach.

I have finally been pushed to my limits.

Perhaps I need to put Marcus Flare to my own modern-day Bechdel Test in which women talk to each other about a man for the sole purpose of deleting him from the script.

I mean, what happens in every romance?

The brutish man-child thrives on confrontation and rejection. He is only tamed by a woman when she does not sting like a bee but acts as sweet as the honey it produces.

Quietly doing her job, the stinger so well hidden, everyone forgets the bee has one.

The times may change, but the plot—in real life and books—tends to follow the same pattern, doesn't it? I'm smarter than

Marcus because I was raised by smart women who hatched plans to better their lives.

And this hen just hatched the start of a great one.

"Ma'am," the security guard asks again. "Are you okay?"

I look the security guard directly in the eye.

"You can catch more flies with honey than you can with vinegar."

He just looks at me, not understanding.

"What I'm telling you," I continue, "is that, yes, I'm more than okay. I am ready to sting."

"That's fine," he says. "Just not here, got it?"

I catch Gretchen watching the scene.

I smile at her and wave to let her know I'm fine.

"Name?" she says to the next person waiting in line behind the rope.

CHAPTER ELEVEN

The buzzing of my cell—over and over—wakes me from a nightmare.

I had been dreaming I was in a World Wrestling cage match with Marcus Flare in Madison Square Garden. My mother was the referee. She made me stand motionless in the center of the ring while Marcus jumped on me—over and over again—from the top rope.

"Don't fight back," my mother kept saying as I lay on the mat. "It'll be over soon."

"No," I said. "I have to fight back."

I grab my cell, which does not recognize my exhausted face. I enter my passcode.

Page Six! You're famous! reads a text from Juice. Well, infamous. Are you okay?

I click on the link she has attached from the *New York Post*'s infamous gossip column.

There is a photo of me tossing my glass of champagne at Marcus Flare. My face is flushed and enraged. I look like a character from a horror movie. Marcus looks calm and innocent standing there. If a jury saw this photo alone, I would be convicted.

I click on the link Juice sent.

FLARE-UP AT LE POMPEUX BETWEEN LIT HEAVYWEIGHTS!
Does Page Publishing Heiress Have Trouble-y with the Bubbly?

My nightmare is real.

I scan the article, my eyes growing with each sentence they gulp.

Sources tell us that Emma Page—the newly minted University of Michigan grad and daughter of Gotham society's Phillip and Piper Page, heads of The Mighty Pages publishing empire—got into a shouting match at Sag Harbor's famed French hangout Le Pompeux with bestselling author Marcus Flare.

"Obviously not over who had more book sales," the source joked.

Page proceeded to toss a glass of champagne on the iconic author, who simply brushed off her assault as if he were editing a chapter of his latest book, The Chase, *which comes out this fall and has already been optioned for a major motion picture.*

Sources revealed to Page Six that Marcus joked to partygoers that Page couldn't hold her liquor and hit on him—"a happily married man," he reportedly said—and that Page's mortified mother had to intervene to calm her publishing progeny, saying, "Please, Emma, I can't tolerate one more lie!"

"Talk about a loaded author attacking a loaded author!" our source joked.

The night was meant to be a celebration of two pub power-houses. Phillip Page announced last night that Flare was launching Books with Flare, an imprint with The Mighty Pages.

If you've read the trades, you know The Mighty Pages needs a mighty shot in the arm, and Marcus was supposed to be the adrenaline.

Truth, they say, is always stranger than fiction (although this is a book we would read!).

Poor Pages.

I stare at the last line.

Literally, I think.

My phone continues to buzz every minute or so, text after text coming like the ocean tide just outside my window.

A text from VV.

Lesson #1 in publishing, Emma: Never lose your cool in public. P.S. You do know who "the source" is, right? He who has no name came out of it smelling like a rose, promoting his new book and movie, and his new imprint. Talk about the triple crown of publicity.

I reply: What should I do?

Well, I certainly wouldn't start my morning sober if I were you. And I'd never waste a glass of good champagne.

I smile despite the indignity.

My phone trills.

"Hi, Gin," I say. "I take it you saw the article."

"Are you okay?"

"I don't know."

I tell her what happened.

"Oh, my God, Emma. That's even worse than I could have imagined. Are your parents going to be okay?"

"I don't know," I say. "What should I do?" I hesitate. "I think that's a question I'll be asking a lot."

She laughs sympathetically.

"What do they always say? Keep your friends close and keep your enemies closer?" Gin asks. "I'd suggest you make faux amends. I was just assigned an important investigative story at the newspaper over a colleague who was expecting to be promoted. Didn't deserve it, but he expected it. And he's tried to make my life a living hell, spreading rumors about me, implying how I 'earned' the story from my boss."

"What are you doing?"

"I'm treating him like my best friend to not only show my colleagues I don't need to play in the dirt but also to ingratiate myself to the person who hates me the most," she says. "What was it you always called characters in books you trusted in the beginning but who revealed themselves to be liars?"

"Unreliable narrators?"

"That's it!" Gin says. "Be your own unreliable narrator. Control your own narrative. That's what I'm doing. I'm a journalist so I'm simply accumulating facts right now and piecing my own story about him together. It's all a ruse, of course, but it's working for now until I can nail him. I tell you, this real-world stuff is real."

I laugh.

"I actually was just thinking of a plan like you outlined," I say. "I miss you."

"I'm only a call, or flight, away."

"I might be on the run, so…"

"Oh, I gotta go," she says. "My unreliable narrator is coming. Love ya like a sister from another mister."

"Back at'cha. Bye."

There is a soft knock my door.

It opens, and Jess appears.

My real sister who seems like more of a stranger.

Jess's hair and makeup are perfect. She's wearing a flouncy summer dress and a statement hat and jewelry, a Hamptons fashionista.

She is holding a copy of the *New York Post*.

"I've seen it already."

"The whole world has," she says. "And they think you're a spoiled brat."

"Living the dream."

"You ruined Mom and Dad's big night," she says. "I'm beyond angry at you."

I stare at her, wanting to explain, knowing I can't.

"I'm sorry," is all I can manage to say.

She exhales.

"I've already started drama control," Jess says, pointing at me with the paper. "I'm hoping we can spin the drama to our advantage. People love gossip. It's what sells a movie, a book, a product. I'm saying this feud was orchestrated as a preview to illustrate the type of books Marcus's new imprint will feature. Lots of drama."

"You're good."

"Now you need to be as well," she says. "Apologize to Marcus."

I open my mouth to tell her everything, to tell her what he said, that I plan to befriend him in order to expose him, but I cannot even get a word out before she screams, "Apologize to Marcus!" She takes a jagged breath. "Somehow, someway."

She turns and glides away saying, "You have to come downstairs to get your own coffee and make up with Mom and Dad. So, wake up, Emma. And I mean every word of that."

This is as much a warning as a request.

I get out of bed and look out the wide windows overlooking the ocean. I open the custom drapes all the way, letting the sun off the water flood the room with light. There is a boardwalk leading to the ocean, and one of the household staff is setting up chairs and umbrellas on the beach.

I have never woken up in a fifty-million-dollar oceanfront mansion.

And, yet, save for location and the price of land, it's really no different than GiGi's cottage in South Haven.

I stare into the ocean and think of GiGi saving me so long ago. I need coffee. Desperately.

I realize I have nothing to wear as I was planning to head back to the city last night. I open the drawers to a beautiful dresser. *Empty.*

I open the stunning wardrobe.

Empty.

I head into the en suite and open the bathroom cabinets. *Nothing.*

"A fifty-million-dollar mansion that has nothing in it," I say to my ragged reflection.

I manage to find a bar of soap and a towel in the bathroom along with a waffle weave robe hanging on the door with *The Ritz-Carlton* stitched on the breast pocket. I run my fingers over the logo of a lion sitting atop a crown.

"Royalty meets financial backing," I say out loud, explaining not only the meaning of the Ritz logo—told to me years ago by my father—but also, in essence, my current predicament. "Power and money make the world go round."

I wash my face a bit too hard—scrubbing away as if it will erase last night—and run my fingers through my hair.

I open the bedroom door. It's quiet. Maybe I can sneak downstairs, grab some coffee and come back and shower without having to confront my parents yet.

I tiptoe as carefully as a cat burglar down the gorgeous bifurcated staircase, admiring the detail of the beautiful balustrades.

I head through stunning room after room, Versailles on the beach.

I round the corner and yelp.

The kitchen is filled with white-uniformed staff.

"What are you doing here?" I ask.

A laugh echoes throughout the cavernous kitchen.

"They work here." Jess is seated in a beautiful banquette.

"I just need some coffee," I say.

"Latte, espresso, cappuccino, Americano, cold brew?" a woman asks.

"Um, cappuccino, please."

In the blink of an eye, a perfect cup of coffee is handed to me.

"Thank you," I say to the staffer. I take a sip. "It's perfect."

"Seems like you got used to that service pretty quickly, Miss I'm So Above All of This," Jess snarks.

I act as if I'm going to toss my coffee into Jess's face to make light of last night's incident, but my parents walk in, and my mother exclaims, "What in the world, Emma? Not again!"

"I have the worst timing," I sigh.

Jess glares at me and raises a perfect brow.

"Mom, Dad... I'm so, so sorry about my behavior last night," I continue. "It was uncalled for, and I want to apologize to you. I feel awful."

Jess clears her throat.

I have to swallow hard. "And I plan to apologize to Marcus as well."

My parents—perfect as always, Michael Douglas and Catherine Zeta-Jones on vacation in East Hampton—look at one another and then me.

"Thank you, sweetheart," my father says. "What is it they say? Any publicity is good publicity."

"You acted like a Real Housewife last night," my mother sighs. "I'm just glad there wasn't a table to overturn nearby."

My mother is not so forgiving.

"And you're dressed like a Real Housewife this morning," she continues.

"I didn't bring anything to wear. I wasn't planning on staying."

"Obviously," my mother says. "Come with me. I can help you find something appropriate to wear from my things."

"I think that you are probably different sizes," Jess says, eyeing me over, smiling at her dig.

"By all means, let's body shame this morning," I say.

"You actually can feel shame?" Jess asks. "I should leak that to Page Six."

"Girls!" my father says as a warning.

He takes a cup of coffee and says, "Today is supposed to be a celebration as well."

I turn and look at my father, questioning. A celebration?

Everyone shoots him a look that I swear reads, *Keep your mouth shut, Phillip. Our girl is not right in the head to hear this right now.*

My mother and sister are acting as if nothing was just said.

Is there another family secret I'm not aware of?

They focus on their coffee.

I want to ask what is happening, but I can read a room, and I don't want an angrier mob. I'm also not sure what to do until I figure out the through line on this story.

"Let's try to act like a happy family," my mother says. "For once."

Instead, I keep my mouth shut, smile and sip my coffee.

My mother takes me by the arm.

"When will you be ready to go?" my father asks. "An hour?"

My mother looks at me for far too long, her lingering gaze shouting the unspoken: *I think my daughter will need more than an hour.*

I am wearing a summery sundress and strappy sandals.

My mother has dressed me in her image, hoping, I'm sure, some of her class might rub off on me.

"Where are we going exactly?" I ask. "And why are you driving, Dad?"

"I told you," my mother says, fingers pecking away on her cell. "It's a surprise."

Her eyes are glued to her phone. In the brief moments they're not, they are glued to the vanity mirror on her sun visor, in which she constantly checks her appearance or pretends to fix her hair without actually touching it.

This is not unusual behavior. But the fact that my father is driving is as rare as my parents inviting VV over for a barbecue and croquet match.

My father *never* drives. I didn't even think he knew how to drive. At the very least, I just assumed he'd forgotten how living in New York.

"I promise you everything will work out beautifully," my father says, always so diplomatically optimistic. "We have a piece running in the *Times Magazine* on Sunday. Jess has been working her magic on social media. This is going to put The Mighty Pages back on the publishing world's radar."

And if it doesn't? I want to ask. *You're still going to lose everything to a conniving hustler, and we'll be living in a motel.*

"We just need an apology from Emma," Jess says with a smile.

My father's eyes meet mine in the rearview mirror, and he nods with conviction, then gives me a sweet wink.

I smile despite the crack in my heart.

What is it about my family? How can they infuriate me over and over, confound and enrage me one moment, but then in an instant—via one simple look from my father—I would do anything to protect them?

I clutch my seat belt and twist it in agony. I have to tell my parents that Marcus wants to ruin them and The Mighty Pages. I have to make it clear to Jess that our family is in trouble. But I also know they trust him way more than me right now. If I said a word in the car, they would all think it's because I'm yet again acting like an impetuous child and refuse to grow up. If my family had trusted me, they would have told me what they had planned with Marcus from the get-go.

My father may be driving, but Marcus is in the driver's seat.

I need proof.

I need Marcus on my side. I need him to trust me as much as my family trusts him. I need a touch more time.

I rub my head.

I also need more coffee and three Tylenol.

The streets leading from the ocean through East Hampton are wide, and marbled sycamores provide a canopy overhead. The landscape is lush, the privets thick or shaped into balls, the hydrangeas otherworldly. This is the result of a place with such history—dating back to the 1600s—and wealth. Homes—if you can even call them that—peek from behind the hedges. Shingled cottages with turrets, contemporary barn-style mansions, sleek modern behemoths that look as if they should be in Palm Springs.

There is money, and then there is *money*.

This is M-O-N-E-Y!

And my parents have always wanted more of it.

This yawning need for more and better—homes, cars, friends, likes, publicity—is destroying my family.

GiGi was very well off. My family has enough money to be happy. Our lives are a gift of her hard work and sacrifice. But my parents aren't comfortable being comfortable. We are poor compared to these Hamptons standards. And they want *this*.

We inch our way through downtown East Hampton—past Gucci, Louis Vuitton, Prada—the traffic at a standstill. I watch hordes of people flock into Citarella, the upscale grocery where you can buy designer ice and forty-dollar prepackaged salads.

My gut is telling me to leap from the car and race into BookHampton, one of my favorite bookstores in the world. When I come to the Hamptons, I escape to BookHampton, spending hours roaming through the aisles looking at the latest releases. I always ask the staff for suggestions and leave with my arms filled with books, just as I did with GiGi.

I could use a book right now.

People lean out their car windows red-faced and angry.

New Yorkers flee the city for the slower pace. They need the Hamptons to detox. We crawl, a mile at a time, until finally the traffic begins to move, and we are in the "country."

But this farmland is not like Michigan's. Here, quaint orchards, farm stands and nurseries are being swallowed up by huge new builds on large tracts of land, FOR SALE signs more prevalent than tomatoes, flowers and trees. Since New Yorkers need this open space, they also require this open space.

Traffic slows as we near another town.

An old wooden sign proclaiming Bridgehampton Founded 1644 greets us, and my father turns on a road that leads away from the ocean and toward the countryside again.

I again want to leap from the car and race to Southampton to Tate's Bake Shop, which makes the most wondrous chocolate chip cookies—crisp and buttery—in the most adorable bakeshop, filled with fresh flowers and carved wooden tables.

I glance at my mother, who is checking her appearance again.

Perhaps I don't hate the Hamptons as much as I like to act.

Perhaps it's the people—and not the place—that gets on my nerves.

My father smiles at me in the mirror. The man can read my mind.

Finally, he turns into a crushed gravel driveway across from a farm.

A behemoth of a house overpowers the lot.

My family jumps out of the car, and I follow, confused.

My mother spreads her arms. "What do you think?"

I furrow my brows.

"Think of what?"

And then I notice the Sotheby's sign, planted in new sod against a row of boxwood just beyond where my mother is standing.

My father's shoes making the quintessential crunch of old money on the white gravel.

"We're thinking of buying this, and we wanted your input and, hopefully, approval," he says. "We need to rethink our future—all of our futures. We're taking big, bold steps with our company, and we need to do the same with our lives."

My father's eyes are hidden behind his sunglasses, but I know they are searching mine, seeking not my input or approval but my acquiescence.

"This is a brand-new home," my mother says, waving her arms dramatically. "This is a brand-new start." She looks like a tiny speck before the moon.

I stare at the modern barn-style mansion. It's undoubtedly beautiful. Through the oversize windows I can see the soaring ceilings, a sleek fireplace, white floors, double kitchen islands. A wall of glass in the back opens to a sleek pool.

Is it what I've come to love about a summer cottage? No.

It's new. It's pretentious. It's yet another modern take on a farmhouse by people who don't even realize that cows live on a farm and a barn is a home for their hay.

"Nine bedrooms, ten baths," my mother continues as if she's a real estate agent trying to make a sale. "Modern, clean." She turns. "See how it's designed? Each of us will have our own suite, our own wings."

My mother loves new, new, new.

She removes her sunglasses and places her hand very close to my arm to replicate the emotion of intimacy.

"You're out of college now, Emma. You're interviewing to work in the city. We all," she says, gesturing to Jess, my father and herself, "spend the majority of our time out East now. It just makes sense to consolidate our lives."

"And leave Michigan behind," I say. "Leave GiGi behind. Leave our history behind."

My father removes his sunglasses.

"Emma, it's getting harder and harder to get back there," he says, his voice a low hum. "It will only become more difficult the busier we become. The people we work with, the people in our orbit, all summer in the Hamptons. If we truly want to stay connected, relevant and reinvent, this is the smartest move to make, personally and professionally. You know how much I love Eyebrow Cottage. It was my home. It was GiGi's heart, but life marches on, and we cannot remain tied to a past that no longer makes sense."

"How much does this cost, if you don't mind me asking?"

My parents look at each other.

"Just a skosh under eight million," my father says.

"Property values only go up here, Emma," Jess says quickly. "It's a lot of money, but you're going to look back in ten years and have a fifteen-million-dollar home at least."

"But we already have a summer home," I argue.

My mother lowers her hand and retreats a step. This is too much emotion for her.

"We're too isolated in Michigan, honey," my father reasons. "We can summer here and still make it back to the city by Sunday night or Monday morning."

"But isolation is the point of a summer place, isn't it?" I ask. "You need to get away from the city and its energy to recharge, reset, imagine, dream." I stop and look at them. "To write."

"We can do that all here, Emma."

Or we can do that in a motel.

If you ever say a word about our little talk with your parents or sister, I will have you in that motel sooner rather than later.

What secret does Marcus have on my family? Just how close are we to financial ruin?

I suddenly see this house sitting on the edge of a dune in Michigan, one that has been eroded by time, rising water and vicious waves. It is perched on the precipice believing it is safe when it's about to collapse into oblivion, and nothing and no one can save it.

Except me.

I'm beginning to feel like I'm the only visitor at Saltburn who sees the danger surrounding them and understands a crazy man disguised as a friend is out to destroy our entire family.

I have to say something even if they don't believe me. I have to tell them what he said. I have to tell them what I know.

But if I do, and they do not believe me, we are toast.

Not fancy avocado toast, but burned-beyond-recognition toast.

I have to write the next chapter myself. Even if it makes them dislike me even more right now.

"I hate you for putting me in this position! How could you?"

"Emma," my mother warns. "Do you even care about our future?"

More than you will ever know.

"Just come inside," my mother urges, turning toward the house. "I know you'll love it."

I do not budge.

"We *need* this as a family," my mother says. "We need to turn the page."

"I don't want to turn the page," I say. "Eyebrow Cottage is a part of my history, too. It means everything to me. It's filled with memories. It's filled with GiGi."

"And this home will be, too," my mother tries to soothe. "Just think of the day when you will be running the business with us, married, your children racing through the house and directly into the pool out back."

That day may never come.

I stop short of stomping a foot in the pretty gravel, but I cross my arms like a sullen child for dramatic effect.

I, at least, can give my family what they have come to expect from me until I have a chance to figure out our next chapter.

"You are such a baby," Jess exclaims. "I can't with you."

She walks toward the house.

"Emma," my mother says, losing patience. "Just come look at the house. Please."

I shake my head. "So? That's it? We've decided?"

"Three against one," Jess calls over her shoulder. "You do the math."

"We wanted to make this decision as a family," my father says.

"When have we ever done that?" I ask.

"Emma—" my father says.

"I'm being serious," I say. "You made the Marcus Flare decision without my input. You kept it a secret. You kept this a secret. You've all obviously looked at this place together without ever mentioning it once to me."

"You have a lot on your plate, sweetheart," my dad says.

"No, stop lying to her, Dad," Jess says, coming back down the driveway toward me, her eyes flashing, each step an exclamation point to her rage. "Let's get real here for once. You're too sensitive. You always choose yourself over everyone else. You're tied to a past that is going to drown you."

Her words hurt. My face tenses. Jess continues, knowing she has me cornered and vulnerable.

"What choice do we have but to tiptoe around your emotions all the time? You need to move on, Emma. You need to leave Eyebrow Cottage. Those memories of GiGi—of how you found her—aren't healthy. They're holding you back."

"I can't leave that place," I say. "I won't let you sell it."

"God, you are impossible," my sister huffs. "No, actually, you're just pathetic."

My mother is done with me. "You have no choice in that matter."

"Emma," my father says, his tone conciliatory. "Take some time. Think about it. Think what's best for all of us, not just you."

"Why do you always have to be the odd bird out?" Jess asks.

Jess is standing in the sun, arms out, questioning my entire existence. I glance at her shadow—dark on the white gravel—which resembles a bird in flight over sun dappled waves. I think of GiGi and *Jonathan Livingston Seagull.*

"Jonathan's one sorrow was that other gulls refused to open their eyes and see," GiGi used to tell me as we floated on the lake. "But you see, Emma. You see. The world will try to make you just like them, but don't you dare follow the masses. You fly, so high, that the only way you know how to get back home is by instinct."

I look at my family, blissfully oblivious to the fact their entire existence is in danger: their company, their finances, their future, their happiness, their homes, their life's work.

Right now, all I want to do is come clean with my family, but they are not ready to see.

Their faces—soaked in the sun—are staring at me, as they always have, wondering, *Where did our little girl go? Is she coming back?*

The only way I know to save them right now is to give them the character they have already written.

I turn and begin to walk down the driveway toward the road.

"Where are you going?" my mother calls.

"Home!"

CHAPTER TWELVE

I am lying on the beach, arms over my head, the book I am reading perfectly positioned to block the sun as well as the thoughts ricocheting through my head.

I feel someone staring at me. I flip on my stomach.

Sun is blinking off the little dormer windows in Eyebrow Cottage. The breeze whistles across the sand. I shut my eyes.

The cottage is saying goodbye.

When I open them, I swear I can see a face in an eyebrow window.

"No!" I suddenly say, sitting up, unable to face the truth.

A woman walking the beach veers into the water, startled by my outburst.

I study the cover of the next S. I. Quaeris book I plucked from my bedroom.

Can a Woman Who Has Lost Everything Find Herself Again?
Secrets of the Shore

The cover image is a woman standing on the beach before a glorious pink sky, her hand outstretched as if she's attempting to grab the setting sun. I narrow my eyes behind my sunglasses. Her other hand is clenched tightly.

She reminds me of…me.

Is she hiding a secret?

I have not heard from my family since my outburst. I *have* heard from a few of my interviews: I have been offered two positions, including one—shockingly—from The Mighty Pages. I think my parents feel as if they must have me close by so they can keep me out of trouble. I have also heard from VV asking for my manuscript.

And I have a plan. Part of it requires doing nothing for a hot moment except keeping my mouth shut. Men like Marcus, I realize, are unnerved by silence. They can bully and pick a fight, but narcissists require attention, even if it's negative. They thrive on it.

But remove that attention—be as still as a gull over the water—and they will crack because they did not get the reaction they desired. I gave him the reaction he wanted, and he won. I remove it, and I believe I have a chance to win. Or at least neutralize his power over me for a moment while this pantser becomes a plotter.

I just hope my parents didn't already buy that Hamptons home yet. I check the Zillow listing every hour, making sure it's still on the market and doesn't show an offer pending.

I think of my parents' love for all that is new: homes, ventures, beginnings.

I glance at the cottage and think of my love for all that is old.

My eyes wander back to the book I'm holding.

Am I too stuck on the past?

But there is just something about vintage book covers, like there is about vintage clothing. Vintage book covers are like old album cover art. Vinyl is back, you know. Everything comes full circle. Even '80s hair and makeup.

Before social media and online design, great thought and skill went into creating book and album covers to create a mood. Artists painted, calligraphers produced ornamental writing. The covers artistically told us what was contained within.

My father's most recent book cover, by contract, was attractive, but it was not original: a burning globe Photoshopped against a baseball glove.

I recently checked my father's BookScan numbers: less than a thousand copies sold.

I can't help but feel as if my family is running out of time before we're placed in the bargain bin and sold off.

How do I deal with Marcus Flare? How do I avert a deal with the devil, and rewrite a storyline straight out of *Damn Yankees*?

Right now, I just need to escape. That's the reason for beach reads, right?

I flip to the back of the book and read the Author's Note.

The Acknowledgments seem so...familiar.

I sit up again.

Wait just a minute.

I grab my beach bag and squirrel through it, digging past a towel, sunscreen, lip balm. There, on the bottom, is the previous novel I'd been reading. I open the book and compare the pages.

Exactly the same. Word for word.

Why would the author do that?

Overwhelmed? Creature of habit? Tight deadline? Superstitious? Simply loved what they had written?

I lie back on the sand once again and continue reading, arms overhead to block the sun.

The novel begins in the 1920s with a young daredevil diving off the top of a thirty-five-foot lighthouse to impress a girl on the beach. The lighthouse keeper runs out in an attempt to shoo him away—worried about his safety due to the current, proximity to the piers and passing boats—but is instead suddenly swept off the catwalk by a massive, surprise wave. The daredevil attempts to save him.

I stare down the shore at the lighthouse.

This is too close to home.

Literally and emotionally.

I flip the pages hurriedly.

The scene, fascinatingly, is not told from the men's point of view at all but rather the two women on the shore—the wife of the lighthouse keeper and the girlfriend of the daredevil—who are watching this drama unfold before their eyes. The book shifts between the current, past and future, omitting names and certain details, leaving the reader wondering if the men actually survive and who the women end up with. Was it either of them, no one or someone else? It's heartbreaking, eye-opening and an allegory about how women were not truly in control of their lives during that era.

I turn my head and stare at the cottage. I can still hear GiGi laughing when I told her of the Bechdel Test in college.

"You don't need a class for that, Emma," I can hear her say. "It's called life. It's always been dominated by men. It always will be. We don't need a test to prove that. We need women who test those rules. And the best way for you to do that is to write that book you always wanted, a book that celebrates the power of women. Isn't that why you're there? To write? To break the mold?"

"I feel like I'm drowning," I say aloud.

"Then let's go for a swim," I can hear GiGi say.

"But you're not here to save me," I say.

"Be your own daredevil, Emma."

I get up and edge my way toward the water. I have waded in the lake, I have run on its shoreline, I have collected rocks and I have floated on an inner tube, but I have not entered the lake alone to swim since…

I step into the water.

I recall the first time I jumped off a diving board at the local pool. It felt like I was jumping off the top of the Empire State Building. I was terrified but thrilled.

I wade into the lake until I'm waist-deep.

Lake Michigan's water still has a chill to it in the middle of summer, and goose pimples explode on my body. I need to recapture that girlish excitement again, that time when there was no fear. I need to tackle my biggest obstacle so that I can be prepared to overcome any obstacle—real or imagined—that stands in my way. I need to trust myself, all alone. I need to jump without overthinking, without hesitation.

And so I do.

I take a breath and leap into the lake.

Water goes up my nose, and I open my eyes to see sand dance beneath me.

I come up laughing and let the sun dry my face.

But there is still one thing more I must do today: I must surrender.

I inhale fully and float on my back.

I can feel GiGi's hands beneath me.

I lean my head up and stare toward the deck of Eyebrow Cottage.

Suddenly, a memory of me and GiGi flashes.

It was a summer day much like this.

I had stayed out too late with friends and slept in one morning. When I finally woke up, it was eerily quiet. GiGi was on the deck, book in hand, head slumped, and I thought she'd fallen asleep. I could see her coffee steaming, and I didn't want to bother her. She got up so early, still worked so hard, got so little peace. She needed the rest.

I made breakfast, took a shower, and when I came back downstairs, she hadn't moved.

"GiGi?" I called.

She didn't respond.

I went onto the deck and touched her arm. She was cold. No heartbeat. I just sat there, weeping, holding her hand, hat-ing myself for all those wasted moments when I could have saved her life.

I was so in shock that I had no idea what to do. I just knew I needed more time with her.

And then I remembered. I knew what she needed. I knew what I needed.

So I did the exact same thing GiGi had done when she found my grandfather: I read aloud to her from the book in her hand. When I finished that chapter, I realized she was almost done with the book, and I wanted her to know how it ended, so I read the next chapter to her, and then the next, until I had finished it.

Then I called 911.

"You saved my life, but I couldn't save yours," I say to the lake.

I lay my head back on the water and fill my lungs with air again.

I feel a shadow cross my face, the sun blocked, and at first I think it is a cloud.

I open my eyes.

A gull is flying directly above me, floating to and fro in motion with my body on the water.

It dive-bombs and lands beside me on the water.

As I float on the lake, it sails on the current.

We stare at one another.

"Jonathan?" I ask.

It cocks its head and stares at me. Its eyes are the color of GiGi's, its feathers and wings her white hair.

"GiGi?" I ask.

The gull opens its beak and mews at me, not an alarmed squawk by my presence but as if I'm an old friend.

In its call, I swear I can hear GiGi say, "You don't need saving. You never have."

And then the bird takes off, flying higher and higher, until it becomes a cotton-candy cloud in the heavens.

CHAPTER THIRTEEN

I am on the deck gobbling up the Quaeris novel I started yesterday.

"Just one more chapter," I keep telling myself.

I still have not heard from my parents or sister since I high-tailed it out of the Hamptons three days ago. I have not responded to any offer.

I feel like this is…

I stare into the lake, which is shockingly flat today, not a wave, a blue carpet stretched to infinity.

…the calm before the storm.

I return to reading and when I finally look up from my chair on the deck, late morning has turned to early afternoon, and the beach is packed.

A good book always defies time.

The lake remains calm, and—from my vantage point—the summer sun has made it look as if I'm peering through a glass-bottom boat.

I can see striations below the surface, children's feet churning sand. The wind whispers through an aspen growing from a nearby sand dune. It is the voice of my past. Not GiGi this time, but the voice of my mother.

They muddy the water to make it seem deep.

My cell trills.

It's my mother.

How is it she can always read my mind?

It rings again.

This is it. The moment I've been waiting for.

It rings again.

I don't want to talk to her. I'm worried my big mouth will make me say the wrong thing, but time is wasting, and if I wait too much longer, Marcus might have done something to hurt my family irreparably. They might have made a rash financial move—like bought that Hamptons home.

I inhale sharply.

"Hi, Mom."

"You're alive."

Another breath.

"One would think a daughter would call her mother to let her know she's made it home."

Vintage Piper.

Don't say it.

"One would think a mother would call her daughter to make sure she's made it home."

Vintage Emma.

I can hear my mother cover her phone with her hand. At first, I think she is—quite literally—muting me, but I can hear her speak to someone in her office in a clipped tone. The staffer must be new because she keeps addressing my mom as "Mrs. Page," which is the equivalent of calling my mother "Grandma," dousing her in a knockoff designer perfume and dressing her in an off-the-rack outfit from TJ Maxx.

"Piper," my mother keeps correcting. "Call me Piper please."

"Emma?"

"I'm still here."

"Did you see the article in the *Times*?" she asks.

My mother has already moved on from the fact we have not spoken to one another since I stormed away. Her conflict resolution is to steel herself with another round of lipstick.

I did see the article. VV sent it to me when she asked about the status of my book.

Remember, she texted. There's never a right time. Only a moment to hold your breath and jump.

"Yes, I saw it."

"Isn't it amazing? So much buzz. Our phones have been blowing up. Everyone wants to work with Marcus. Everyone wants to work with us. With book sales slowing, I think we have momentum and a new path into accounts."

"That's great, Mom." My tone is as calm as the lake.

"You know, Marcus actually asked about you."

It's go time.

"I was just about to apologize," I say.

"Marcus doesn't want an apology," she says.

"What?"

"He wants to work with you."

It worked! My silence worked! The narcissist couldn't take it.

"What?" I blurt again, acting surprised.

"I was as surprised as you are considering what transpired."

"But…why?"

"He said he admires your book smarts and tenacity. He said you are a very strong woman. He forgives your breach of etiquette and said it was nice to see such passion in a young person today. He'd like to help you mature."

I'm sure he would.

My mother takes a breath. "It's also because he's a kind man. I hope you will eventually see that one day."

He's a liar, Mom! I scream inside. *He wants to hurt you.*

I suddenly want to throw my cell into the lake and start a tidal wave that will reach New York, but I realize that's sort of impossible considering it's a Great Lake and my phone only weighs a few ounces.

My mother continues.

"Honey, I'm sorry we didn't tell you about the deal with Marcus, but we were under a confidentiality agreement."

"But Jess knew?"

"She's part of our company," she says, keeping her voice even. "She has a relationship with Marcus. She needed to know. And it all worked out perfectly."

For him.

My mother continues. "I know this is a very uncertain time in your life, a time of great transition. You just finished college. You're unsure of your future. You miss GiGi."

She pauses. I can hear someone say something to her. I can hear her whisper, "Shoo!" She continues, her voice soft as a kitten's purr.

"But a bright future awaits you in publishing, be it with us or someone else."

Oh, she's good.

How do I respond?

Like the character who just learned a valuable life lesson.

"Thank you for saying that. And you're right, everything after college just seems like I'm walking a tightrope with my future, and I just don't want to take the wrong step."

"You won't," she says, "because you are the most amazing woman I know."

The tone of her voice touches me. *What is going on with my mother?*

"Um, thanks, Mom."

"May I make a suggestion?" she asks. "As a temporary solution?"

"Of course."

"We need readers to go through the onslaught of manuscripts we're receiving for Books with Flare. Marcus asked specifically for you. Would you consider culling them? It's sort of what you would do with She Who Has No Name, should you choose to be an agency assistant. It's what you would work your way up to do with us should you join our team with the offer we extended. It would sort of allow you to test the waters before making a final decision. I think it may be the perfect temporary solution for you in so many ways."

I sit up in my chair.

This is working out better than I imagined.

I'm catching more flies with honey than vinegar.

Or, am I being set up? What does he want? To keep an eye on me so I don't ruin his plan? To drive an even deeper wedge between me and my family before he ruins us, so I literally have nothing when he's done?

But shouldn't I keep an eye on him?

Or is my mother playing me like Marcus is playing her?

I feel trapped between two very heavy bookends.

Think, Emma.

"I still don't understand why he would want me to do that," I explain. "We, um, don't have the most amicable relationship. And he made me look like a fool in the press."

My mother clears her throat as if to silently say, *You did that yourself, sweetheart.*

"As I said, he knows you're smart," she says instead. "He knows you know books. He said he needs a young, savvy reader and confidante who has her finger on the pulse of what's going to be hot. You understand both commercial *and* literary fiction, Emma. You know classics *and* our cultural zeitgeist. You are the biggest and best reader I've ever known. He trusts you, Emma. So do we."

He doesn't trust me. He despises me. And our entire family.

"We are a family, but this is also a business. We have a lot riding on this deal." I hear her exhale. "Including our entire future."

You have no idea.

"So no pressure," I joke.

She releases a hollow laugh.

"How bad is it, Mom?" I ask, suddenly serious. "Please. I need to know. I think I deserve to know."

She sighs.

"You are my daughter, and our children should not carry the burdens of their parents. And yet no matter how hard parents try to keep their babies safe, we still place our boulders of burden upon your hearts."

My mother's unfiltered—albeit erudite—semi-honesty stuns me.

"I will say this—we are facing the same pressures all of the major publishers are facing," she admits. "But we do not have the cushion they do, so we've had to release a little air from our financial tires. But we will rebound. We always do. We are a resilient family."

Gut punch. Mom wins.

"You'd just be reading manuscripts and offering your thoughts. Oh, and Marcus said he will be paying you nicely for it out of his own pocket."

Hush money.

"It's essentially what you're doing right now anyway, right? Reading for pleasure?" she presses. "And no matter what decision you make about your future, this will look great on your résumé. I mean, you're helping decide which books will be part of the debut list from the hottest new imprint in publishing. It's a win-win."

"Would I have to deal directly with Marcus?"

My mother laughs, hard this time.

"God, I hope not."

I laugh, too.

"It feels good to laugh again with you," she says. "I missed you while you were at college. We used to have such great debates. Jess was my let's-go-shopping girl, and you were my let's-go-there girl."

My mother missed me?

"I envy that you had the quintessential college experience," she says. "Not the one I would have chosen, of course, but you made great friends, had a great time and received a great education."

"Has someone kidnapped my mother?" I ask.

She laughs again.

"Let me know what you think," she says. "We will need a decision about Marcus by the end of the week. And we'll need a decision about your future with us..."

If you have a future.

"...by month's end."

She hesitates.

"You don't want to upset Marcus?" I ask sweetly.

"I don't," she says. "We can't."

"And you think I can help?" I continue.

"I do."

"You know I'd do anything for this family."

And I have no choice. I must play a game of cat and mouse with Marcus, who fell for my silent catnip. Saying yes is the perfect way I can stay in the know and help protect my family until I can figure out what Flare has planned for our family in his burn book.

And yet I can't just give Marcus a yes that easily. I want him to know I'm good at playing games, too. A little more silence will completely unnerve him and convince my parents I haven't altered my entire being.

"Can I think about it?" I ask instead. "Just for a day or two."

My mother sighs. It's not the answer she wanted, but it's not completely unexpected either.

"Until the end of the week," she says. "That's it, okay?"

"Okay."

My mother clears her throat.

"I also want you to know how sorry we are that we sprung the Hamptons house on you, but we didn't want you to leave without knowing what we envision for our future," she says.

"I appreciate that. I'm sorry about how I reacted."

"I understand, Emma. Eyebrow Cottage is a wonderful part of our family's history, but I do think it's time we consider creating new memories together," she says. "There is a lot of pain associated with the cottage for you, for all of us, and I'd love us to start new lives in a new place where we're not surrounded by death at every corner. You need a new start, Jess needs a new start, we all need a new start, don't you think?"

My heart pangs.

I look around the deck.

GiGi found Grampa here. I found her.

Am I chained to this place by love or guilt?

Does my mother actually have a point? Or is she writing a story she knows I need to hear?

I think of Jess, Capote, her Swans, his Swans, Marcus.

It's always hard to trust a writer.

My eyes scan the beach, lake, lighthouse, horizon.

"You know there's a big ol' ocean and beach here, too," she says, reading my mind again. "And your family, most importantly. We love you." She pauses. "I love you."

Emotion from my mother. My heart melts just a little bit more.

"I love you, too, Mom," I say. "I just think I need a touch more time regarding that decision, too. This still feels like home to me. It's the only stable place I've ever really known."

My mother sighs again. This is also not the answer she wanted either, but it's not the one she perhaps expected to receive either.

"*We* should be home to you, Emma, no matter where that is."

"I know, but I grew up here," I say. "Going to boarding

school, I never really felt like I had a landing spot. This was always it for me." I try to soften my reaction with a joke. *"Jonathan Livingston Seagull's* landing spot."

She doesn't laugh.

"Are you angry with me for boarding school?" she asks. "For sending you away?"

Her tone has changed.

"No," I say. "But GiGi…"

"I allowed GiGi to be the hero in your life, Emma! It wasn't easy for me to be the bad guy all the time."

My heart jumps.

Where did this come from all of a sudden?

I can hear my mother stand and shut her office door.

"Someone had to make hard decisions, Emma. GiGi wanted you with her all the time. Yes, you can get a wonderful education at a public school, but that was not my experience. GiGi never had a formal education. You needed to see the world. You needed to be around peers and faculty that challenged you. What's so wrong with a mother wanting to give her daughter every opportunity she never had?"

"Mom," I say. "Please."

"I speak the truth," she says. "You speak your mind all the time whether we want to hear it or not."

My face flames.

"GiGi made her own way, Mom. I admired her for that."

"Your grandfather lifted her out of her circumstances."

"No, she did that on her own. She changed her life. You're the one who was lifted out of her circumstances, by Dad. GiGi made all the money that *you* are now spending."

I wish I could take it all back as soon as I say it. What happened? We were doing so well.

"Emma," my mother says, her tone now a warning despite being the one to start this new war. "It's not like I just sat back and crocheted all day. I instilled a vision into your father. He needed me, or he would have ended up in that house and that town forever, being..."

"Happy?" I quip.

"Trapped!" my mother snaps. Her breath is ragged. She inhales deeply. I can almost hear her counting to ten. "This is not the way I intended this conversation to go, but since it has veered in this direction, I'll be the one who needs to say what everyone is thinking. Don't throw your life away. You need to think about your future, Emma. It's not there in Michigan daydreaming about trying to bring a dead woman back to life. It's not there fantasizing that old books are going to give you the happy ending you want. It's not there pretending that the novel you were writing in college is a masterpiece."

A dagger to the heart. I won't let it hurt me.

"How did you know?"

"Your friends talk to me, Emma."

"Why are you so cruel?"

"I'm honest, Emma. There's a big difference. You need to learn that difference. Your future is here, putting your expensive degree to work and contributing to the dream I thought we all shared. You've always painted me as the villain simply because I wasn't GiGi, and that's not fair."

"I think you sort of primed that canvas and painted that self-portrait all on your own, Mother."

"GiGi gave you advice, and you listened. You never have with me."

"Because she loved me!"

"She also needed you because she no longer had a captive audience of boarders in that house who treated her like she was their savior. She basked in that glow. And when it was gone, she tried to make us her minions."

I am so angry I can no longer see the beach.

"Stop it, Mom. Stop it. Please. You cannot just sell your entire history and reinvent your life overnight. It doesn't work that way."

"But it does," she insists. "You have been so blessed, and yet you are so naive. How do you think most people make it through this existence? They sell off their bad memories of childhood and family like the last ugly chair at an estate sale and move on so the past doesn't consume them whole." My mother takes a deep breath. "You will leave that cottage, Emma, and restart your life, or, God help me, I will force you out of it. I've played nice long enough."

I end the call and scream into the sky.

Tears of frustration rise, but I will them to stop. I will not cry. Instead, I take the book and bash it against the deck a few times to release my frustration.

I lift my face to the sky.

"Help me, GiGi," I whisper. "What should I do?"

Children scream happily in the lake water. They are kicking up so much sand that the clear lake looks like a muddy river.

"They muddy the water to make it seem deep."

I didn't understand this Friedrich Nietzsche quote my mother used to say to me as a girl, but I do now: deliberately trying to make a situation more confusing and complicated than it really is.

I stare at the lake until it clears. I sigh.

Uncomplicate it, Emma.

I pick up my book and escape once again into its pages where, for a moment, I can be safe. And that's when I see it: the edge of a leaf peeking from the pages.

A tangible time stamp.

I open the book to reveal the leaf. It is dry, crumbling and yet still intact. I scan the pages the leaf has marked. My eyes swim when I come upon a passage that makes everything muddy again:

An acorn is like a secret: whether or not it ever grows to see the light depends on how deep you bury it.

Word for word, just like GiGi used to say, just like the sentence in the Marcus Flare novel.

Word for word, just like the author's acknowledgments.

Did S. I. Quaeris plagiarize?

But this book was written *before* Marcus's novel.

Did Marcus?

Or was this simply a favorite quote from a favorite author that GiGi loved?

I mean, I quote authors all the time.

I get this tingly, creepy, out-of-body feeling that Marcus has been playing me since my college days, before I even knew him.

My mind spins in confusion.

My cell trills.

And then it twirls even more.

Incoming call: Jess

My mother has already called in a hostage negotiator.

CHAPTER FOURTEEN

"Mom's worried she might have been a little rough on you."

"A little rough? Have you seen *Mommie Dearest*?" I ask. "Joan Crawford was way sweeter and showed more remorse."

"The vampire does have a pulse," Jess says. "It just beats very, very slowly."

She laughs to herself.

"And you know she doesn't own a wire hanger."

I can't help but smile.

Is my sister siding with me for once?

"So true," I say. "And her clothes get way more love and attention than I do."

"What happened?" she continues. "She was Shakespearian in her explanation."

I tell her how it went downhill quickly from a Disney movie to a Rob Zombie film.

"Did you know swans are often vicious toward one another and will kill within the family?" she asks. "We see them as these elegant creatures—beautiful, long-necked, gorgeous plumage, bright-beaked—and yet they are naturally aggressive to each other. Their instinct is to maintain power as well as protect the flock." Jess waits a beat. "Sometimes, their instincts—and messages—get mixed."

The world seems to change color before my eyes. Did my sister name her BookTok group as an homage to Capote's Swans or as a subtle swipe at our mother?

"Did you…" I start.

"Aren't words magical?" Jess asks instead, cutting me off before I can finish my question. "How we use them? Which ones we choose and why? We really only require a few words in life to make everything better. *I love you. I'm here. How can I help? I will never leave.* And yet we always seem to choose the wrong ones. Especially this family of wordsmiths. The magic of an author is to pick the right words at the right time. That's why I love books, Emma, even though you think I do it only for the money. The beauty of a book is not to hide from the world but rather our second chance to make it right. We can reimagine and reinvent, see the world in an entirely new way simply by turning a page."

I can hear her breathing. Then the sound of a metal top popping open and what I can only assume is a mint going into her mouth.

"Turn the page on Mom," Jess finally says. "Reimagine her. Reimagine *us.*"

Jess's unexpected honesty and tenderness takes me off guard, but I am still leery of getting attacked by my own flock.

"Why aren't you still angry at me over how I treated Marcus and stormed out of the Hamptons?" I ask.

"I am, Emma. I'm still really pissed at you for being such a brat."

"But?"

"But I want my sister back."

A heave from somewhere deep inside, a tsunami of hidden emotion tidal waves from my gut, and I push my cell into my leg to cover the sound. I gasp.

I watch two girls on the beach burying one another in the

sand. I can see me and Jess playing and laughing—simply being sisters—before the world began to hurt us, and we began to hurt one another.

"Why now?" I ask.

"Our family has always prided itself on its independence, and we both have always taken pride in that, too," Jess says. "But now I'm worried our flock is becoming isolated, and it's hard to protect each other when we're swimming all alone and other predators are able to infiltrate."

"You're sort of freaking me out," I say.

"Would you just listen to me and check your mouth at the door for a moment?"

Ouch.

"Yes."

"I want to tell you a story," Jess says. "About someone you know and don't. Me."

I shift in my chair and watch the two girls wash the sand off one another in the lake.

"I've been drowning my whole life, Emma. Do you know how lucky you are to know that someone loved you unconditionally, more than anything else in the world? You were the center of GiGi's universe. Yes, I know GiGi loved me, but I also know I wasn't you. Parents and grandparents say they never have favorites. The world looks at someone who dares think that as if they have two heads. But they do. They just never say it out loud. You were just like GiGi—brash, outspoken, independent, never caring much what the world—and men—thought of you. And I know how scared you were when you got caught in that rip current as a girl and how angry you were at us for not racing to help, but, Emma, you were in the best hands possible. GiGi would never have let anything happen to you. And you probably don't remember this, but she got to you in a matter of seconds, carrying you home, her little seagull. But I've always been out there in the lake slowly drowning, no one watching. I was the firstborn, Emma. The firstborn is supposed to be the golden child, but you came along and broke all of the rules without giving a damn about what you said or what anyone thought. I think you're so angry at the world after GiGi's death because now you know how the rest of us feel—totally adrift, utterly alone."

"Why didn't you ever say something?" I ask.

"Because you've always had friends."

"You have friends," I say. "Babe."

"She is a friend," Jess says. "But she's a friend I pay a salary. And you always wonder inside if they love you for you or if they love you because there's a paycheck attached."

"Oh, Jess," I say.

"It's always been easy for you to make friends, from boarding school to college. You're actually more like Mom than you like to imagine."

"Hey!" I say.

"It's true," Jess says. "You're a fierce protector of your flock. You bite when you get threatened. Have you ever thought about how men treat me? I'm an object, like an expensive car that they want to touch, drive, be seen around town with, own. But it's even worse with women. Do you have any idea how they treat me?"

I am speechless at Jess's revelation. I always believed my sister had it so easy in life. I thought her looks unlocked every door. I was always jealous of her, and I now wonder if I locked her out of my life without considering what she might be dealing with.

I did lock her out.

When she asked if she could hang with my friends, I'd say no.

When she asked if she could read next to me on the sofa, I'd say no.

When she asked if she could play a game with me, I'd refuse.

I didn't mean to shut her out, I just invented a storyline for her that wasn't close to reality.

"No," I finally say.

"They make an impression of me based solely on my looks before they even get to know me. I'm a snob, a bitch or a slut. And I guess I've gotten used to leaning into those stereotypes to prove them right. I have a disease to please, and I know it's not healthy, but all I want is to feel seen and loved. It's awful, Emma, and it eats away at my soul like rat poison."

"Jess, I'm so sorry."

"I know," she says. "I'm sorry, too, because I know you get treated a certain way for speaking your mind. All women get treated a *certain* way. I'm just tired of being sorry."

"But look at all The Swans who follow, admire and love you, Jess."

"They love an image of me, Emma. They have no idea who I really am." She sighs. "I think there's only one person who sees me as clearly as I see myself."

"Who?"

"You."

I watch the two girls reach into the lake and—together— pick up a large, colorful stone and toss it in the air. It makes a huge splash.

I feel as if a weight has been lifted from me and against my better judgment, I ask, "Can I tell you a story now?"

"Of course."

And so I tell her about what Marcus said about destroying our family.

"I know you might not believe me, but I'm telling the truth, sis, and I'm terrified," I say. "I'm scared for Mom and Dad, you, the company, the future of The Mighty Pages. I'm worried about the future of our family. And I'm sorry I didn't tell you, but you wouldn't have believed me a few days ago." I hesitate. "I'm worried you still won't."

Her unnerving silence makes me think I shouldn't have told her. She doesn't believe me.

Now she has locked me out.

"Babe found a photo on social media someone took of you and Marcus," she finally says. "It wasn't the salacious one Page Six used of him looking so abused, it was one taken right before that. He is glowering at you, saying something to anger you. Someone else told Babe she overheard Marcus mocking you. I do believe you, Emma. Now I know why you threw a drink in his face."

"Why didn't you say something?"

She sighs deeply. "Because he's threatened me, too. He's warned me not to say anything to you or Mom and Dad. That's why he wanted to talk with me at Liber. I told you, our flock is being isolated. He's playing us against each other."

"What does he really want?"

"I don't know yet, but maybe we can figure it out." She hesitates. "Together.

"I need my sister," Jess continues. "Now. More than ever."

"Come home," I say. "Please. The front door will be unlocked."

"I'm booking my ticket as we speak."

CHAPTER FIFTEEN

I realize I have not—due to my nerves, a jitter that arrives from out of nowhere every so often and shakes my body like an internal earthquake—consumed anything today except coffee and water.

I feel like Jess.

I suddenly remember a writing professor I had in college—a well-respected author—who always asked the following question to writers to ground them and their works in reality: "When does the main character eat?"

It was meant to remind us—no matter if we are writing fantasy, young adult, historical fiction or memoir—not that our protagonists literally needed to be shown eating a meal but that they had to be human, connected to the reader and the world in a deeply personal and very real way.

"You need to eat, Emma," I tell myself in the silence of the cottage's kitchen.

I am famished.

My stomach growls and a hunger headache is playing a drum solo on my temples.

I open the cabinets.

Pasta, but no sauce. Cereal. Oatmeal. Tea. Coffee. Chips. Crackers.

I open the refrigerator.

Wine. Champagne. Pellegrino.

The cheese is moldy. The asparagus rubber.

I toss it into the trash and open the freezer.

"Still a college girl," I mutter. "You had time to go to the store."

My mother is right.

It's time for me to grow up. I can't live the rest of my life expecting dinner to be ready in the commons, or GiGi to have whipped up a summer barbecue.

I open the freezer and search inside, tossing icy packages this way and that.

And yet I am just a young woman trying to find her footing and place in this cold, cold world.

I smile.

A creative, driven woman.

"App night!" I yell.

A plethora of frozen food greets me—spring rolls, mac-and-cheese bites, mini meatballs and street tacos, pot stickers and puff pastries—all leftovers from my father's launch party. I look at the food, trying to piece together a meal that makes sense from disparate pieces. I decide on pot stickers, spring rolls and some jasmine sticky rice.

Perfect.

I turn on the oven to preheat and pull two tins from a side cabinet. I take a seat in an armchair by the hearth and pick up my latest read, yet another S. I. Quaeris novel from the stack in my bedroom.

To say I'm obsessed with these books would be an understatement. I no longer know if I'm reading them for escape or comfort, or to discover...

Something.

What that might be, I have no clue.

An eyebrow window of information…

Or am I just trying to bring a dead woman back to life?

After finding the leaf bookmark and the exact same quote in the Quaeris novel that was in Marcus's book—a quote my grandma was fond of using—as well as the exact same Acknowledgments in each Quaeris novel and then talking with my sister, I feel as if I'm trying to finish a puzzle that only has the edges complete.

The new book I'm reading is entitled *Autumn Harvest*. Even though there is no fire in the hearth and the leaves have to turn, I picked it up because of that leaf and the acorn I picked up in college from Julie Andrews that still sits in a jewelry tray on my dresser.

I picked it up this morning and could hear that thespian's voice in my head:

Let's start at the very beginning… A very good place to start.

I feel like I need to start at the beginning again, in so many ways.

And so I do.

I pick up the novel and flip to the Author's Note yet again. Exactly the same.

I read the novel's first page.

At one point in time, if your first or last name had a Z in it, if your skin were darker than the Dutch ancestors that surrounded you, then you were not welcome in this world. You were not to be loved.

That is why I chose God.

And even He seemed to reject me.

I stop.

Profound silence.

So loud that I hear buzzing.

I glance at the cover of the book again. This is *not* a typical romance novel. But what is typical? Why am I stereotyping, like Marcus Flare and my own family, a certain genre of books? Perhaps books—like women, like my sister, mother and me—defy categorization.

Call it a beach read, a summer sizzler, chick lit, feel-good fiction, a love story…

A damn good book is still a damn good book.

Period.

I continue reading, lost in the pages.

The preheated oven and the doorbell buzz at nearly the same time knocking me into the present.

My sister is not scheduled to arrive until tomorrow and yet she could have jumped on a plane to surprise me. I'm sure she's accumulated enough bonus miles to fly first-class to Fiji.

"Jess?" I call. "Coming!"

As I round the corner, I see two women—one who is perhaps in her sixties and another, much older, leaning precariously on a walker—standing beyond the screened door.

"Hi," I say. "Can I help you?"

"Does Pauline Page still live here?"

I look at them curiously.

"GiGi?" I rarely heard anyone call her by her real name. "No, I'm sorry, she doesn't. I mean, she did." I stumble trying to explain. "She passed away a couple of years ago."

"Oh," the younger of the two says. She bends down and speaks loudly into the other woman's ear, "Pauline died, Mom! *¡Muerta!*"

The older woman clamps a shaking hand to her mouth and whispers, "*Que descanse en paz*," before crossing herself.

"Did you know her?" the daughter asks.

"I'm her granddaughter," I say. "Emma."

"*Lo siento mucho*," the two women say, giving their condolences.

"Thank you."

They stand there for a moment, the mother looking around the yard, her hand a butterfly over her heart.

"It has not changed," she whispers.

"How did you know my grandmother?" I ask.

"My mother was a boarder here," the daughter explains. "A lifetime ago. We now live in Detroit. She doesn't have much time left, and she always told me stories about this place and how much she wanted to return one last time to see it…" She stops. "To see your grandmother."

My heart begins to pitter-patter in my chest.

"I'm so sorry to bother you, but would it be possible if we had a peek inside?" she continues. "We came so far, and I know it would mean so much to her."

Her mother's hands are clamped tightly.

"Of course," I say. "Please, come in."

We help the older woman into the house, and she stops in the entryway, looking up the staircase she can no longer navigate. She shuts her eyes and begins to talk, quickly, in Spanish. When she is done, she opens her eyes. They are filled with tears.

"My mother wants you to know that she moved to Michigan with her parents from Mexico when she was a baby. My grandfather worked the local blueberry farms. It was hard work, a hard life, but better than what they had. No one treated them particularly well, and my mother felt like an outcast at school. She had a tough time learning English, and no one would play with her. She had visions as a girl, and kids thought she was strange. My grandparents believed it was God speaking to her."

Her mother lowers her head as if in prayer.

"When she was eighteen, she decided to become a nun," her daughter continues. "But, after a few years, she knew that wasn't her calling, and she left the church. My grandparents were staunch Catholics, and believed she had turned her back on God and shamed the family. They refused to take her back. She had nothing. Someone told her about your grandmother, and she came here with a single bag. Your grandmother helped her with her English by reading books with her. She eventually helped her get a job at a local pie pantry, and my grandmother made fruit pies by hand."

Her mother mimes she's crimping a crust.

"She met a man there who came in every Sunday after church to have coffee and blueberry pie with his family, who he visited every weekend. He worked for Ford. They eventually married, my mother moved with him, and they had a family. She has always credited your grandmother's strength and kindness for saving her life."

"*¡Ella era un ángel!*" her mother says.

"Yes," her daughter says, "Pauline was an angel."

"*¡La biblioteca!*" the mother says, pointing.

We help her into the library. She shuts her eyes and inhales.

"She has always loved the smell of books," the daughter explains. "I read to her every day. She had a stroke a few years back, and she now mostly speaks in Spanish again, as she did as a girl, but, as you can tell, I know she understands what's going on." She looks at me and mouths, *She has congestive heart failure.*

The mother points a shaky hand around the library.

"No," she says. "*¡Todo ha cambiado! Sin color.*"

"She says 'everything in here has changed. No color.'"

"You're right. My parents took down all of GiGi's—I mean, Pauline's—books and replaced them with their own. They're publishers."

The woman nods.

"*¿Ceja?*" she asks me. "*¿Ceja?*"

I look at her daughter, not understanding the word.

"She's saying 'eyebrow.'"

I smile. "Yes, she called this Eyebrow Cottage."

The mother points up. "*¿Su oficina? ¿Ceja?*"

"Her office?" the daughter translates. "Eyebrow?"

I nod. "Yes, her office is still there. I was never allowed in-side. No one was."

The daughter translates, and the mother points at herself emphatically.

"I was!" she says very slowly. "I gave her stories!"

"I don't understand," I say. "*No entiendo.*"

"*¡Tu abuela fue una gran autora!*"

"She says, 'your grandmother was a great author.'"

"No, no, she wasn't an author," I explain. "She was a great reader, though."

"Sometimes, she mixes words up and gets confused," her daughter says. "I'm so sorry."

"I understand."

"May she see the kitchen before we leave?" her daughter asks. "She helped your grandmother cook meals for boarders and has such wonderful memories. She said making pies with her changed her life. My mother used to be such a wonderful baker. I try, but…"

"It's not the same," I finish. "I get it."

I lead them into the kitchen, and the old woman looks around, pleased that—unlike the library—nothing much has changed in here, save for the countertops and appliances. She leans against the counter and stares at the lake, shaking her head.

"Mom?" the daughter calls. "Are you ready? I think we've taken enough of this young lady's time."

She turns and nods. She begins to move toward the entry-way again when she blurts, "*¡Mi libro! ¡Mi libro!*" She veers un-steadily toward the hearth and points at *Autumn Harvest*.

"*¡Mi libro!*" she continues. "*¡Mi historia!*"

"That's not your book, Mom. That's Emma's." The woman looks at me. "I'm sorry. I told you she gets very confused, and it's already been a long day of travel for her."

"It's okay, really," I say.

We head to the front door, the older woman still muttering, "*Mi libro.*"

Her daughter escorts her out the door, turns and says, "Thank you for this. I can't tell you how much it means to me and especially my mother."

"It was my pleasure," I say.

As they turn to leave, I ask, "I didn't get your names. I want to tell my father, Pauline's son. He might remember stories his mother told him about your mother."

"My name is Maria," the daughter says, "and my mother's name is Zarela, Zarela Cruz."

"How beautiful," I say.

"It is, isn't it?" the daughter says. "It means 'fruit of the earth.'"

They navigate carefully down the gravel path and turn to wave when they reach the gate. The mother blows me a kiss. I pretend to catch it on the wind. She stops, bows her head, mumbles as if she's saying a prayer and then crosses herself again.

I wait until I hear their car drive away.

I head back to the kitchen and line an assortment of frozen apps on the cookie sheets. I slide them into the oven, set the timer and then return to the hearth and pick up my book.

I reread the opening lines of the book.

My heart stops.

Z.

Zarela Cruz?

My book! My story!

"She was a great author!"

I close the novel and stare at the cover featuring an orchard.

A puzzle with only the edges complete.

I drop the book. It hits the floor with a loud thud, which echoes throughout the kitchen.

CHAPTER SIXTEEN

I am reading *Autumn Harvest* as quickly as I can on the beach as if my life depends on it.

My beach chair is positioned directly on the shoreline, my feet in the lake, but my mind is elsewhere.

The sun's reflection on the waves creates a zigzag pattern of diamonds. They spell out one, large letter:

Z.

I consider the book.

Is this really her story? Or was she, as her daughter said, simply an old woman with a fuzzy memory?

I couldn't sleep, so I woke with the sun and ran at dawn, under a sky of pink and purple. There were a few beach walkers this morning, a woman doing yoga, a few rock hunters, but I was the only one who seemed to be running from both her past and her future.

The beach is still largely empty.

I'm drinking coffee from one of GiGi's favorite mugs, which is perched in the sand, and states Reading Is Dreaming with Your Eyes Open!

I take a sip of coffee, staring at the faded art on the mug.

I reach up and remove GiGi's cap that I'm wearing and place it on my lap.

My sister is coming home.

What do I think will happen?

Nancy Drew and the Hardy Boys will solve The Mystery of Mean Marcus?

That only happens in books, right?

If I work with Marcus, I will likely say or do the wrong thing. I could end up living the rest of my life knowing I helped stick the last knife in my family's back.

Or, are Jess and I as savvy as the Swans? Can we, too, take down a prolific writer who always seems to get away with his outlandish behavior?

"I think you have your seasons confused."

I am in shadow.

I look up.

Jess is standing over me, pointing at the cover of the novel I'm reading.

"I'm just confused in general."

She laughs.

"Welcome to the clown car," Jess says. "I'm driving."

I stand, and we hug.

"Why didn't you call me?" I ask. "I told you I'd pick you up from the airport in Grand Rapids."

"I needed a car anyway," she says.

"Two control freaks," I say. "I missed you so much."

She smiles.

"Me, too," she says. "Let's try to not screw it up again." Jess pauses. "Until tomorrow."

She holds me at arm's length and looks into my eyes, as if trying to make sure this is all real.

"I'll try," I say. "But you know me." Jess doesn't laugh. "And I'm sorry about, well, everything, sis. I mean it."

"I forgive you," she says. "Let's start there, okay?"

I nod.

Jess looks around the beach. "It's good to be back. There's nothing like Michigan in the summer."

I look at her to make sure this is all real, too.

"I mean it," she says. "I can love the ocean *and* the lake. It's like having two lovers, one in the city and one in the country."

"I have a lot to fill you in on," I say. "A lot."

"That sounds more ominous than our last conversation," she says.

"Have a seat," I say.

"Hey, before I lose this glimmer of nostalgia, I had an idea on the drive here. Why don't we decorate the cottage for the Fourth of July just like GiGi did. Remember? It was something we all did as a family every summer. We have a couple of days before the holiday. We don't really celebrate holidays like that anymore."

"It's so warm and fuzzy to go to Tavern on the Green for Thanksgiving, isn't it?" I tease.

"Can you imagine Mom stuffing a turkey and making a pumpkin pie?" Jess laughs.

"I can imagine Mom making reservations at Tavern on the Green," I say. "Come on. I know where GiGi keeps everything."

"I had another idea on the ride here, too."

I look at her. "Yes?"

"Can I surprise you?"

"No."

She laughs.

"I just want one day of fun—one summer evening in Michigan—before we talk about Marcus and the real world. Is that bad? Just one night?"

I shake my head.

"I think that's a great idea."

She smiles. I continue.

"And I think I already know where you want to go."

I grab my things off the beach and put GiGi's hat on Jess's head.

She touches the brim and closes her eyes for a moment.

"C'mon, Emma," she says. "The Page sisters will show this town how summer and the Fourth of July is done."

There is nothing that a Rum Runner from Captain Lou's in South Haven can't fix.

Or two.

Captain Lou's is an old, shingled shack with an outdoor bar and live music on the weekends that overlooks the river and the harbor, where you can sit and watch boats idle by all day long.

Jess motions for the waiter—who has yet to take his eyes off my sister since we arrived—to bring us another round.

"You have a lot in common with VV," I say.

"Them's fighting words," she says. "And after another of these I'll be ready to fight."

"Here ya go!" he says. "With a floater. My treat."

A floater is an extra shot that Captain Lou's "floats" on top of their famed frozen drink. We need it like we needed the onion rings at Clementine's—another of South Haven's famous haunts—which come homemade and piled high on a post as if you just played ring toss with them. My sister said we needed the grease to soak up the booze.

The waiter sets our drinks before us. He is about my age, very tan already, hair bleached by the sun, eyes like the lake. His arms are marble, and his biceps make the sleeve on his T-shirt scream in both delight and exhaustion.

"Anything else?" he asks. "Like my number?"

My sister laughs.

"Subtle," she says. "Thank you, but I'm not dating."

"You? Why not?"

"I'm happy being single right now."

"I could make you happier."

He smiles, and it's such a heart-stopping, earnest smile that—even on a perfect summer day in Michigan—the world dims in its brightness.

"Maybe after one more Rum Runner," my sister says.

He bows and walks away from our table backward, still soaking in my sister's beauty.

"Cheers again," she says. "To Michigan!"

I clink her glass.

"What?" she asks, noting my stare. "I just said that to appease him."

"You've always done things to appease others."

"Like I said, I have a disease to please."

"But you don't need to," I offer slowly so as not to upend the delicate balance of understanding we've just achieved.

"It's hard to unlearn," Jess says.

She takes a big slug of her Rum Runner and eyes me further.

"I'm detecting judgment," she continues. "I had nothing to do with his initial response."

"I know that," I say, "but you have this aura."

"I'm just Jess," my sister says, leaning back with force, her chair scooching away from the table. "What am I supposed to do? Wear a mask?"

She sighs.

"This is what I was just saying to you on the phone, sis. I'm judged every day by women, by men, by…you. By things I say and don't say. God, it's exhausting. The last thing I need is to hear it from you when I'm trying to forget our lives for a hot second. Give me a break please."

"I'm sorry," I say.

It's too late.

"You're a book that's always been judged by its pages. I'm a book that's always been judged by its cover. Since I was a kid.

Girls were jealous. Guys were flirts. And I felt ugly compared to Mom."

"You? I always felt like Weird Barbie compared to you and Mom."

"But you always had GiGi, Emma. You always had friends." My sister looks over the deck at the boats drifting past. "Books were my only friends. You get shut out of the game for so long, you don't want to even play anymore."

Her words somersault me back in time.

When my sister and I were young, we shared a room at Eyebrow Cottage.

We could have had separate rooms, but we wanted to be together after being separated at boarding school.

"Summer's short, like you," Jess always said, mussing my hair, when we'd arrive and settle into our room. "Life's long. One day, we won't be able to do this."

We would push those two twin beds next to each other in the middle of the room and make our own girl camp. We read books that scared the bejesus out of us—Stephen King, V. C. Andrews—with flashlights under the covers, we did each other's hair…

We didn't need anyone else in this world.

And then Jess went through puberty, and a little girl became a beautiful flower.

That's when the knocking on the front door began, which turned into late-night texts on her phone. Jess began to spend more time with boys than with me.

Oh, I tried to make them see me, but the knocks, the texts were always for her.

And it was so effortless for her. Ten minutes before the mirror, and she could stop a train. My attempt at perfection required an hour and a half, a can of hairspray, an array of makeup and a facade of confidence.

One night when she was on the phone talking to a boy instead of talking to me, I grabbed all my stuff. I didn't yell, or go to another room. I went to the basement.

"Where are you going, Emma?" Jess asked.

"As far away from you as I can."

GiGi heard the commotion and followed me to the basement.

"May I ask why you're so upset?"

"She doesn't know I exist. She hates me."

GiGi came over to the old Jenny Lind bed in the corner of the drafty basement and took a seat on the squeaky mattress.

"She doesn't hate you," GiGi said, "and you are—and will always be—your sister's world. But, at this point in her life, her world is very, very different from yours. You'll understand one day."

I didn't want to understand.

Nearly every week after that—and for the next few summers—my sister would randomly appear at night on the basement stoop in her pajamas holding a stack of board games.

"I got Uno, Monopoly, Operation, Clue, Scrabble, Which Witch?, Trouble, Sorry!, a deck of cards for Hearts and—your favorite—Yahtzee!" she'd say. "Your pick!"

"No, thanks," I'd say, turning back to my book or my journal, head down until I heard the stairs creak and door shut.

I stayed in the basement until my sister began to spend more time away with my parents. When she'd return, we not only had separate bedrooms, we had separate lives.

I had GiGi.

Jess had my parents.

I had friends.

Jess had boyfriends.

Eventually, she just didn't want to play with me anymore.

I had shut her out.

I open my mouth to address our childhood rivalry—which has always been the wedge preventing us from shutting the door on our past—but my sister now has her chair turned toward the water, her elbows on the railing, chin resting in her hands.

"Remember GiGi's boat?" she says wistfully, trying to keep the door closed on our conversation.

I nod.

"Why do you think she rarely took us out on it?" Jess continues.

I watch the boats—sailboats, whalers, cigarette boats, yachts—drift on the water.

GiGi had a tritoon named *The Ni-Ko-Nong* in honor of South Haven's history and sunsets.

And that was the time GiGi typically took her boat out, summer evenings, when the hordes had returned home for a nap and dinner, the winds had died down, and the lake was hers and hers alone.

Once *The Ni-Ko-Nong* was out of the channel, GiGi would gun that little boat toward the horizon. She'd venture out about a mile, turn off the motor and float, either reading or filling her journal with notes. She'd watch the sun set, and then motor home—lights on—hat perched atop her head, singing Sinatra's "Summer Wind."

I accompanied GiGi out on the boat more than Jess, but—my sister is right—those days were rare. Most times, she'd sneak off on her own, without a word, as if the horizon were the only friend she needed in the world.

"I always thought she just needed her own time," I say. "I went out with her on occasion…"

Jess lifts her head from her hands and shoots me a glance that reads, *Of course you did.*

"…*rare* occasion, but, most days, she'd sneak off by herself."

"What happened to that boat?" Jess asks.

"Dad sold it, remember? Said it was silly to keep it and pay for insurance, the slip, winter storage and maintenance since no one used it."

"I really wish we'd kept it," Jess says. "Sometimes, I think you have to be on the water—way out, like GiGi—to really appreciate the reason you're here. To get away from the world until it's just you and the horizon."

It's as if she, too, can read my mind, like Mom and Dad.

"Me, too."

The waiter returns, and Jess keeps her head turned toward the harbor.

"Just the check," I say quickly.

He walks away, head down.

Such is the magic—and devastation—Jess has on men.

We walk at dusk through downtown South Haven, the streets bustling with resorters. As we walk, our arms and hands bump together, just as they did when we were girls and were so tired from a day at the beach that we didn't think we could take another step to walk home and ended up sort of leaning against one another to make the other stronger, whole.

We collapse into the porch swing when we get back to Eyebrow Cottage, unable to make it all the way inside, and let the night breeze blow us to and fro.

GiGi's solar lights suddenly pop on in her garden, and her beautiful flowers—still tended to by her longtime lawn care company, a husband and wife now in their sixties—are illuminated.

The hydrangeas are starting to pop—electric blue and soft pink—and they sit next to GiGi's beloved peonies, which have already come and gone.

"I can see GiGi tending her garden," Jess says, as if reading my mind once again. "It's like she's still here."

"She is," I say.

Jess knocks my leg with hers, a sisterly truce.

"She always loved peonies the most, you know," I say.

Jess is quiet.

"Thank you for saying that," she finally says. "Remember what she used to say?"

I shake my head. "No."

"Hydrangeas bloom off old wood and are a wonder of color and endurance. Peonies exhaust their stems with their short-lived beauty. But you can't have a garden without both."

I smile.

"See? I listened to her."

"We were there for everybody else, but not for each other," I say. "Nobody can tend to our own weeds but us."

"I thought it was easy for you."

"I thought it was easy for you, too."

The lake breeze catches the swing and we rock in silence.

Jess grabs my hand. I put my head on her shoulder and we rock back and forth in twilight. The sky grows colorful.

"The final wink," Jess says.

"Wanna go play a game?" I ask after the color dims.

She turns to look at me, her face covered with the most wistful smile. This time, she puts her head on my shoulder and whispers, "I'd love that."

I stand and extend my hand.

"But I still get to pick!" I say.

CHAPTER SEVENTEEN

"Why did I think this was such a great idea yesterday?" Jess asks.

She is lathered in sweat, her hair plastered to the side of her face and her back.

"Because you weren't hungover," I say.

"And why is this garage 700 degrees."

"Because now you're hungover," I say.

She laughs.

"I couldn't do this without you," Jess says.

"I wouldn't do this without you."

"Because you'd kill yourself," Jess says. "Why do the tallest members of a family always have to risk their lives?"

Jess is teetering on the top step of a shaky ladder handing me red, white and blue containers filled with festive flags, bunting, banners, streamers, tablecloths, plates and wreaths.

"Remember how Dad and I would always have to be the ones to grab a can of soup from the top shelf in the pantry or perch ourselves on a footstool to reach a book on a top shelf in GiGi's library," Jess continues, "and we'd always say…"

"How did it get up here in the first place," we say in unison, laughing.

Jess stops, wipes her brow and gestures at the endless stacks of color-coordinated bins for Halloween, Thanksgiving, Christmas and Easter.

"I forgot how much she loved a holiday," she says.

Her face is caught between a smile and a frown, as if she's sad that she had forgotten but happy she finally remembered.

"I think that's it." Jess climbs down the ladder and takes a slug from a bottle of water.

We carry the containers into the front yard. I open up lid after lid, and it's as if memories are being released like genies into the summer air.

I drape American bunting around my waist.

"She used to wear this as a skirt to the fireworks, remember?" I ask. "Mom and Dad were mortified."

"She had a knack for embarrassing them," she chuckles. "Remember the blueberry pie eating contest?" I nod. Jess catches my eye. "You have that knack, too."

Jess helps me drape the white picket fence with the bunting, and as we do the same off the shingled front porch, I finally tell her what transpired the night before she arrived.

As I recount the story of the grandmother, how she believed GiGi was an author and that she inspired *Autumn Harvest*, I segue into telling Jess about the same line GiGi used to quote that was in both the S. I. Quaeris and Marcus Flare novels as well as how GiGi's favorite author never changed a single word in their Author's Note.

I am talking so quickly that I don't realize Jess has taken a seat on the front steps and her half of the bunting is draped across the hydrangeas fronting the porch.

I take a seat by her.

"Sorry," I say. "That is a lot of intel."

"It is," Jess says. "Can I say something without you blowing a gasket?"

"No."

"I will anyway," she says. "You're a writer. Yes, I know all about the secret novel you wrote in college. Mom told me. Your friends have talked to her about it. GiGi told Dad."

I keep my mouth shut.

"It's not a shock, Emma. You always wanted to be a writer, and GiGi always pressed you to be one as if you were going to finish a chapter she never had the chance to complete," Jess says. "Are you done with it?"

I nod.

"Is it good?"

"I don't know."

"Yes, you do."

I nod.

"I'm proud of you."

"Really?"

"It's sad you have to ask that of me," she says, knocking me with her knee as she did last night. "Really."

"Thanks."

"Is that why you met with VV?"

"Not at first," I say, "but it led in that direction."

"She's a great agent."

I do a hammy double take and stare at Jess. "Are you still drunk?"

"No, although she usually is. She's still the best in the business. Mom and Dad have always been in a battle with her. It happens in publishing. Some agents and editors don't see eye to eye." Jess looks at me. "And it's hard to look her in the eye with those Mr. Magoo glasses."

I laugh.

"So," Jess continues, "do you think—as a writer with a great imagination—perhaps all of this is just a story you've created in your own head to make sense of all the drama that is going on in our lives right now? A way to cope and explain the unexplainable?"

"Maybe," I admit.

"Right now, we have to deal with Marcus and get to the bottom of why he wants to hurt our family," Jess says. "I'm still unsure what his motive is. I mean, major publishers are teaming up with famous and celebrity authors and starting imprints like wildfire—Sarah Jessica Parker, Gillian Flynn, Kwame Alexander.... What does he have against us? I mean, I know Mom and Dad can be a lot to deal with, but to want to destroy us? It's like he's got his TV shows confused. He's mistaking *Schitt's Creek* for *Succession*, and I just don't get it yet."

Jess hesitates.

"And?" I ask.

"And Marcus is a snake. Is he just a snake in business, or is he truly dangerous? He came out of nowhere and seems ruthless in his approach to people, which is such a shocking juxtaposition to the fiction he writes and the persona he presents to the public. Something just doesn't add up for me. We need more pieces to solve the puzzle.

"And," she continues, unprompted. "I feel like I need to shower every time I'm around him. The way he touches me, looks at me, circles me, almost like a predator. I've been going along with it because I know the trouble Mom and Dad are in financially and how much this deal means to them. We need him. We need the money. If it works, it could change everything, Emma, and I mean *everything*. I know Mom and Dad often seem like characters sometimes..."

"You think?" I say, cutting her off. "You just said it! Moira and Johnny Rose from *Schitt's Creek*."

"And you're Alexis," I add at the same time Jess yells, "And you're David!"

We laugh hard like we used to—tears streaming down our faces—when we believed we were sisters whose hearts wouldn't be complete without the other half.

"I know Mom and Dad seem like characters," she continues, "and they can drive us crazy, but wouldn't you do anything for them?"

I narrow my eyes. I consider the awful things Mom said to me.

"Emma," she continues. "They're all we have in this world."

I then think of what else Mom said: The only thing parents and grandparents want is the best for their children and grandchildren. They hope to raise them right—no matter how many mistakes they make along the way—in order to leave the world a better place.

"I would," I say. "But you have one thing wrong."

"What?"

"Mom and Dad aren't all we have in this world," I say. "We have each other."

"God, you're a good writer," she says.

Jess opens her arms, and we hug for the longest time, rocking back and forth.

"I promise this will all make sense," Jess says. "I think some time away from the city and the pressure will provide some clarity."

"And you'll be able to add holiday decorator to your résumé," I say, standing. "Ready to finish?"

I extend my hand, and she pops up.

We hang wreaths on the gate and front door, stick sparkly ting ting in window boxes, and plant a big American flag in the bracket off the giant sugar maple in the front yard. I salute when the lake breeze catches it, and the flag flaps in the wind.

I walk over and begin to open container after container.

"Hey, are the Michigan flags in any of your bins over there?" I call to Jess. "There should be two of them—the University of Michigan flag GiGi started hanging when I started college there, and a state flag because she loved Michigan so much. GiGi kept them out during the summer for visitors and then in the fall for football. Remember?"

"Yeah," Jess says, digging.

"Found the Maize and Blue!" she yells, holding up the university flag. "Isn't that what you insane Michigan fans call it?"

"Insane means passionate, right?"

I race over and dig under a stack of plastic tablecloths and hold up the state flag. "Found this, too!"

Jess and I head to the porch, where brackets for the flags are adhered to columns on each side of the steps.

I hang my U-M flag and begin to sing "The Victors," Michigan's famous fight song that anybody who has ever turned on a TV during the fall will recognize. Jess moves to the other column and hangs the state flag.

"If you seek a pleasant peninsula, look about you."

Jess stares at me. "Are you sure you're not the one who's still drunk?"

"No, I'm impressing you with my state knowledge." I point at the flag. "You grew up here, too. You should know this."

I hold out the flag and study it closely. I rarely remember taking the time to look at our state flag even though it's everywhere in Michigan.

The state coat of arms is a blue shield featuring the sun rising over a lake and peninsula with a man, hand raised, holding a gun. The shield is flanked by an elk and a moose, an eagle on top, with a white banner beneath it.

"I don't see where it says anything about a peninsula," Jess says, studying the flag, too.

"They didn't teach you Latin at the fancy boarding school *you* attended?" I ask. "It's just the root of all the romance languages. Nothing important."

"Ewww, you're insufferable, David."

I laugh and continue.

"*Si quaeris peninsulam amoenam, circumspice,*" I say, pointing at the script in the banner. "I'm probably mispronouncing the hell out of that, but I do know it's a Latin phrase meaning, 'If you seek a pleasant peninsula, look about you.'"

"How did I never know that?" Jess asks. "It's so sad that we never really stop to take the time to look at what's right in front of us." Her cell trills, and she grabs it quickly and begins to text. When Jess finishes, she looks at me. "Guilty!"

"As punishment, why don't you start taking a few bins back to the garage?"

Jess glares at me.

"You're the tallest!" I continue.

She jokingly flips me off, stacks two bins and heads toward the garage.

I go inside, grab a bottle of water, return, and take a seat on the front porch swing and admire the work we've done.

"It's not the Fourth until the world is dressed in red, white and blue," I can hear GiGi say.

Autumn Harvest waits for me on the striped cushion of the porch swing. It's good, but the visit yesterday makes it seem like I'm reading someone's diary. I feel compelled to finish, and this would be the perfect spot to do that this afternoon.

A sudden gust off the lake catches the two flags and stiffens them.

I stare at the white banner set against the dark blue fabric.

I glance down at the novel.

My head pivots back and forth between them.

"Do you need an exorcism, Linda Blair?" Jess asks as she returns, heading up the stairs.

I jump up, sending the porch swing flying.

I grab the flag and read the Latin words.

"*Si quaeris peninsulam amoenam, circumspice!*" I whisper.

"What?" Jess asks.

I grab the novel and hold it up in front of Jess's face.

"*Si quaeris!*" I say, pointing at the flag and then the cover of the novel. "S. I. Quaeris."

"What in the hell are you talking about?" Jess asks.

I don't answer. I don't know how I didn't figure this out. I don't know how anyone—especially in Michigan—never put two and two together. But who reads Latin in a flag? And this was all in a time before the internet and social media. The secret was hidden in plain sight.

"Hello?" Jess asks again.

I flip to the Acknowledgments.

There, right in front of me, is the answer. It's been right there in front of me—in front of the world—forever, just waiting to be discovered.

I see the first letters of each paragraph now as if they are in bold and glitter and lit from within:

I first must thank my readers. Without you, I would not be able to live my dream. Writing is what keeps me sane, how I make sense of an often senseless world. Books are the great connector. They bring us closer, bridge the gap, remind us that we have more in common than what divides us. My novels are about family, friends, the wisdom of our elders, the overlooked women in our lives, the overlooked soul within you, and I write them to remind you that you matter, and that it is the little things in life that mean the most: A sunrise. A sunset. Love. Happy endings. Each other. My little novels are meant as threads of hope and beacons of light for those who are drowning in the world. Know there will be a better day. And that can start right now by escaping into a better one.

A big thank-you as well to my team: Harlequin (and now Silhouette), you are the best publisher an author could dream of having. You give a voice to women, their issues and their hearts, and I could not be more proud to call you my home away from home and my literary sister.

"Men know best about everything, except what women know better." That's a quote from George Eliot (aka Mary Ann Evans

who wrote Middlemarch*) and a favorite of my editor. I keep that in mind with every book I write.*

Gratitude. This is the motto by which I live. I am grateful for each sunrise and sunset. I am grateful for each day I get to watch my family grow and laugh. I am grateful, that my simple stories will, hopefully, live forever, something none of us can do.

I am eternally grateful for my friends and family, who inspire me daily and support my dream. I'm also grateful they continue to speak to me even after I've written about them (names were changed!).

Grateful for you. Every single one of you. Your letters that the publisher forwards to me are hugs, constant reaffirmation that my novels are touching you, helping you, changing you.

I must also thank my "invisible team," who helps me write two books a year. They plot while I "pants." They edit as I write. They are young—and keep me young—but are the foundation of this big, beautiful dream.

Page by page, word by word, sentence by sentence…that is how each and every one of my glorious days are filled (oh, and with some coffee and wine, too!). I race out of bed every morning, excited and humbled to begin my days. I get lost in my stories. I become my characters. And, oh, what a glorious way to live!

A final nod to home, a place I love (and never leave) more than any. This place inspires me, fills my soul, and when I sink my toes in the sand, or dive into the crystal water, I know I am part of this place, and it is a part of me, and we will forever be intertwined.

Go now and read! Anything and everything! Hug your librarian! Support your local bookseller! And go to places you never imagined, be people you never dreamed, walk in shoes you thought you'd never travel, and be changed. It is a privilege to evolve and change. We should never be the same people we were. Books help us on that journey.

Eliot again writes, "It is a narrow mind which cannot look at a subject from various points of view." Books saved my life. And I believe they just might save the world. *XOXO!*

"I am GiGi Page!" I yell. "The Acknowledgments never changed because the author was telling us who she was in each and every book."

Jess looks at me, still confused.

"S. I. Quaeris was our grandmother!"

CHAPTER EIGHTEEN

"How did you get that?" I ask. "*Where* did you get that?"

Jess and I are standing outside GiGi's office. She is holding the skeleton key GiGi used to wear around her neck.

"Do you actually think Mom would let GiGi be buried with this around her neck?" Jess rolls her eyes. "She waited until everyone was gone and took it."

"I don't know whether to be mortified or thrilled at her foresight."

"With Mom, it's totally normal to feel both emotions."

"And?" I ask. "Where did you find it?"

"It's always been in the safe in Mom and Dad's bedroom here. Mom told me about it one night after a martini and three glasses of wine."

"How do you know the code to their safe?"

"It pays to be nice to Mom," Jess says with a smile. "And she's a total narcissist anyway. The code isn't a number, it's the name of her first book, *Tethered*."

"You're good," I say.

"You're just starting to appreciate my unique talents."

"I feel like an intruder standing here," I say. "Like I shouldn't be here. Have you ever been in here before?"

"Of course," she says. "I snooped around after GiGi died."

"Why didn't you tell me?"

Jess points at my mouth and makes a big circle around it with her hands.

As Jess inserts the key, the GiGi-Marcus quote echoes in my brain: *A secret is like an acorn: whether or not it ever grows to see the light depends on how deep you bury it.*

"I'm nervous."

"I think you're going to be shocked."

Before I can ask why, the old, thick, heavy door creaks open in an appropriately creepy, Stephen King sort of way. I flinch as if GiGi is on the other side waiting to catch us.

I expect a rush of ghosts and spirits to fly out and enter my body as payback for disobeying GiGi, but her office looks, well, like an office.

"Told you," Jess says. "Super boring."

It's dusty for sure, and a few cobwebs billow in the corners for effect, but GiGi was meticulous, as are my parents, and even without much use the last few years, everything looks as if my grandmother just stepped out for lunch.

There is a row of file cabinets of varying size that look as if they were plucked from Dunder Mifflin stacked along the tallest wall away from the dormer. Wooden bookshelves are perched beneath the angled walls. These, surprisingly, are not organized. Some shelves are stacked with books, one atop another, while others resemble piano keys, with spines jutting forward as if they were pulled out and replaced quickly. Tucked into an eave is a closet.

And then I see it.

My grandmother's desk.

I've only seen it in person a few times in my life. Once, when I came charging in when she'd forgotten to lock the door.

"Out, scout!" she had yelled, without turning.

Another time, South Haven experienced an entire summer of nonstop rain: cold temperatures and lake effect precipitation drenched the coast day after day. The roof began to leak into my grandma's office, and workers were in and out of the house for weeks. My grandmother was so unnerved she got shingles. My father had to come and stay with her, and the two of them hid away in her bedroom, Jess and I delivering meals while my mother stayed in the city.

"I have too much work," I could hear GiGi say to my father. "Too many deadlines. Help me."

A roofer looked at her one afternoon and said, "Geez, lady, just sit in your beautiful kitchen and work."

"I can't work in *public*!" she cried.

There is only one photo I know of that captured GiGi sitting at her desk. It was in an old shoebox I found crammed in the back of her closet after she died. I wouldn't let anyone touch GiGi's belongings. I went through the pictures, one by one, as if my life depended on it. I nearly threw the shoebox away, thinking it was empty. But there she was, young, raven-haired, bewitching, intense, hunched over a mountain of papers, fountain pen in her hand as if she was about to use it as a sword to vanquish the invisible demons that surrounded her.

And on her lips? The most knowing smile.

And her face? The most knowing look.

I kept that photo on my desk at college. Now I keep it in a box awaiting a future desk of my own. One like hers.

GiGi's desk is placed directly beneath the eyebrow window. Light pours in through the small window, illuminating the arched wood that surrounds it.

I run my hands over its surface.

It is a vintage rolltop desk, burnished wood, large and imposing. GiGi once said it took four men to get the desk in here, and that they stopped—midway up the steps, backs breaking—until she agreed to double their wages.

The desk has four drawers on each side of the kneehole. A wooden chair on brass casters—with a pretty floral cushion—is pushed beneath it.

I place my hand on the rolled top and speak directly to it.

"Why would the author's name be part of the motto of the state flag? Why would every book's Acknowledgments spell out *I Am GiGi Page*? Why would that old woman say GiGi wrote her story? Why would GiGi quote this author? And why would Marcus Flare use the exact same quote decades later?"

I take a seat in GiGi's chair.

"Tell me, GiGi. Please."

For the first time, I realize this is the only room in Eyebrow Cottage that doesn't have expansive windows or a beautiful view.

As if she didn't want an ounce of distraction.

Or attention.

I look at Jess, take a breath and roll open the desk.

Nothing, save for a pen sitting all alone.

"Told ya," Jess says.

I open the drawers on each side.

Files, categorized: bank, electric, gas, taxes—federal, state, property—car. Each filled with old bills. GiGi never went electronic. In anything.

I get up and walk to the file cabinets along the wall.

More files, these organized by the names of GiGi's boarders over the years, paper statements with PAID stamped on them, old checks.

"Nothing," I say, my voice lifeless.

"I mean, this can't be coincidence, can it?" Jess says. "She was spelling out her name for the world to see. What are *we* not seeing?"

I feel beyond helpless, so perplexed that my legs feel weak.

I take a seat, cross-legged, on the Persian rug that's as faded as the type on those old statements. Jess joins me, and we just sit in silence.

See, Emma. See something!

I look beyond Jess toward the bookshelves that are home to the S. I. Quaeris novels that used to line her library. The covers call to me like a siren. I crawl over to them and begin to pull the novels off one at a time, studying them before turning to the Acknowledgments that recite the same thing over and over: *I AM GIGI PAGE.*

"What are you doing?" Jess asks.

"I have absolutely no clue."

"Do you think maybe you're just coming to terms with selling the cottage, and this is a final goodbye to GiGi and all its memories?" Jess asks.

"I don't know. Maybe." I look up at Jess and smile wanly. "Maybe."

I mindlessly continue to pull book after book from the shelf, stacking them before me, touching each one.

I get up and walk over to the closet.

"Ouch!"

I bump my head on the sloped ceiling, as GiGi always seemed to do, emerging from her office rubbing a knot or sporting a Band-Aid on her forehead.

"How you doing, Grace?" Jess asks, repeating the line GiGi would say whenever someone would trip.

I open the closet. It is deep and oddly shaped. At the front, there are rods holding hanging blankets and quilts, sweatshirts and hoodies.

"What's in there?" Jess asks. "I forgot."

"Stuff to keep GiGi warm when she worked early in the morning or late at night."

"Oh, yeah. She was always chilly, wasn't she?"

I reach out and touch an old football blanket—plaid and

square—that GiGi used to carry around the house like Linus on chilly, damp days. A vintage Michigan hoodie catches my eyes. I pull it free, thinking I might wear it when I write. I grab the hanger and turn to Jess.

"No wire hangers!" I yell, impersonating Faye Dunaway doing Joan Crawford in *Mommie Dearest*. "No wire hangers *ever*!"

"Save that so we can give it to Mom for Christmas," Jess jokes.

I laugh and turn back into the closet.

And that's when I see it.

I lift the hanger as I need to use it as a weapon.

At first glance, I thought it might be someone standing in the back of the closet, but as I lean closer, I see that it is a standing safe. A big one. Hidden behind the rows of hanging quilts and hoodies.

"A safe?" I say, the words coming out as a husky whisper.

"What?" Jess asks.

I find my voice.

"A safe!"

Jess comes running.

"Ouch!"

"You banged your head, too, didn't you, Grace?" I joke, calling her by the name GiGi would use when we'd do something clumsy.

"Oh, my gosh," Jess says when she sees the safe.

We pull the blankets and sweaters off the hangers and squeeze into the open space.

"Safe cracking is obviously your superpower!" I say.

"GiGi's birthday?" she asks.

Jess spins the lock left and right and back again, ear close, listening.

She shakes her head. "Nope."

"My birthday?" I suggest.

"Narcissist," she laughs.

Jess tries again.

"Nope."

"Try Dad's," I say.

Jess enters the code. Nothing.

I then remember what she said about Mom and Dad's safe.

"It's not a number, it's a name," I say. "Try S. I. Quaeris."

I hear a soft click. The safe pops open.

I pretty much shove Jess out of the way.

I grab my cell, turn on the flashlight and shine it inside.

A shoebox sits in front. I pull it free.

"Look!" I say.

Phillip is written in GiGi's script on top.

I open it.

There is a Polaroid of my father sitting at a childhood desk—both tiny and adorable—holding a fountain pen. *Phillip's writing desk* is written in the white frame of the photo. There is another Polaroid of my father holding a wrapped present in GiGi's library beside the giant grandfather clock that used to stand sentinel. It looks like Big Ben next to my tiny tot of a dad, and he is pointing at the time: 7:30. *Phillip's 5th Birthday! On the dot!*

Beneath the photos is a Bible with my father's name inside, a well-worn copy of *Jonathan Livingston Seagull*, also with my dad's name inside the cover, plus an old journal. I open it, and every lined page is filled with a poem or story.

"Can you believe it? This was all Dad's," I say. "He was a born writer." I look at Jess. "He actually had a Bible? Logical, analytical Dad? And he's always made fun of how simplistic *Jonathan Livingston Seagull* is. He used to chide GiGi for reading it to me." I hold up the journal. "Look how prolific he used to be."

I throw a hand over my mouth to hold back a scream of surprise.

"He wrote a poem called 'The Beach Is My Happy Place.'" I read. "'Hello, Mr. Sun, We are going to have so much fun.'"

Jess laughs.

"What did they do with our father?" she asks. "I'd love to see the poetry that he and Mom wrote when they were young." Jess catches my eye. "But these are just family mementoes, Emma, that GiGi squirreled away like any grandmother would do. Hidden memories that meant something to her. Nothing more."

I set down the box filled with my dad's childhood, and I shine my flashlight into the safe again.

Nothing.

I go deeper into the safe with my hand and the light.

I gasp.

"What?" Jess asks.

"Look!"

The back of the safe is filled with a stack of paper, hundreds of pages, all written in fountain pen, held together by a rubber band. I pull them out to show her.

First draft
The Summer of Lost & Found
By GiGi Page

"Oh, my God!" I yell. "I was right, Jess! She was S. I. Quaeris."
She grabs the cover sheet from me as I sift through the pages.

"How can this be?" Jess asks. "How could she keep this a secret her whole life?" Jess looks at me. "Why would she keep this a secret? It makes no sense."

I cram an arm into the safe, which reaches deep into the wall. I sweep the remaining contents free.

A total of four manuscripts, two a year, a fall and summer novel, and Christmas and spring, are freed. Each is filled with editorial notes and proofreaders' notes.

"This manuscript is dated 1975!" I gasp. "Are you telling me GiGi wrote her entire life? Since Dad was a baby?"

"She must have started right after Grampa died," Jess says.

"Is that really how she got so rich?" Jess continues to stare at me. "What is happening?"

I quickly google S. I. Quaeris again, along with her editor's name, searching for pertinent information.

Her editor. Dead. For many years.

"Her last book was published the year Mom and Dad started The Mighty Pages," I say. "There has to be more manuscripts. I bet this is only the start."

I pull more manuscripts free. I recognize them from published books I have read, novels now sitting right in front of me.

"Did Mom and Dad know?" I ask.

Jess raises her brows, gives me a look that says, *How could they not know?*

I again reach my hand into the back of the safe. A manila folder. I pull it free and open it.

"What is this?" I ask, handing it to Jess.

"It looks like some kind of police report," she says. "And a magazine article."

She reads in silence, flipping the pages of the article, then the report.

"What?" I finally ask, unable to take the suspense.

"There was a death threat against GiGi," Jess finally says. "A very real one."

"You're kidding, right?"

"I'm not," she says, shaking her head. "It looks as though GiGi published a rather provocative essay in *Ms.* magazine in 1973 about a woman who loses her husband at a young age. She doesn't want to remarry—as she realizes her late husband was the love of her life and that she's happy living alone and on her own terms—and yet she doesn't want to..." Jess hesitates "...how should I put this? She doesn't wasn't to stop having sex either."

"What?"

Jess scans the article.

"A Michigan man named Ignatius Marcuzzi was so outraged by the article that he stalked GiGi. Apparently she woke up one night in bed to discover him over her holding a gun. Boarders in the house heard a commotion and tried to overpower him, but he brandished the gun and escaped until he was eventually apprehended. Ignatius told police, 'That woman is a disgrace to our state. I would kill her to protect people from her filth and ideas.'"

My astonishment turns to rage. I think of GiGi, alone and scared.

Slowly, that rage turns to a rush, a thrill of discovering that GiGi and I have always been connected more deeply than I ever imagined.

We are both writers.

"S. I. Quaeris," I whisper, glancing at the books that surround me. "That's why she chose a pen name, Jess. It was her only option. She wanted to write, she had to write, but she also had to protect herself and her family, and the only way to do that was with complete anonymity. GiGi did what so many female writers had to do in the past: Use a pseudonym to protect or disguise her identity and get her work to be taken seriously in a world that didn't like the ideas women championed. And she chose a name that paid tribute to the place she loved and wrote about. She was telling the world who she was in every single book."

"Has anything changed in life or literature?" Jess asks. "I mean, really changed? God, I've been fooling myself by thinking what I'm doing has been making a difference."

Her words send me back to the University of Michigan when Juice asked the same question.

Jess hands me the folder. I read the report, newspaper article and magazine essay in silence.

"Are you okay?" she asks.

"I don't know," I say. "I'm processing in real time. You?"

"I'm beyond stunned right now. I thought I knew everything

about GiGi. It turns out I didn't know a thing. The truth was right before our eyes, and yet we didn't see a thing. No alarm bells ever went off."

"Should we call Mom and Dad?" I ask. "Tell them what we discovered? Confront them?"

"I don't think so," Jess says. "Not yet. I feel like we're standing on quicksand, and we need to get on solid ground to think clearly. This is like the ultimate literary *Victor/Victoria*."

I wonder if there's more. I stoop and again shine my light around the safe. There, at the back of the safe, on the opposite side, are shoeboxes filled with letters from readers. On top one of them is a small business envelope. I open it. Inside is a single flash drive.

GiGi was computer savvy after all?

I race out of the closet, avoiding hitting my head at the last moment, and from the office and return—out of breath—with my laptop.

I insert the drive and hit Open.

A list of files appears, page after page.

"Jess," I say, my voice hushed. "This contains her whole history." I read. "Including emails between GiGi and Dad over the years. Get over here."

I open one.

Re: Lost & Found on the Shore

Mom:
Please find my and Piper's notes below. This is a great story. We strengthened the middle a bit, as it seemed to lag, and we also added a bit more Michigan history.

We have an idea for your next winter novel. We will outline, and—knowing you need a bit more assistance now keeping up—rough out the first few chapters. So excited.
—Phil

I blink in slow motion, my lids suddenly made of concrete.

"They *knew!*" Jess says. "Why didn't they ever say anything? To protect her from what happened? I just don't get it."

I open email after email.

I stop at this:

Mom:
Piper and I co-wrote a summer novel based on an old boarder tale you told us. Let me know what you think.
—Phil

Dear Phil:
I love the concept, but I don't think it's really ready for my editor to review. Needs a lot of work and doesn't really have my "style." I'd love to see another draft.
—Mom

"GiGi turned down Mom and Dad's work!" I crow.

"No wonder the strained history between them," Jess says.

The emails between Dad and Grandma turns into a folder titled *Query Letters/Agents, Rejections.*

Dear Mr. Page:
We regret to inform you...

Dear Mrs. Page:
While I love the concept of your novel...

Dear Mr. and Mrs. Page:
While your writing is strong, there is something missing here for me: A voice. You write beautifully about setting, but there is a genuine lack of emotion. It's as if you've put your characters on a shelf and are pulling them down to analyze them but never let them come to life. I'd suggest going back and writing from your

heart and your soul. Listen to that voice that is talking to you. Writers tell the same stories; it's voice that sets them apart, that brings those stories to life, that makes the personal universal, that connects us all.

Best of luck, and please reach out if you consider redrafting.

Regards,
Vivian Vandeventer, VV Literary

"That's why they hate VV," Jess says.

"Mom and Dad couldn't get published," I add. "Their own work was rejected. Is that why they started The Mighty Pages? To have a way to publish their own work? Is that why they call themselves *New York Times* bestsellers...because of *GiGi's* books and their part in writing them? Do they want to sell this cottage and leave Michigan and GiGi's memory behind because it's a reminder of what they can't face? They never found their true voice. This place haunts them because they still feel the sting of rejection."

"It all sounds very Piper, you can't deny that," Jess says, shaking her head. "I'm in shock. I can't believe they knew all along."

At the end of the flash drive is a folder that reads NEVER SHARE, PHIL! EVER! PROMISE ME!

I take a breath and open it.

Phil:
Received call from a woman, who said: 'I know who you are. I've figured it out. S. I. Quaeris is Pauline Page. My offer to you is this: Help me become a writer, or I will finish what Ignatius Marcuzzi didn't. I need your ideas—lots of them—and your influence. If I receive that, you and your family will remain safe.'

"Oh, my God!" Jess says, her voice echoing in GiGi's office. "She was blackmailed. After everything she went through."

I click another email in folder.

"Dad wanted to go to the police," I read. "GiGi refused."

I scan the folder.

"No more emails about it between Dad and GiGi," I continue, "but…"

"What?" Jess asks.

"GiGi took notes of the calls with the woman." I read those. "'I can help you. I have some ideas to kick-start your first novel and career, and I've written a first chapter for you as well. Once we have a manuscript, I would be happy to introduce you to my publisher. Just don't involve my family. Please. I beg of you. They're all I have in this world.'"

We both pick up our cells, fingers flying.

"Ignatius Marcuzzi went to jail for what he did to GiGi," Jess says, showing me an old newspaper article. "Eight years. It was his third offense and home invasion all targeting women in the area." Jess reads. "Oh, my gosh. He died mysteriously in prison."

She continues.

"His wife lied to give him an alibi," the article says. "Said he was home with her, although GiGi and the boarders identified him."

"What was his wife's name?" I ask. "Does it say?"

Jess scans her cell, eyes darting back and forth.

"Jeannette," she says.

I google Jeannette Marcuzzi.

"Ooh, I found an article that mentions her," I say. "She had a son named Avery who won a poetry contest as a kid. It was about how he missed his father in jail."

"Sad," Jess says, coolly. "But I don't think that helps us."

I stare up at the light glimmering through the Eyebrow Cottage, a shimmering blur of sunshine and the lake.

I look down at all of her books, a family legacy unearthed.

S. I. Quaeris.

"Latin," I say.

"What are you talking about?" Jess asks.

I look at her.

"It's not a dead language at all," I say. "It's still speaking to me."

"Are you okay?"

I do another Google search.

"Oh, my God," I say.

"What?"

"The Latin word for fire is *ignis*," I say. "Ignatius means fiery."

"I'm not following," Jess says.

"Ignatius Marcuzzi," I say. "Marcus *Flare*. Get it? Fire is the common denominator. Marcus Flare is a pen name to honor his father, Jess! He used his mother to call and threaten GiGi on his behalf. He still wants to destroy our family because he believes GiGi destroyed his."

"Oh, my God, Emma. Are you sure? That sounds…insane."

"Why else would he use the exact same quote in his book that GiGi used decades earlier? Even you said he came out of nowhere. Why would a man like Marcus Flare write fiction for women? Because GiGi helped him start. His books may still be popular, but why do many readers and critics find them to be so poorly written now? Because she's not here to give him any more ideas. His goal is to ruin our parents' literary reputation with this secret, which will taint their company and legacy. Then he can do what he wants."

I look at Jess and continue.

"And that's why he wants to ruin our family! We took his father away. Now he still wants revenge even though GiGi made him who he is."

"The swan protecting her flock," Jess says.

"What do we do?" I ask. "We have to tell Mom and Dad everything."

I grab my cell.

"No, not yet!" Jess says. "They have a legal contract with Marcus, which I know that his lawyers largely drafted because Mom and Dad were so desperate. I heard our attorney say it was ironclad, and protected all of Marcus's interests. What if they tried to call it off, and he sued them? He could win. At the very least, he could outspend and outlast them in court."

"But the media would call him out," I say. "We have proof."

"And America trusts the media these days?" my sister asks facetiously. "As a social media pro, I know he would spin it on us somehow, revealing who GiGi was and that Mom and Dad were ashamed of her, or tried to steal her work. I mean, it's not completely untrue, is it?"

"So what do we do?" I ask.

"Call Mom and accept the offer to work with Marcus. We need to stay as close to him as we can."

I pick up my cell.

"Hi, Mom," I say when she answers. "Jess is here, and she's talked some sense into me finally. I know, can you believe it? And I'm thrilled to say I've come to a decision and that I'd love to accept the opportunity to work with Marcus and learn from the best. Hopefully, that will lead to a job with you."

My mother actually screams in delight.

"Oh, I have another call," I lie, not wanting to say the wrong thing when my head is spinning in a million directions. "Talk soon. Bye!"

When I hang up, I look at Jess.

"What next?"

"We're going to utilize GiGi's game plan," Jess says. "And yours to stay close to Marcus as well as mine."

"Meaning?"

"Meaning we're going to school Marcus. A little old school coupled with a little new school. We are going to do what women have always had to do to win over the years—break the rules while playing within them. Is your book really as good as you think it is?"

I remember VV's words.

"I do."

"Send it to me," Jess says calmly, "and then—God, I can't believe I'm going to say this—I want you to send it to VV."

"Is this the right time?"

"We have no time," Jess says. "So, yeah, it's the right time."

"And then?"

"And then you and I are going to gather our swans," she says. "And we will remain elegant until we need to turn vicious. We have to do it the right way, or we will lose to this monster."

She picks up one of GiGi's books and looks at the cover before holding it before her like a shield.

"We will protect our flock no matter what," Jess says. "Nobody fucks with our family unless their last name is Page."

PART TWO

Second-Person Perfect

CHAPTER NINETEEN

One Week Later

At first I think a mosquito has slipped between the screens on my windows, woken me from a dead sleep and is buzzing around my ear.

I open my eyes. It is still dark.

I flap my hand wildly around my head and give my ear a hard slap for good measure.

The sound stops.

A few moments later, the buzzing returns.

I roll over. My cell is flashing. It's 5:07 a.m.

It is not a number I recognize.

"Spam," I mutter, ignoring it.

It immediately buzzes again. I pick up and yell, "Stop calling me! It's still the dead of night. I don't want to take your stupid survey or save five dollars a month on my AT&T bill!"

I start to hang up when a man's voice says, "Emma Page? My supersecret Solar Flare!"

My blood runs cold. I know that hiss.

Marcus Flare. He doesn't wait for me to answer.

"First, it's not the dead of night. It's morning. We're both on Eastern time. I've already done a five-mile run, showered, had breakfast, written four pages and answered emails. This is the time of day when highly successful individuals achieve the most. You must start your day with intention if you are going to work with me."

I wake up quickly.

My intention is to gut you like a pig.

"Now is the time when most adults would say something in return," he says condescendingly. "It's called the art of conversation, a skill set your generation has lost looking at your cell phones all day and not actually speaking to a live human. The thing I look most forward to in our working relationship is your witty repartee. If I were you, I'd use your voice while you still had one."

I sit up in bed now fully awake.

"How did you get my number?" I finally ask. "And why did you really ask to work with me?"

"I got your number from your parents. They're so grateful to me for believing I'm saving their ass that they'd give me your social security number if I asked," he says with a dismissive laugh. "They also believe that I can save your sorry ass."

"They're good people," I say.

He laughs again, harder.

"No, they're not, and you know that," Marcus says. "They're the worst kind of rich people. They did nothing to achieve their status except inherit their wealth."

"No, they took great risk starting their own company," I say, shocked that I'm now defending my parents with such fervor. "They could have just sat back and done nothing with their lives. They followed their passion."

"The Pages think they're untouchable and that nothing will ever knock them from their pedestal," Marcus says. "Well, I brought a sledgehammer to the museum."

My head spins. I want to tell him, *I know everything, and I will destroy you!* but I remember what Jess said: we remain elegant until we need to turn vicious in order to protect our own flock.

I take a breath.

"Why are you doing this? Just tell me so I understand. I deserve a little clarity, don't you think?"

"No, I don't. That would spoil the surprise ending, wouldn't it?" he purrs. "I used to love O. Henry. But I will answer your question and tell you why I specifically asked to work with you. Do you want to know?"

"Yes," I say.

"Yes, who?" he asks.

"Yes, Marcus?"

"I prefer Mr. Flare actually. Try it."

My heart is in my throat. I feel sick.

"Yes, Mr. Flare."

"Good job, Emma. You *can* obey like a toy poodle. I'd ask you to bark, but I know you prefer to bite, so I'll limit my training to one lesson a day." He exhales, quite pleased with himself. "Now for the fun part. Why did I ask for you, Emma?"

"Yes," I say.

He doesn't respond.

"Yes, Mr. Flare."

I nearly choke on my words.

"I want you to help me find the absolute worst manuscript in the world for my new imprint," Marcus says, his voice as chipper as a child's on Christmas Day.

"What?" I ask. "Why would you want to harm your own imprint right out of the gate? It's your name on the line."

"You're so slow," Marcus says impatiently. "I thought you said Michigan was a good university." He sighs. "Okay, let me explain. I want to torpedo any chance your parents have of saving *The Mighty Pages* right out of the gate. And the only way to do that is to hit them in the gut both financially and critically. You know how much your parents value their image."

He's got me there.

"They must be humiliated in business and embarrassed in the press."

"But you can't make the decision to publish unilaterally," I argue. "There's a team involved, and my father—for all his faults—knows a good book. He would not allow a bad one to be published intentionally."

"He might hate it, but he won't have a choice," Marcus explains. "It's my imprint, and—contractually—I have final say on what is and isn't published. When the book fails, which I will ensure, I will say that I couldn't get Piper and Phillip to change their rather stodgy literary ways, but I believe so much in what they started that I plan to step in and take over. They'll need the cash just to get out of the hole they'll have dug by then, and I will step in to buy and rename The Mighty Pages to Marcus Flare Books: Fiction That's on Fire."

Fire! I was right!

My heart races.

Stay cool, Emma.

"But a big publisher would likely step in and buy," I say. "They would offer a good price and want to take on many of my parents' established authors. You have no leverage against the big boys."

"It's part of my contract, sweetheart," he says. "I get the first chance to buy before anyone else. Your parents agreed to nearly every single detail of my contract because they need saving that badly."

He continues.

"I think you are forgetting exactly who you're dealing with here. I am the world's bestselling author, meaning I make my publisher millions of dollars every year. People don't doubt what I say or do. They can't because I am the closest thing publishing has to a home run with every book I write. Publishing is a business and a game, Emma. I can tell you right now which books you and the world will be reading next year and the next. I know before you know because I see where the money is invested, who the books are marketed to and, as a result, I can predict what readers will buy. When I say that your parents no longer understand what sells and that I'm stepping in to save independent publishing with my money, instincts and fame, publishing will believe me. When I take over The Mighty Pages, people will cheer. Now, do you have something handy to take notes?"

"Yes," I lie, adding, "Mr. Flare."

"Good. You seem a bit out of sorts. I talk fast, and I have three more calls before six. That's when I cut off contact with the world until noon so I can write."

When I don't respond, Marcus asks, "Are you there?" in a clipped tone.

"Yes," I say. I know what to add to soften his tone. "Sir."

"Good. Here goes. Our new imprint has already received countless submissions since it was announced in the *Times*. Every major literary agent wants to publish with us. Every new writer in the world wants to be discovered by us. And you get to help decide who that will be...with a twist: Find me the worst book out there, one that is so poorly written, one that defies explanation, one that should be burned upon reading. Caveat, Emma—the premise and opening of this novel must actually be decent as that is all I will be showing your parents to win their approval. Think of the book as you do your mother. A beautiful face with a rotten inside."

My blood boils.

"The writer you discover will become infamous." Marcus is silent for a second before emitting a wicked chuckle. "Perhaps you should submit your own novel. It's probably your only shot to get published."

"I understand completely, Mr. Flare," I say.

"Attagirl!" he says, his tone sounding pleased by my quick submission. "No pressure. It's only a daughter working to destroy her own family behind their backs. It's really everything you ever dreamed, isn't it?"

How can this man be so evil and yet see our family weaknesses so clearly that he knows exactly how to prey on us?

"Now go find that golden ticket," he says, quoting *Charlie and the Chocolate Factory*. "Good luck, sweetheart."

He hangs up.

Silence.

His final word buzzes in my ear just like the make-believe mosquito.

Golden ticket.

Golden key.

I turn, and a soft golden glow grows on the horizon. The lake is waking up. The birds are dancing along the shore.

I focus on the soft lapping of the waves.

Just as my head begins to calm, my laptop dings. I open it. An email from Marcus, with all of the manuscripts attached in a zip file.

There's no need to open the file because the world's bestselling author just gave away a winning plot twist to an unpublished writer. He may have just saved us as GiGi saved him.

"Two of us can play this game," I whisper to myself. "*Sweetheart.*"

CHAPTER TWENTY

I head onto the deck just as a pop-up thunderstorm storm passes over South Haven.

The weather can be such an ironic little bugger, can't it, knowing exactly when to match your mood?

A line of clouds marches toward the shore. Lightning flashes, and the lake illuminates as if being lit by a strobe.

An errant firework pops near the lighthouse and its boom echoes over the lake. I see the silhouette of a boy dashing about in circles, excited that his contraband Fourth of July loot can still be used.

The wind gusts, and an acorn from a towering oak hovering over the house ricochets off the deck.

"The acorn wasn't buried deeply enough, GiGi," I say out loud. "Let's start at the very beginning, shall we?"

Over the water, the horizon brightens.

A sign?

Another firework explodes.

The little boy is armed and ready.

My cell rings. *Jess.*

Do we have enough ammunition to win a war?

As soon as I answer, I tell her about my call with Marcus, word for word.

Then I tell her of my plan.

"You actually might be smarter than he is," she says. "And by smarter, I mean demented. Emma, that's genius."

"Thanks, I think."

"And I have a plan of my own. I rented the Hamptons house Mom and Dad wanted to buy through Labor Day."

"What? Why?" I can't deal with the thought of selling Eyebrow Cottage right now.

"Hear me out," Jess says. "Someone had to take it off the market until Mom and Dad came to their senses. They think Marcus is their savior. They were going to buy the house, Emma, and that would have been a nightmare considering what's happening. I signed a short-term lease to give us some time."

"How did Mom react?"

"Let's just say I now know what it's like to be in Mom's line of fire. She actually told me that you were the grown-up now."

I laugh.

"She's coming to her senses," I say. "But how can you afford to rent that place? I'm sure it was outrageous."

"It was," Jess says. "But it's better than losing everything. And I just signed some big, new clients." She waits a beat. "Actually, Marcus signed me to help with his new book, and he's paying me well. I think he not only wants to stay on top more than ever but that he wants to keep me under his thumb until this is all a done deal. He thinks he has the Page sisters all figured out, but we're a chapter ahead."

"Are we?" I ask weakly.

"For now," Jess says. "I do think the Hamptons house is a good ruse. I casually mentioned to Marcus that mom and dad signed a lease-to-own deal. He laughed, saying how bad their credit must be, but now he believes they're still spending wildly, still about to buy the house and have zero concerns about any-thing. It also makes it look like you haven't said a word either."

Jess takes a breath and continues.

"You said that we were going to go old-school on him and new school on him. What's that mean exactly?"

She explains, and I laugh.

"You know what you need to do next, don't you?" she asks.

"I do. I'll call VV immediately. I've been waiting for your Bat-Signal. But I will have to tell her everything. You know that."

"I do, and you know what's ironic?" Jess asks. "I actually trust her. She may not like me, or Mom and Dad, but she hates Marcus even more. And she's old-school. She's ethical. She knows the difference between right and wrong." Jess hesitates. "Just tell her to stay sober. I worry what she might say after a martini." She hesitates again. "Or four."

"Right," I say. "That'll be easy, like telling a Swiftie to boy-cott Taylor's music."

CHAPTER TWENTY-ONE

"I know it's shocking for *me* to ask *you* this, but are you sober?"

I laugh, and VV continues.

"Lord knows I've had a Bloody Mary or two for breakfast that's turned into a champagne brunch that's turned into a night where the cab driver has had to wake me up yelling, 'Ma'am, you're home!,' but this seems insane, even to me."

"I'm sober," I assure her. "But this all certainly does feel like a drunken night out where you wake up the next morning thinking, 'What happened?'"

"Well, I'm sorry for all you're going through, and I'm sorry for what your grandmother went through," VV says. "My God, what women endure at the hands of men." She pauses. "It explains so much about why your parents started The Mighty Pages, the books they publish, the wall they build around themselves. I thought it was snobbery. Now I realize they're just like the rest of us. They're scared to get hurt and rejected."

I can hear her jewelry jangle in the background.

"So, let me get this straight," she continues. "You're ready to send me your manuscript and, in return, you want me to send you the worst manuscript I've ever received?"

"Yes," I say.

"Hold on one second," she says. I can hear her tap on her keyboard. "Oh, I just got one. And another. And another."

I laugh.

"I promise it will never see the light of day and that the author will not be hurt," I explain. "I just need it to fool Marcus long enough for me and Jess to finalize the plan I told you about. And I want to use a pen name on it just to make the irony even richer."

"But of course. As if this isn't crazy enough. What are you thinking?"

"C. Bell," I say. "For Currer Bell."

"Very clever," VV says with a chuckle. "The pen name Charlotte Brontë used to first publish *Jane Eyre*. No one knew until she visited the publisher and revealed her true identity."

"I thought a gotcha moment might be fitting. Every great book needs one, right?"

"I don't think Marcus will get that pen name reference considering how tone-deaf he is to the history of women in publishing," VV says. "But he's clever, Emma. Don't underestimate that he probably has a gotcha of his own waiting."

"But we know all of his secrets."

"Where there's one body buried, there's many," VV warns. "I've worked with a lot of assholes in this business, blowhards with egos the size of a shopping mall. Oh, you're probably too young to remember a shopping mall. They were fabulous, by the way. I could buy and eat anything in one place, and also get a perm. But I digress…not even an iceberg could take down those jerks. Men can say or do anything, and yet there is a limited societal appetite for what women are allowed to do. You do too much, and you are tasteless. Tread carefully."

"I will," I say. "And after you send the manuscript to me and I send it to him, I have another favor to ask about mine."

"Oh, God," she interrupts. "Now what?"

"Try to get it to go to auction."

"It's got to be five o'clock somewhere doesn't it?" VV gasps. "You're actually driving me to drink. Do we think we're Marcus Flare now?"

"I know that's a big ask," I say. "And I know you still need to read it, but if you think it is good enough, I would love you to represent me and work your magic."

"I am not Houdini, honey," she says. "Although that word-play does give me an idea for the type of novel you're seeking."

"You're the best, VV."

"I know I am," she says, "but I'm the best for a reason. I'm grounded in reality."

"If you believe in my book then I know you can get enough buzz going about it." I hesitate. "And, after it goes to auction…"

"If!" VV says. "You do realize what you're asking me is the equivalent of telling an owner of a Jack in the Box franchise to get a Michelin star or he's fired."

I finish my thought, undeterred by reality.

"I'd like to give it to my parents." I pause for effect. "For free. No advance. If they even want it, I mean."

"So I'm risking my reputation and the ire of the world's bestselling author for nothing?" she asks, her bangles creating a cacophony. "You do realize 15 percent of zero is zero, right? You do realize agents make a living selling books. I can't pay my rent with air."

"Please," I beg.

"Well, I can't tell them I'm selling it for free at first," she says. "They would be suspicious and never believe it was me. That part would have to wait."

"I want to save my parents and The Mighty Pages," I say, "and I believe a book they would never publish—a book written in GiGi's honor—has the chance to do just that. Wouldn't that make for a happy ending?"

"We can dream, my dear," VV says. "And what name, pray

tell, would I use when submitting your work? I think I need to take notes now to keep track of all the lies, but I know that Emma Page or GiGi Page would sort of let the cat out of the bag, right?"

"Ignatius Marcuzzi."

"Good Lord. Is your novel entitled *Goodfellas*?"

I laugh, explain and continue.

"Just make sure Marcus doesn't see it or..."

"Or he'll get'cha," VV finishes. "God, I admire your chutzpah. You remind me of when I started out in this business, brash, ready to take on the world, when I had a thyroid that functioned and skin that didn't wave hello every time I lifted my arm." I can hear VV exhale deeply. She continues. "I don't know if your plan is genius, or the *Titanic*."

I hear the lake call beyond the kitchen windows.

"At one time, the *Titanic* was genius."

"Okay," VV finally says. "I'll try my damnedest, but that's like asking me to stay completely sober for the four Zoom meetings I have this afternoon."

"I can never thank you enough," I say.

"I haven't done a damn thing yet," VV says. "I could fail."

"You never fail."

"God, I hate you," she says. "Hey, I have a joke for you. How many publishers does it take to screw in a light bulb?"

"How many?"

"Three. One to screw it in, and two to hold down the author."

I laugh.

"I'm trying it out on the team at Knopf today," VV says. "They're *very* serious." VV rattles her bracelets as if to make sure I'm listening. "Emma?"

"Yeah."

"Don't get screwed."

CHAPTER TWENTY-TWO

Marcus Flare is a solar system unto himself. Planets rotate around *him*, the moon his own face which reflects light back onto its creator.

I stare into the Michigan predawn sky.

Five planets are visible this early summer morn: Mercury, Venus, Mars, Jupiter and Saturn.

It is a rare sight, one I have not witnessed for years—since GiGi was alive and standing next to me—and I feel blessed to witness it.

It is clear and humid. I stand on the deck, which is slippery with dew, and stare into the sky.

The world is mine for a moment.

I glance at my cell: *4:59 a.m.*

I might as well become a barista at Starbucks considering my hours. I now wake before dawn simply to field Marcus's calls. He has made me part of his solar system.

I am waiting for him to call as he does every morning between 5 a.m. and 5:10.

At first, I composed updates and sent automated texts to him at five, but he did not like that.

"I need to hear your beautiful voice," he told me.

Yes, he wants to hear my voice.

He wants me live because he enjoys playing with his prey.

Marcus Flare is not simply an author. He is his own universe of books, movies, TV series, speaking engagements, product and clothing lines, development deals, nonprofits, an imprint…

A publishing house.

Marcus Flare is a star. He lives in a rarefied world. He has global power.

Staring into the sky, I feel the gravity of my situation for the first time. I am not messing with any ordinary being; I am messing with a force of nature.

He could crush me like a meteor.

What am I doing?

Stars twinkle.

I am protecting my universe.

How many ideas did GiGi send him? What must it have been like for her to live on a knife's edge of success and fear every single day, in a middle realm between being safe and being caught, of having it all and losing everything?

VV confirmed to me—confidentially, of course—that Marcus employs ghostwriters to help him pen his books with the promise he'll support them when they are ready to publish their first novels. All sign NDAs. Their names do not appear on the cover. They do not get any credit. VV says this is a known fact in the back rooms of the publishing world, but readers do not know any better.

They believe he does it all himself.

They believe he has always done it all himself.

VV said a source at Marcus's publisher told her over a multi-martini meeting one night that none of his ghostwriters have yet to publish a book. He simply profits off their talent and hard work. He stands on their backs to reach a higher level.

And now he wants to break my family's back.

My cell rings.

I will become Jamie Lee Curtis and take Michael Myers down if it's the last thing I do.

"Good morning, Mr. Flare."

"You sound like you're actually saying it with respect for a change," he says, his voice absolutely giddy. "Good girl. Update?"

"I'm reading like crazy," I lie. "I've become friendly with my mom's assistant, and she's given me access to the slush pile at The Mighty Pages. I told her it's research for a book I want to write."

"You're quite sneaky."

"Thank you," I say. "I'm sure I'll have something soon."

"I love it, but time is ticking," he says. "I want to make my big first launch announcement later this summer while we have the media still buzzing. As you know, we'll need a year to build that momentum before we stick a spear in the dying dragon."

"I promise," I say. "Nothing's been *quite* bad enough yet. I want to find you the perfect manuscript, the literary equivalent of *Showgirls*. The buzz that leads to the bomb."

"My God, you *are* good," Marcus says, his voice growing giddier. Then it deepens. "Why are you being so cooperative now, Emma?"

Think fast.

"Because I want to be successful no matter what it takes," I answer, voice as cool and calm as the lake. "I will do anything to become a writer like you."

"Keep this up," he purrs, "and I just might hire you to work for me after I acquire The Mighty Pages. Or maybe I'll take a look at that manuscript of yours. For real. If it's passable, you could become one of my ghostwriters."

He gasps dramatically.

"Oops, I said that out loud. Ghostwriters! I guess I'm be-ginning to trust you. Don't make me regret that, or it won't be pretty."

Yes!

I want to scream, but I keep my mouth shut.

"You heard me, right?" he presses.

"Yes, sir."

"I know it's shocking, but I actually require some assistance writing three books a year. But I will sue you if you say a word publicly. But you won't have a penny to pay me so that won't do me any good now, will it?" he laughs.

I remain silent.

"You're actually considering my offer, aren't you?" he asks.

What? Am I? Is that why I hesitated? Do I hate my family that much?

No. Just more Marcus mind games.

"I would definitely be honored by your consideration," I say. "Thank you for your friendship and mentorship, Mr. Flare."

"Friends? We're becoming friends?"

He says it like a cartoon cat might when it has a frightened mouse cornered. He continues.

"But this is exactly why I asked to work with you, Emma. I knew from the moment we first met that you were a chip off the old block." Marcus sighs. "People think we shouldn't hate, but it's one thing in this world that fuels our collective fire. It's what makes the world go round. It's what makes people interesting. And that will never change." Marcus blows into the phone. "The only thing hate needs is oxygen, then—poof!— if will ignite. The hate you have for your family—which you mistakenly directed at me in the beginning—was just waiting for oxygen, and I have finally given that life. Doesn't it feel good? You're welcome, Emma. We'll talk tomorrow."

He hangs up.

I stare at the lake, still dark and sleeping. But on the horizon, a rim of light.

"Which one is family?" I ask out loud. "The one who loves us unconditionally and protects us from the world, or the one who seeks revenge?"

I already know the answer. Marcus has taught me one thing at least.

Family can be either, depending on who is helping us write our story.

CHAPTER TWENTY-THREE

I sit in the dark reading the letters that GiGi's readers sent her over the years.

Some are handwritten, faded ink in looping cursive. Some are typewritten. Postcards contains notes and photos.

There are letters from women who have lost their parents or children. Women whose husbands and sons died in war. Men who had lost their jobs. A woman who could not have children; another whose child had been stillborn. So many women undergoing chemotherapy.

But most readers simply wanted to reach out to my grandmother and say thank you.

Thank you for your books!

Your books gave me hope!

Your books made me forget!

I found your books when I needed them most!

The envelopes were sent from every part of the US, Kansas to Kentucky, Maine to Missouri. Letters were sent from all over the world as well.

Marcus writes for power. GiGi wrote for connection.

All of these readers—so very different—sought out my

grandmother's words as a way to make sense of this often sense-less world.

And they were calmed. Given hope. A reason to go on.

I touch the handwriting on the letters and envelopes, wondering how many are still alive. How many are still being touched by GiGi's stories.

I wonder how my grandmother lived with such strength and wrote with such power even though she must have felt trapped her entire life.

I hear a flapping noise outside.

There's a moth trapped in a porch light I forgot to turn off last night. I watch it flail wildly, banging itself against the light.

There is only one way free, but it can't seem to find it, and so it repeats this pattern of madness over and over.

Is this a sliver of how GiGi felt every day of her life? Waking up expecting to see the man who was trying to harm her and her family, then desperately seeking any light she could find?

Her family was her light, her source of power.

I go outside to the porch light.

I cup my hands together gently and capture the moth.

"You're okay," I say, setting it free.

I head back in and turn on the TV, waiting for another morning of Marcus. For the last week, he has been popping into my world to wreak havoc like Beetlejuice. The light from the television bounds eerily around the cottage.

I mindlessly click the remote.

The movie *Wild*, based upon Cheryl Strayed's memoir, is on.

I think of my father, and realize I have to tell him—in this rare instance—the movie was as good as the book.

I mean, how often do you read a book or see a movie where the main character ends up with no man, no money, no home and yet has a happy ending?

"I'm about to find out," I say out loud again.

I watch for a bit and then click the remote again and happen upon *Legally Blonde*.

It's all Reese this morning.

I turn up the volume.

Most current books and movies still fail the tried-and-true Bechdel Test, but not *Wild* and *Legally Blonde*. The main characters rely upon themselves to make it.

So must I.

Marcus is my Pacific Crest Trail. He is my Professor Callahan.

And no one in their right mind thinks I will come out on top. Save for, perhaps, my friends.

Gin and Juice used to tell me that most Michigan students were book smart, but that wasn't enough.

"To be successful in life," they said, "you have to be street-smart as well. And you, Emma, are both."

I grab my cell and text BAT SIGNAL! Good morning, Angels! Can we FaceTime?

Gin and Juice—up as early as I am—immediately call. I smile when I see their faces. Their expressions droop when they see me.

"Are you okay?" Juice asks. "You look awful."

"Thanks," I say.

"Oh, no," Gin adds. "Another monstrous morning with Marcus?"

I nod. "But that's great use of alliteration for so early in the morning." I scan their faces on my cell. My heart hiccups. "I miss you two. And I need your help?"

"Anything!" they respond at the same time.

"Is there any way you two might be able to use your street smarts and book smarts to get some intel on Marcus Flare?"

Juice actually cackles. "My whole life has led up to this moment. What do you need?"

"I can't say too much yet, but, Gin, I'm looking for you to

use your journalistic skills to dig up any info you might be able to find about a Jeannette Marcuzzi from Michigan whose son was named Avery. Her husband was Ignatius. He went to jail."

"I'm on it!" Gin says.

"And, Juice, I know this is a long shot, but I'm wondering if there's anything you can find out about Marcus's finances. I know you know people who know people who know things about very rich people at your firm, but I don't want you to get in any trouble."

"Let me worry about that," she says. "What do you need?"

"We know he's rich, but does he have debt? How much? Is he overextended with his business ventures? Does he owe people money? I actually have the name of his financial advisor and attorney in New York. My sister got them from the contract he signed for the new imprint. *Anything* you find might just save my life and my family's life."

"Well, that's no pressure at all," Juice says with an anxious laugh.

"Are you in danger?" Gin asks. "I mean, real danger? Because I will cut a bitch."

"And I will help bury the body," Juice adds.

"And now we're all going to jail," I say. "I am in some danger. And I'll likely be in a lot more very soon."

"Remember, 'there are certain rules that one must abide by in order to successfully survive a horror movie,'" Juice says with a smile, reciting a line from *Scream*, which we watched every Halloween as we got dressed up to head out to the parties.

I smile.

"'Not in my movie,'" I say reciting Neve Campbell's famous line where she finally takes down the killer. "Or should I say *book*." I nod convincingly at my friends. "I know what I'm doing." I stop. "I think."

They laugh nervously.

"We will do anything we can for you," Gin says.

"Anything!" Juice adds.

"Thank you for taking my SOS," I say. "I know you have to go. Have a great day!"

They blow kisses, and the call ends.

I put my cell down, relieved to have friends who would do anything to protect me.

Street-smart. Book smart.

If there's anything I've learned in my life, it's this: you better bury a body way deeper than any acorn.

CHAPTER TWENTY-FOUR

My cell rings at exactly 5 p.m.

I already know who it is: Marcus may be a 5 a.m. kind of person, but VV is an it's-five-o'clock-somewhere type of person.

"I asked for three blue cheese olives!" VV is saying when I pick up. "Martini math is very simple, young man, three blue cheese–stuffed olives, drained and patted dry. Three ounces of quality vodka—four if you want to get lucky—one ounce of good vermouth and one teaspoon of olive brine. If you can't do that, then a tumbler of Four Roses, straight up."

"Where are you?" I ask. "It sounds like the subway."

"I'm trying some new hipster bar frequented by all the young blood in publishing," VV says. "I'm trying to stay current, but I feel like I'm in an episode of *Euphoria*. Everyone is wearing a napkin and drinking Red Bull. The bartender thinks I'm harassing him. What is wrong with your generation? You act like every joke is a nuclear insult on your entire being. You don't think *Seinfeld* was funny. What are you going to do when you're my age and you have no sense of humor to deal with every ache and pain and downpour of crap life has to throw at you?"

"We'll google the answer," I say.

"Ha! Anyhoo, I wanted to avoid Liber so I didn't run into Marcus."

"Why?" I ask. "What are you up to?"

"I found the ideal manuscript for your dastardly plan."

"You did?"

"When you said Houdini the other day, I remembered a manuscript I received a couple of years ago from a magician's assistant, and my assistant, Leo, dug it up," VV says. "It's about a magician who uses that old trick to make his assistant disappear onstage. You know the one. He says, 'Abracadabra!' or whatever magician's say—you know, they freak me out, don't you, along with clowns?—but I digress. She's supposed to disappear through a trapdoor onstage, but his incantation brings back an evil spirit while the assistant goes back in time and pops up onstage with Harry Houdini and is witness to his mysterious death."

"That actually sounds kind of good," I say.

"Exactly!" VV yells. "I thought I'd discovered the next Stephen King when I read the first chapter. I called the author and asked for exclusivity and the rest of the manuscript."

"And?"

"It was a nightmare," VV says. "A cosmically, comically horrific nightmare of a book. The author has chapters that are supposed to be set in the 1920s but everyone is using cell phones and driving Teslas."

"Was it supposed to be…?" I ask.

"No!" VV roars. "It was not supposed to be funny, ironic, dystopian, time traveling. It was just plain ol' bad. I mean, there's a chapter told from the point of view of the protagonist's cat. It makes no sense at all. But if one were to just send a first chapter—say Marcus used that to tempt your parents—then I could see them going all in."

"It sounds perfect. I don't know how to thank you."

"Yes, you do," VV says. "I'm about to read your manuscript,

and I trust it's going to be as good as you think. That will be your thank-you to me. That, of course, and a movie deal, so I can actually make some money off of you. If your manuscript is as good as you believe, I will be calling you again to celebrate with an even bigger martini. And, if it turns out to have a cat—or be anything like *Cats*—I will kill you before Marcus has a chance, I promise you that."

I hear her take a sip of a drink. "This martini is horrible! Four Roses immediately. Emma, I have to go. A young editor from Hachette is making out with a not-so-young editor from Macmillan. One of them is married. Both of them have a manuscript I sent them. I need to go say hello just for fun. This place is suddenly taking a turn for the better! Leo should have already sent you the manuscript, and I'll be in touch about yours."

Before VV hangs up, I hear her say, "What's your name? And please don't tell me it's Arlo or Beck, or some hipster monstrosity."

"You did it," Marcus says to me a few days later. "I'm impressed. The manuscript is believably brilliant in the beginning and ludicrously awful after that. We can tease the opening and when the galleys are finally sent, critics will kill it before it even has a chance. Then I can turn the final page on the Pages."

I gulp hard. Guilt swallows me whole. This is all becoming very real.

"I'm glad you're pleased, Mr. Flare. But I'm worried about embarrassing the author. I didn't think it would go this far for some reason."

"Oh, my God, Emma. I didn't think you had remorse. Bury that emotion right now." He inhales. "Leave it to me when it gets to that point. I'll get the author to sign an NDA, pay them handsomely, tell them we'll use a pen name on the galleys so no one will ever know and that I will consider their next novel as a thank-you for their willingness to play along. Any publicity is good publicity, right? You should know that by now."

"I understand. And no remorse."

"I think I do want to hire you, Emma. It will be the nail in the coffin for your family."

"Well, I have turned down every other offer except for yours and my parents'," I say.

"Good girl! Go ahead and take your parents' offer," he says. "You'll be the only one I retain on payroll."

"I will," I say.

"You're just like me, Emma, whether you like it or not."

He hangs up, and I call Jess.

"You know it's almost Shark Week on TV?" I ask. "The things you learn by watching TV at five in the morning."

"I'm not following."

"I've hooked the fish, Jess," I say. "The shark is on the line. He quite literally bit on the manuscript I sent him. He told me to take the job with Mom and Dad. He said I'd be the only employee he retains."

"It's time," Jess says. "Book your ticket to New York. We'll celebrate your new job with Mom and Dad at the Hamptons house, and we'll celebrate the manuscript discovery with Marcus at Le Pompeux. That just seems fitting, doesn't it?"

"And then?"

"We have to get the shark on the boat without getting eaten alive."

CHAPTER TWENTY-FIVE

"I don't think Marcus has liked anyone this much in ages."

Except for his own reflection.

"That's quite the compliment, Dad. Thank you."

My father shuts his laptop.

We have been talking with Marcus on Zoom about *The Magician's Assistant*, the debut novel for Books with Flare. As I watched Marcus talk, his face a mask of genuine excitement, I couldn't help but watch my own as it happily went along with his lies. I felt like I was the magician's assistant who needed to disappear. I kept smiling, trying to act normal, but no one looks normal when they try to act normal: I felt like I resembled a killer on one of those true crime shows who tries to act way too cool and proclaims her innocence while being grilled by the police in an interrogation room with blood all over her blouse.

My mother claps her hands.

It echoes in the cavernous Hamptons open living room.

"And I don't think I have loved the opening of a novel so much in ages," she says. "It's both literary and commercial. It has that big book vibe. I feel like I did when I was reading *Horse* by Geraldine Brooks. I was absolutely thrilled and enthralled by the chronological and cross-disciplinary leaps she made in that work. Of course, we didn't get that manuscript because we couldn't play with the big dogs, but this is why we got into business with Marcus. His name, influence and monetary support will make all the difference this time. It will allow us to be players."

"I just don't know why he's being so secretive with the rest of the novel," my father says. "I can't publish something I haven't read."

"Like Marcus said, we're working with the author right now before it's turned over to you," I lie. "I'm helping with the edits. I guarantee the rest of the book is as great as the opening. Trust me."

Jess gives me a side-eye that implies she's both impressed and shocked at my ability to lie so well. I involuntarily scratch my nose, worried that—like Pinocchio's—it is growing.

"I do," my father says. "Implicitly."

"You are just full of surprises," my mother says. "I'm so impressed, Emma."

I know she wants to say, *I'm so stunned considering our blowout fight*, but she takes the high road. So do I.

"Thanks, Mom. I also have another surprise I wanted to wait to share until we were all together."

My mother sits up. "Go on."

"I'd love to accept your offer to work at The Mighty Pages."

"Oh, honey," my dad says first. "I'm so thrilled."

He stands, and I hug him.

"Oh, Emma," my mother says. "We're going to make a great team!"

She stares at me for the longest time shaking her head in disbelief. "I don't know what to say. It's like you've taken a page out of our family book. Let me call Diane. She will be so thrilled. And then we can celebrate!"

"Why don't we all go outside by the pool and do that," Jess

suggests, attempting to move the focus off me for a moment. "It's a beautiful day, and I rented this house to be enjoyed."

"But not purchased," my mother says.

I give Jess a look of gratitude.

"I think you already spent enough money on Botox and filler this week, don't you, Mom?" Jess jabs to keep the focus squarely on her.

"My appearance is solely due to yoga, rest and lots of lemon water, young lady," my mother says, standing and finishing her glass. "Plumps the skin."

"Uh-huh," Jess says with a laugh.

We move to our respective wings to change and then head outside to the pool.

It's linear and sleek, with a tanning shelf at one end. A teak deck encompasses the water, and a small pool house cum makeshift bar sits at the far end. The doors are open to reveal nostalgic Hamptons coastal decor: vintage beach banners and buoys hung on the wall, a rope chandelier, a small table filled with antique barware.

I open a large storage container hidden behind the pool house and retrieve a floatie. I pull out a pump and begin to inflate it, a magical unicorn slowly coming to life.

I toss it in the pool and jump in.

Jess struts toward the pool looking perfect and carrying a bottle of rosé.

I clamber atop the unicorn. Jess looks at me.

"You've changed," she says. "No fear of the water now?"

"I overcame it this summer," I reply. "I overcame a lot." I smile at my sister. "Thanks to you."

"Thank you," she says. "We have just one more obstacle."

"Nothing me and my magical unicorn can't overcome," I joke.

Mom and Dad walk down the floating stairs in the glass atrium.

"When should we tell them about what's going on?" I continue. "I'm having trouble keeping my lies straight anymore."

"You sure seem like a pro at it," Jess says with a laugh. "We just need to sharpen that unicorn's horn a bit more. We're almost home."

"Or we might need a home," I add.

My mother appears in a black swimsuit with a gold trim cutout in the middle.

"You look amazing, Mom," I say. "I think I hate you."

She stops on the teak deck and lowers her sunglasses.

"Life is a fight to the finish," she says, "not a casual stroll."

My father is carrying his laptop, my mother a manuscript. Jess follows them into the shaded pool house, opens the wine and pours four glasses. I paddle over to the edge of the pool, and she hands me a glass.

"I don't think anything could sum you up better," my father calls. "A unicorn on a unicorn." He laughs.

I think back to when my father told me as a girl that writers were unicorns in this world.

I take a sip of rosé.

Jess takes a seat in the warm pool water on the tanning shelf.

And then I do something I've done my whole life: I watch my parents read.

When a passage strikes either of my parents, they will read it aloud to the other. One will nod and remark on the meaning of the passage or brilliance of the author, and a few moments later, this literary tango will be repeated.

I watch my mother's eyes grow misty. The most unemotional woman in the world is showing emotion the only way she knows how: reading a book.

My father chuckles. The man who is always in control of his emotions lets loose a staccato of boyish giggles.

My father catches me watching. He glances up, lowers his sunglasses and gives me a wink.

My heart flutters like the hummingbird currently fascinated by the bright, rainbow colors of my unicorn. My dad returns to reading alongside my mom.

I think of a conversation I had with my mom when I was a girl and reading *Flowers in the Attic*.

"Is your mother mean like the grandmother in this book?" I asked. "Is that why I've never met her?"

"Yes, Emma," she said. "They didn't lock me away in an attic, but they did steal my childhood, and they tried to steal my future."

"How?" I had asked.

"We were poor, but that had nothing to do with it," she sighed. "They were just miserable people. My father hated my mother, my mother hated my father, and I was the lightning rod for all their anger. What's the old adage? Happiness isn't a state of mind, it's a habit? Well, misery was their habit. I worked my entire childhood—babysitting, delivering newspapers, working at McDonald's—to make enough money to go to college, start a new life and get away from them. My father told me one day he wanted to start an account for me at the local bank to protect that money. He cosigned with me, and I put all of my money into that account, year after year. When I was accepted to college and went to the bank to retrieve my college fund and make my first tuition payment, the money was gone. All of it. The teller told me my father had come down and withdrawn it all earlier that week and that he had rights to access it as a joint owner. My father went out, got drunk and gambled it all away in one night. The robber was in my own home. He might as well have locked me in an attic."

"What did you do?" I asked, shocked.

"I left and never looked back," she said. "GiGi took me in. She didn't charge me a dime at first. I worked my way through college. And then, one summer, I met your father. He was so handsome, but it was more than that. He was smart, and he was kind. I never knew kindness. I'd never met someone so genuine. He listened to me. He *saw* me. When I graduated, he asked me to marry him. I was jealous of your grandmother's relationship with your father. I couldn't understand how a parent could be so...good. She isn't perfect, but GiGi is a force of nature, as you know. She is a fierce protector of people she loves, especially you. Oh, Emma, the pain we carry around from our childhoods. You believe you can sling it off like an old coat when you grow up, but it's not like that. It's not just that you carry it around, it's that pain becomes a *part* of you, embedded in your DNA. You can't get rid of it. You try to burn down your past, but a fire scar remains on your soul."

"You're a good mother," I had said.

She had laughed, hard.

"No, I'm not," she said. "We'll see how I did in a few years. Hopefully, I won't screw you up too much. I just don't want to hurt you like I got hurt, so that's why I'm distant sometimes. Being a mother has never come naturally to me, but I want you to know how much I love you and always will, and I promise that I will keep trying to do better. I'm not in your father's league, I'm not in GiGi's league, and I never will be. I try to be with all my clothes and makeup and attitude, but they're light-years ahead of me in unconditional love because I was never shown that. We all have some *Flowers in the Attic*–sized mysteries in our pasts, Emma. What we cannot do is lock our hearts away to protect ourselves, and yet that's what we end up doing. Promise me you won't do that. Break the mold."

"I promise. I love you, Mommy."

"And I love you, my dear, sweet girl more than you will ever know and more than I will likely ever be able to show."

Now I continue to watch my parents read.

We are a family, like so many, distanced by the ghosts on our shoulders.

We want to hug, we want to reach out, and yet we are paralyzed by our pasts.

Books may not allow us to reinvent the people we've become, but they can remind us of the people we can be.

The people we want to be.

Jess jumps into the pool and my unicorn bobs toward the edge.

I set my wineglass on the deck, jump off my float and walk toward the pool house.

I lean down and hug my mother.

"What in the world, Emma," she says, flustered. "You're getting my book all wet!"

But after a moment, she sets down her wine, lays the manuscript in her lap, clasps a hand on mine and leans her head against my body.

I hold on tightly and do not let go. I want to give my mother the hug that she never received as a child, the one she rarely gives as a mother, to let her know I can protect her now and that she hasn't screwed me up too much.

CHAPTER TWENTY-SIX

"I have some news."

VV's voice sounds strangely subdued.

I tiptoe out of the living room where my family is gathered reading in silence before we head out to dinner.

"Are you okay?" I whisper as I walk. "You've been so quiet lately."

"I had a chance to read your manuscript," she says with a sigh. "We need to talk."

This is not good.

She takes a deep breath and continues.

"You know how difficult publishing is these days. I'm afraid I didn't accomplish what I'd hoped."

She hates my book.

Not only that, I'm a naive narcissist, the worst combination. Who am I to think my novel was any good? Who I am to think a twenty-two-year-old child could save her parents with a little trickery? I believed I was Superwoman. I wasn't even Batgirl.

I am standing in the hallway clutching my cell so hard I think it might disintegrate in my hands. My knuckles are white.

Moreover, what if—it finally dawns on me, the haze of illusion dissipating—that Marcus has been playing me? What if he's been recording our conversations, tells my parents I want to work for him, it crushes them, and they just give up, and the company is his before we even get a chance to finish our plot? He's been so excited for the Le Pompeux dinner Jess arranged that I wonder if he's going to turn the French table on us?

"Let me cut to the chase," VV says. "I loved your manuscript, Emma. It was lyrical and heartbreaking, an ode to sisterhood, family, first love and first loss, a tribute to all the ways family shatters us and yet protects us. You obviously have GiGi's genes."

It is the news I wanted to hear my entire life. These are the words I dreamed an agent would say to me one day. I always believed if I ever heard these words, I would fall to the floor, screaming, weeping, in joy, and then pop a bottle of champagne although there would be no need to drink it because I would already be drunk from the news.

VV continues.

"I sent your manuscript to ten editors I believed would love it and see it as the big book I do. I received a number of passes."

Um, these are not *all* the words I dreamed an agent would say to me one day. VV loves it, but no one else does? That's like being runner-up to Miss America. Being nominated but not winning the Oscar. I feel like a debutante who ends the social season in a beautiful gown but no husband.

The world around me begins to fall away.

This is over. It's all over.

"Oh," is the only word I can finally manage to choke out.

"I also received a number of offers," VV says. "It was only three offers from three *huge* editors at three *huge* imprints. I wanted to go ten for ten, but batting .333 will always get you in the Hall of Fame. You are going to auction, Emma! Congratulations!"

★ ★ ★

In an instant, my dream is no longer some ethereal flash that comes to me before I fall asleep. No, it is now reality. And that reality is suddenly completely overwhelming.

I now feel as if I'm falling from the sky.

I am a published author.

I say it again in my head.

I! AM! A! PUBLISHED! AUTHOR!

"Hello?" VV asks. "Did I lose you?"

"No," I stammer. "I just don't know what to say."

"Ah, a dream coming to life. That first deal for an author is as shocking as that first slap on a baby's butt."

"I actually thought you were going to say my book was a disaster."

"What?" she cries. "No. I'm sorry. I'm a little distracted. I'm getting a manicure, and some young thing is trying to talk me into having flowers painted on my nails. Does VV look like she would ever put flowers on her nails much less wear a floral print? I'm not an ingénue. I've never been an ingénue. And the only flowers I prefer are Four Roses bourbon."

"Thank you," I say. "I can never thank you enough."

"You're the one who worked her ass off writing a book while going to college," she says. "By the way, I sent the novel without any name attached. The manuscript was so good I didn't need to play any games. I said it was penned by a young writer honoring her late grandmother and who wished to remain anonymous for the moment. That captivated them even more. But we will have to reveal your identity at auction. I told everyone we're still waiting for one more response."

"From whom?" I ask.

"The Mighty Pages."

Falling again.

"What did they say about the book?"

"Phillip and Piper have not changed a bit," VV says. "They're playing it all very close to their vests. Still reading. Still taking their sweet time."

I peek my head around the corner and look at my parents.

Are they reading my manuscript *right now*? Have they been reading it right in front of my eyes? Is that why my father was laughing and my mother was tearing up?

"This is all starting to feel very real," I whisper to VV.

"You got yourself into this. Enjoy the ride. Albeit your ride is a bit more Six Flags roller coaster than most," she replies.

"*You've* been to Six Flags?"

She laughs. "Do I look like I eat funnel cakes? I'm more a Four Seasons gal. It was just a damn good analogy." Her voice suddenly raises. "And do I look like Hannah Montana? If I see a flower come close to a finger, you are dead, and I will be acquitted by a jury of my peers when I show them my nails."

"You have no peers," I say. She cackles.

"I told your parents that we have offers on the table and that they will need to let me know by Thursday."

"This week?"

"That's how a calendar works, Emma."

"What if they hate it? What if they say no?"

"Then I have to go to another publisher and hope you find a plan B to drum up lots of income for The Mighty Pages to take down Marcus Flare," VV says. "If so, I will try to get you as big an offer as I can so maybe you can help them that way. And—I can't believe I'm going to say this—but I won't take a commission either."

VV continues.

"But I know it's more than that, my dear. I know this is personal. I know how much you want your parents to love your novel, and I know how much you also want a touch of familial vindication. You want the type of novel they couldn't write and do not publish to be the savior of their elitist publishing house. You want your grandmother to posthumously receive the attention and accolades she never did in life. You want to prove to Marcus that you are writing a book he never could and honoring a genre that doesn't need 'inventing,' because stories of love and family will always resonate. But sometimes life and the best books don't give us an easy, happy ending. Sometimes you can be healed but still carry around a scar forever."

I look back out at my mom.

Fire scar.

"I'll let you know as soon as I hear anything from them," VV says.

"I will, too," I add.

The last thing I hear her say before hanging up is, "A *daisy*?"

I lean around the wall and watch my parents. I study every nuance of their faces, trying to calibrate their reactions to what they are reading. My life—their lives—hang in the balance.

"You're like a Roomba, Emma," my mother says, eyes up, catching me spying. "Come into the living room and settle down before we go to dinner."

I reenter the room trying to act casual. I take a seat in a sleek, modern chair that was made to be admired but not used. The low chair consumes me.

"Forget how to sit?" Jess asks me.

My family stares at me.

Jess is wearing a multicolor striped cutout dress that looks as if it was papier-mâchéd onto her torso. My father is wearing dark jeans, Gucci loafers with no socks and a crisp white shirt with a sweater around his shoulders. My mother is wearing a short, knit dress in buttercream that fits her body like a glove, and pink heels.

"You all look so nice," I say as innocently as I can.

"Thank you," my mother says.

Why are you acting so weird? Jess texts from across the room.

I think they're reading my manuscript!!! I reply.

I catch her eyes. They are wide.

"What are you guys reading?" Jess asks casually.

My parents lift their heads.

"I'm reading Marcus Flare's newest manuscript," my sister offers, giving me a look as if to say, *This is how you act cool.*

"And what do you think?" my mother asks.

"Vintage Marcus," Jess says.

"That's very nonspecific," my mother says.

"You know what you're getting," Jess replies.

"I'm actually reading a new submission," my father says. "Actually, we both are."

"What do you think?" I blurt. *Subtle.*

"I never like to comment until I've completed a book," my father says.

"Who's the author?" I press.

"We don't know," my mother says. "Part of the mystery. It's a fascinating backstory."

"VV sent us the manuscript," my father adds.

"And it wasn't laced with anthrax, if you can believe it," my mother says wryly. "I actually have no idea why she would send us this to be honest. We have our first Flare book. This is already going to auction. We need to watch our budget. Not to mention, it's nothing we typically read or publish. But—"

My father grabs his cell.

"Our Uber is here," he says, interrupting her.

"But what?" I press my mom. "But what?"

"We have to go," my mother says. "No more work talk. Tonight's a celebration! Off we go!"

PART THREE

Third-Person Perfect

CHAPTER TWENTY-SEVEN

"It's too bad your sister and parents came down with something," Marcus says to me on Wednesday when we meet at Le Pompeux. "That's what you get for eating at a truck stop. But they'll have to get used to microwaved burritos, won't they?" I smile as he continues. "But I'm glad they didn't spoil the night for us. We'll all see each other later this week anyway. I think the universe planned it this way. Please."

He motions for me to sit. I take a seat on one side of the banquette.

"You're so far away," he pouts, sliding around to the center. "Le Pompeux celebrates the passion of food and intimacy of ingredients. We will be sharing a lot tonight." *Creepy.* "Food that is." He pats the banquette seat beside him. "Closer."

I slide a bit farther and as I do, he slides, too. Our shoulders meet.

My stomach turns, and I want to run away, but I force my body to stay put.

"Now we can finally get to know each other better," he continues. "I feel like you've become a big part of my life. I start every morning with Emma Page." Marcus looks at me, waiting until I meet his gaze. "And now, finally, I'm ending a day with you."

That night on the beach at my dad's book party seems like a lifetime ago. I'm still the same age, but I feel much, much older.

Our waiter appears, and I want to leap into his arms to thank him for the interruption.

"A bottle of Veuve," Marcus says, smiling at me. "No plastic flutes tonight."

"Would you care to start with anything, sir?" the waiter asks.

"We'll share Le Tartare de Thon and Le Crab & Avocado, please," Marcus says.

"Very good, sir. I'll be back in a moment with your champagne."

I focus my gaze on the harbor outside the open patio doors.

It is a twinkly summer night.

Star light, boat lights and car lights dance atop the water like an ethereal Fred Astaire and Ginger Rogers from GiGi's favorite late-night movies.

Through the front windows, a snaking line outside Le Pompeux glimmers as well: people, young and old, decked out in sequins, diamonds, sunglasses (yes, worn at night), cell phones shining.

"You're an insider that's always felt like an outsider," Marcus says out of the blue.

He's been watching me. "I was always an outsider looking in." Marcus points at the line of people.

"You always seem so confident," I say. "I'm shocked."

"We all wear a suit of armor," he says. "Just look at your parents." Marcus smiles and looks outside. "I feel as if we were destined to meet at that allegorical velvet rope. Both of our families were instrumental in making us the people we are, both of our families propelled us to this moment, right here, right now."

You have no idea, I think.

The champagne arrives, and the waiter pops the cork. He

pours us two glasses and then nestles the bottle in a bucket of ice on a stand by our banquette.

"To family!" Marcus toasts. "To honoring it and destroying it. Cheers!"

He raises his glass. I raise mine. Marcus recoils as if I'm going to toss it in his face and then laughs.

I actually want to smash the bottle over your head.

"Cheers!" I say.

We clink glasses and chitchat until our food arrives.

"You must taste the tuna," Marcus insists.

I pick up my fork.

"Oh, no, no, let me feed you."

He cuts the tartare and captures some tuna and wonton, swirling it in the sesame dressing.

"Open wide," he says.

I feel both sick and like a fool. I open my mouth.

"Isn't it delicious?" he asks.

"Mmm-hmm," I say, chewing.

"The perfect combination," he says. "Like us."

I start to choke. I grab my champagne and take a big sip, remembering I need to keep my wits about me.

"Are you okay?" he asks.

I wipe my mouth with my napkin. "I'm sorry. It's just so good."

"Your mouth has very good taste."

I am now screaming inside so loudly that I'm sure whales in the nearby ocean can hear me.

Marcus takes a bite of the tuna and then a sip of his champagne.

"I also have very good taste," he continues. "In books, in business and in people. So let's discuss your future."

"I would love nothing more."

"Good," he says. "It seems we have your father convinced our terrible manuscript is a masterpiece. You are still completely confident in that assumption after spending the weekend with them, correct?"

"I do," I nod. "We were just talking about it. They are ready to leap."

"Good, good. I plan to leak the first chapter to the press, which will force your parents to get behind it and expend some capital before they ever see the final manuscript. They trust us both so much now."

"They do," I say.

"Then we ruin them," he says. "They'll have no option but to sell to me at a bargain basement price, and I take over and publish the books I know will make money—mine."

"Yours?" I ask, nearly choking again. "I didn't know that. How exciting."

"And maybe yours," he says.

Marcus moves so close I can feel the heat from his body.

"For a price."

"A price?"

The waiter appears and tops off our champagne. "Are you ready to order your entrées, sir?"

"Not quite yet," Marcus says. "We're enjoying the appetizers and each other's company. Both are quite delicious."

I smile.

"So," Marcus continues after the waiter departs as quietly as he came, "you want your book published, you want to work with me, and you want a career as an author, am I right?"

"Yes. More than anything."

"There is a price to pay for everything that matters in this world, it just all depends how much you want it," Marcus says. He again nods to the line outside the windows. "You're either waiting in line your entire life for that dream, or you're granted entrance and never have to wait again. I prefer not waiting for what I want."

"What is the price, Mr. Flare?"

He places his arm on the table so that it's touching mine.

"Say my name again," he purrs. "I can't tell you how much I love hearing it come out of your mouth."

"Mr. Flare."

He trembles.

"Let's recap what you have in your shopping cart, shall we?" He clears his throat. "For all that you dream, I have two simple requests. First, you sign the NDA my attorney has drafted that I have waiting in my house on Lily Pond Lane."

"Haven't I proven myself to you already?" I ask.

"You have," he says, "but that's not enough, because I do not trust anyone in this life, even you. Sadly, the human race is inflicted with guilt and remorse, emotions I thankfully do not have but know are still racing around in those Page veins of yours. To truly have someone's trust you must own them in some way. They must fear you. They must stay awake at night thinking of how they can be hurt if they do not perform as asked. I learned that from the earliest of ages."

Marcus looks at me and smiles.

"People are simple creatures," he continues. "We are taught that we require only a few things for happiness—family, love, a home, a little money, safety, a feeling of warmth. So when those things are threatened, simple creatures will follow basic rules."

"What is your second request?" I ask as calmly as I can muster, hands now under the table so Marcus will not see them shake.

"That, after you sign the NDA, you sleep with me."

I can feel my heart pulse in my temples. My jaw clenches. I grip my hands as hard as I can to keep myself together.

"I've recorded our conversations, and you will become a pariah if I publicly release what you've done to your parents behind their backs."

"But you… " I start.

"No, I wouldn't, Emma. Everyone in the publishing world

knows I'm saving your parents' asses, and they're thrilled I am trying to keep an indie publisher alive in a world of mega publishers and shrinking options for authors. Your parents haven't had a hit in ages. They may present a perfect image, but their business model is flawed. Furthermore, no one in publishing would touch one of your books, save, of course, for me. Your parents despise the type of book you've written, too. And, as I've told you before, I hold a secret that will destroy your parents' entire reputation."

"And what is that, exactly?" I ask. "I think we've played cat and mouse long enough, don't you?"

"Oh, no," Marcus says. "Not until we seal our deal."

"But why would I do that without knowing the actual dirt you have on my family? Why would I just agree to your conditions without some sort of proof?"

I force myself to be quiet for a moment and challenge him with a lingering stare. Marcus does not do well with silence.

He shifts in the booth. I know I can go further.

"I mean, you could be bluffing," I add, knowing, of course, he's not.

"Oh, no. You're smart, but not smarter than me," he says. "Quid pro quo, Emma. You know what that means?"

Oh, I know my Latin, mister. Believe me.

"Something for something," I say.

"Very good!" Marcus says. "Yes, there must be a reciprocal exchange of services—or, in this case, favors—and that starts with your signature and your accompanying me home tonight. Once you—pardon the pun—sign on *my* dotted line, I will tell you every last juicy piece of dirt I have on your parents while we're enjoy another glass of champagne. Words are words, actions are concrete, just like NDAs."

Marcus holds up his champagne glass.

"I'm actually saving you," he continues, "from every construct society has placed upon your shoulders...love, family, playing by the rules."

"You're *married*," I say, barely able to hide my disgust.

"And?" he says with a sudden, howling laugh. He lowers his glass. "Another construct, Emma! My God, that's what I'm trying to teach you."

"Does your wife know?"

"Of course she knows! And I know, too. I mean, after three years of tennis lessons with a pro who looks like Rafael Nadal, you think she could actually have learned to return a serve."

"Why do you stay with her?"

"Because she's beautiful, and it's the story people want, Emma," Marcus says. "And Rebecca gets anything and everything she's ever dreamed of."

"But not love."

"Goddammit, Emma, there is no such thing as love! When will you learn that?" His voice echoes. People turn. Marcus waves at a couple. He turns back to me, his voice low. "That's what I'm trying to make you understand through all of this. We've all been taught to believe in love, but it's a ghost, Emma. It's not real. Family is not real. Happy endings are not real."

Marcus takes a sip of champagne and glances around Le Pompeux.

"Why do you think the world searches for love, reads books about love, watches movies about love, dreams of happy endings? Because no one has it, and no one ever will. We spend our lives searching for something that does not exist and the search for that makes us miserable. I write about it solely because I know it's profitable."

"How do you know love isn't real?" I ask.

"Because all we do in this world is hurt one another," he says, "and then we seek this magic elixir to make all that pain go away, but it's a self-perpetuating cycle. Love shouldn't hurt. Family shouldn't cause you pain. Once you stop believing in love and learn that it's a business like any other, the world is yours."

Marcus skews his eyes at me. I look into them, deeply.

I am no longer afraid.

I no longer see an evil man, just the decayed soul of a lost boy who was never told that he was loved. I suddenly realize why his writing has never resonated with me, why it's so different from GiGi's. It's because he doesn't know a damn thing about love. It's a mystery to him, and he writes about it like a setting he's never actually visited.

Marcus is wrong: love is real.

And love can hurt.

They are not mutually exclusive.

I am living proof of that dichotomy.

Love can only hurt when you love back.

That's *why* it hurts.

But we must love or what else is there?

An eternal void.

A hole as big and dark as the one in Marcus's heart.

But love can only start when you are shown love, when you love yourself, and if you're incapable of that, you are incapable of loving anyone at any time.

And that is the difference between me and Marcus.

Despite my family's eccentricities, I was taught to love myself, believe in myself, honor myself, and that takes root in a family and grows through generations like the rings in a tree.

I glance around Le Pompeux and then look outside. I no longer see people behind a rope. I see young and old, those who are privileged and those scraping together enough cash for a special night out. They are here to celebrate birthdays, anniversaries and one another.

I realize Marcus is staring at me.

"As a young, smart, progressive woman you should fight

against all of the societal constructs you've been taught to live by in America," he declares. "Let me help set you free."

I again see a boy whose father is in prison, a boy who will never be free.

"May we get the check?" Marcus asks as the waiter returns. "We'll get some dessert to go to enjoy together later." He looks at me. *After*, he mouths.

"Of course, sir," the waiter says.

I begin to scratch my arm, harder and harder.

I cough.

"Excuse me?" I call to the waiter as he begins to leave.

"Yes, ma'am?"

"Was there papaya in the Crab & Avocado appetizer?"

"Yes, ma'am."

I know this, of course.

"Oh, my God," I say. "I'm allergic to papaya."

"Do you require an EpiPen?" the waiter asks. "A doctor?"

"No, I carry one in my purse in case of an emergency like this," I say. "Please excuse me."

I stand and hurry to the bathroom.

I take a seat in a stall and wait.

My cell trills after a few moments.

He left…of course.

When I return to the banquette, Jess is sitting where Marcus just was. She is pouring Veuve into a new champagne glass.

The waiter returns.

"Mr. Flare paid for dinner and left you a note," he says, handing me a piece of paper. "I hope you're feeling better, ma'am."

"Much, thank you."

The waiter leaves.

"Marcus is a true gentleman," Jess says. "Paid for dinner but left without saying goodbye when he thought you were sick and knew he couldn't sleep with you."

I open the note.

I'll be back in the Hamptons on Friday. See you at seven. One Lily Pad Lane.

"He's like a dog with a bone," Jess says. "And I mean that literally."

"Did you get everything?" I ask. "I will kill you if you didn't. I can't go through this again."

Jess places her cell against the bottle of champagne on the table and hits Play.

The entire nightmare of an evening is replayed before my eyes.

"This footage is so close," I say. "How did you get it all so clearly?"

Jess grabs her cell and begins to text. A moment later, Babe and Gretchen appear.

"You can thank our two friends from college," Jess says. "Gretchen got Babe a table right in front of you. Her face was hidden by that massive vase."

"The Swans will always protect their flock," Babe says.

"Thank you," I say. "What do we do now?"

"Finish this champagne," she says, "and then tell Mom and Dad everything."

CHAPTER TWENTY-EIGHT

"I don't think you've been in my office since FDR was president!" VV says with a big laugh. "Please, please, have a seat."

My parents turn to take a seat.

They nearly fall over the coffee table when they see me and Jess seated before them.

"What is going on?" my mother asks. "Is this another trick of yours, VV?"

"All in due time," VV says. "I'm too old for tricks. And no one can pay my hourly rate anyway."

My parents do not laugh or move.

"Please," I say. "Have a seat. I *promise* this will all make sense in a moment."

My parents look at one another and then, very slowly, take a seat in the chairs at each end of the coffee table, their eyes trained on us.

"Would you care for anything to drink?"

"I was originally thinking sparkling water," my mother says. She continues to eye me and Jess. "But now I'm thinking hard liquor is the way to go."

"I knew I liked you!" VV pours glasses of bourbon and sparkling water. "You always need a chaser," she continues, setting the glasses before my parents, the jangling of her jewelry the equivalent of a trash truck.

"Thank you." My mother takes a sip. "So, why did you ask us to meet after all these years? We could have handled everything over the phone. I feel like we've been set up."

"Not at all. I thought it was time to mend fences," VV says, taking a seat. "And, yes, I've been watching *Yellowstone*."

My father finally cracks a smile.

"I thought it was best we take this meeting face-to-face," VV says. "So did your daughters."

"Why are we here?" my mother asks. "Why are *they* here?"

She doesn't as much stare at me and Jess as she stares through our souls.

"Let's start with your first question, Piper, shall we?" VV asks, her voice calm and shockingly diplomatic. "The manuscript I sent you."

"I'm curious why you sent this manuscript to *us*?" my father says. "You know it's not what we publish. It might be something we'd consider in the future after we complete the acquisition of our first novel for Books with Flare, which will be in the works soon, and get a more solid foundation. We do need to move in a more commercial direction, if you can believe I'm saying that out loud. But, right now, I'm not sure we're in a position to make an offer on this one, especially considering all of the competition for it."

"May I answer your questions with a question?"

"Shoot."

"Very *Yellowstone*, Phillip," VV says. "When was the last time you read a book just for enjoyment?"

My parents look at one another and then give VV a curious look.

"Like you, the majority of time we read for business," my father says. "When we discover a great new book, it becomes not only enjoyment but also the most incredible journey of our lives."

"Was that your experience with this manuscript?"

"Yes," my father says.

My heart somersaults.

"May I ask why?" VV leans toward my father, peering through her fun-house glasses.

"It's a novel for a reader of any age who has ever loved and lost, and—even decades later—can feel that sting as easily as the first frost," my mother says. "It's about family rivalry, and how women—and sisters—can hurt one another but, ultimately, have one another's backs."

"It's also about family on the shores of Lake Michigan, and that speaks to me even more personally," my father adds. "For me, reading this novel was like coming home."

"But, again, as Phillip said, I don't think we're in a position to buy without Marcus's input and final approval," my mother says, "and I don't think we'll have the financial firepower right now to match the other offers at auction."

"What if I told you the author only wants to sell to The Mighty Pages?"

"What?" my mother asks. "Why?"

"Why don't I let her explain?"

My parents look at VV, waiting for clarification.

"Aren't you going to call her?" my mother asks.

"There's no need," VV says. "The author is right here."

Everything moves in slow motion. The turning of my parents' heads, trying to understand what is happening. The jangling of VV's jewelry. How tightly my sister's hands are clamped together. The ragged heartbeat in my ears. The formation of a final breath.

"The manuscript is mine," I say.

Silence.

"I don't understand," my mother finally says.

"And I can never thank you enough for the words you just said about it," I continue. "I think I've waited my entire life to hear them."

"*You* wrote this book, Emma? Why didn't you just tell us?" my father says, looking baffled.

"Because we know," Jess says. "*Everything*."

My parents look at us, faces contorted in confusion.

"I figured out GiGi was S. I. Quaeris. Jess and I found the safe in her office," I say.

"And all the manuscripts, the flash drive that revealed GiGi was being blackmailed, everything," Jess adds.

My mother leans back in her chair and takes a sip of whiskey. "I knew it would come out one day, Phillip."

"We only kept it a secret to protect GiGi and both of you," my father says. "It was GiGi's sole wish."

"I know," I say. "But we found out something else."

"Something you never knew," Jess says.

"The man who blackmailed GiGi was Marcus Flare," I blurt. "And he wants to destroy our family and take over The Mighty Pages as revenge for what we did to his family."

My parents search each other's faces and then the room, as if there might be hidden cameras and this was all a joke.

"No," my mother says. "No. No. No. I don't believe you."

"Emma? Jess?" my father asks, his voice firm. "This sounds like a plot from a Harlan Coben novel. I understand this is a very unsteady time for all of us—our business, our family, our future—but I can't understand why you would pull something like this."

"We're not pulling anything, Dad," Jess says. "Please. I know it sounds insane, but you have to believe us. We're your daughters. We'd do anything to protect you."

"Would you?" my mother asks. Her words are as pointed as a bullet. "Emma, I know you don't like Marcus. And I know you don't like us being partners with him. I also believe you would do anything to get him in trouble to end our working relationship. But that train has left the station."

Anger flashes inside me, but I swallow hard to keep my emotions inside. If I act like a child—which is what my parents expect—Marcus will win. Jess and I will be dismissed. All our effort will be for nothing.

I watch my father watch me. He knows my soul. He knows his mother, and all she endured. In his eyes, I know he knows. I know he believes us.

"How do you know?" he finally asks. "Once more. With every detail."

Jess and I go through the entire story again, detail by detail— how we found out, what Marcus said to me, how we planned this ruse, the faux manuscript he sent to them and why VV worked so hard to get my manuscript to auction.

"To save The Mighty Pages," Jess concludes.

"To save our family," I add.

My parents are again quiet.

"Marcus Flare," my mother says. "Very clever. Very evil."

"That's why he didn't want us to read the rest of *The Magician's Assistant*," my father says.

"Believe me, you don't want to," VV says in a deadpan, grabbing her whiskey and taking a sip.

"He wanted to ruin us from the outset," he adds.

"But we're DOA, Phillip," my mother says, her skepticism turning to panic. "We've invested *everything* into Books with Flare. He was going to be our savior, but we trusted the devil."

"He has first right to buy The Mighty Pages if we fail," my father mutters. "He knew that all along. That's why he pushed for it. How could I have been so stupid? We fell for his plan."

"But we have a better one," Jess says with a smile.

She explains what we have planned next.

"I want The Mighty Pages to publish my novel," I say. "For free."

"With all the buzz it has right now going to auction, I can spin this into a big story in the trades with Jess's help," VV says. "Then when it's published, whatever it sells will be pure profit after your initial investment and overhead to print, ship and conduct your marketing and publicity campaigns. I know that could be significant at first, but you would have no advance to recoup. And the breakout potential for this is huge."

"But it's not what we publish outside of Marcus," my mother says uncertainly.

"No, but it's what you need to publish," I press. "Especially once we change Books with Flare to the new imprint Jess, VV and I have in mind."

We tell them.

"God, we're good!" VV crows. "And I promise to send you the best manuscripts for it."

"You know," my father says, "we actually started The Mighty Pages for the right reasons. And the wrong ones, too." He looks at his hands as he continues. "We wanted to do things differently and give voice to authors who we believed weren't being heard and given an equal chance of being published. Your grandmother was a trailblazer in literature, and I personally wanted to honor that and create a diverse list of authors, stories and books. And I think we succeeded and were far ahead of the publishing curve. I also felt if I got in the game, I could stay in it until I could rectify what happened to her. That's why I wrote my most recent novel, Emma. I became fascinated with the game of baseball because of her. It's the only sport that doesn't have a clock attached to it. The game isn't over until the last out."

My heart is in my throat.

"I still need to be convinced," my mother—always my mother—says. "If we weren't in such financial straits, I would never have agreed to publish commercial fiction with Marcus."

"Always such a literary snob, aren't you, Piper?" VV says. "I think the whiskey is already kicking in. Sorry."

"No, you're not," my mother says with a wicked laugh.

"No, I'm not," VV says.

"Mom, why don't you try to think of this new endeavor… like GiGi's garden?" Jess says.

"I'm not following," she says.

Jess continues. "Hydrangeas bloom from old wood. They are the classics of a garden. Hardy. Reliable late bloomers. Long-lasting. That's what you've always tried to publish. The new imprint would be like the peonies in GiGi's garden: the flowers everyone wants to bring inside their homes the moment they bloom because of their beauty." Jess nudges me and then smiles at our mother. "A garden requires both varieties to make it through the season."

"You should be the writer," I whisper.

"I had some help."

My father perches on the edge of his chair.

"But, Piper, you cannot deny that we've also been elitist in our thinking that anything commercial, like romance, would not be well received critically and undermine our aura of only publishing literary fiction. Every house at the time was publishing blockbusters. We thought we could build a mighty list from smaller titles. It worked for a while. But then publishing changed, and our egos got in the way. Our stubbornness to expand our list was rooted in the fact that we could not write those types of books well, and I, especially, was envious of how easily it came to GiGi. She was one of a kind. She wrote simple stories that spoke to people's hearts."

My mother sips her whiskey in silence.

"Your grandmother was a gifted writer," my father continues. "And so, so driven not only to write but also to protect her family and give us a life that was free of the grief and worry she dealt with every day. We needed to publish commercial fiction because we were losing so much money, and Marcus knew that. I believed that if we were successful, we'd have an imprint where our commercial list could receive the critical acclaim it often lacks and help fund a literary list that needs to find a bigger audience. As you just said, Jess, we need to tend a garden for all tastes and seasons."

"Sometimes we forget why we read," my mother says as if to herself. "Sometimes it's to walk in someone else's shoes for a while. Sometimes it's to travel to a place or time we never will. Sometimes it's to get angry or more informed. And sometimes it's simply to escape, smile and be offered a little bit of hope so it's possible to go on in this world. Your novel reminded me of that, Emma. I, too, need that, and so do many readers. And if that's a start in the reeducation of Piper Page, so be it."

"Mom."

That's all I can say.

"And we are so proud of you," my father says to me. "Your grandmother is smiling from heaven."

"Now, we need to go through our plan for Marcus," Jess says. "We only have one chance."

As Jess is talking, I receive a text from Gin and Juice.

BINGO! it reads in caps. WE GOT HIM!

A stream of texts appears, and I smile.

"Remember," VV says, "that any plan to kill Marcus must include wearing garlic and a crucifix around your neck."

"What if we don't succeed?" my father asks.

VV stands and opens the door to her office.

"Leo!" she calls. "We're going to need a bottle of something strong! And a wooden stake!"

CHAPTER TWENTY-NINE

The Mighty Pages conference room is silent save for the *tick-tick-tick* of the antique clock that sits in the corner.

The clock is GiGi's, the one she had in her library, which chimed on the hour and whose pendulum always somehow seemed to speak what went unsaid.

I used to wonder why it was here. Why would my parents go to so much effort to move this single heirloom so far from a place they no longer wanted to be?

And now I know.

Because my parents have always honored family more than anything.

But their story was silenced for a long, long time.

The clock suddenly strikes ten, and I jump.

My mother paces around the grand, wooden conference table like a beautiful caged leopard. She checks her reflection in the window, smoothing her hair. She is dressed as if she's going to appear on *Today*. Piper always dresses for a fight.

Marcus Flare appears in the wall of glass, and my mother turns to look at each of us as if we're about to skydive and have entrusted the safety of our parachutes to one another.

"Who's ready for a life-changing Friday?" Marcus announces as he enters the conference room. "How are you, Phil? Pipes?"

My parents wince. They despise nicknames. You might as well serve them a bologna sandwich, Cheetos and a Mountain Dew for lunch.

Marcus extends his hand to greet each of us. He is drinking a venti Starbucks and is so amped up it appears as if it's his third coffee of the morning. He winks at me.

He's accompanied by a man I recognize as his attorney, a handsome, younger man in a suit that is much too tight.

"Greg Matthews," he says by way of introduction, extending his hand to all.

"It's nice to see you, Greg," my father says. "I didn't realize you were attending the meeting today. It's just to discuss initial steps for the first Book with Flare."

"The more the merrier, Phil," Marcus says. "You never know what might come up. Shall we get started?"

We all take a seat, and Marcus beams looking around the table. He takes a moment to look us each in the eye.

"Everyone's here," he says, sounding a bit too much like Hannibal Lecter. "The whole family for Sunday dinner."

He wants to eat us alive.

"So," Marcus rubs his hands together. "I know you've had a chance to read the opening of our first book together. It's quite a stunning debut, isn't it?"

"Stunning," my mother agrees without a hint of sarcasm.

"As you know, Emma and I are working with the author to perfect the manuscript before you see it. However, I know you trust our judgment implicitly, and I'm hesitant to wait any longer as time is ticking. My writing and travel schedule is insane. We still plan to publish in a year, correct?"

"That is the plan," my father says.

"Fabulous!" Marcus says. "I think we should make an offer

to the author and then set our marketing budget for the book. I'm thinking a million-dollar advance."

"For a debut?" my mother questions.

"We need to show we're serious," Marcus says. "Not only to the author but also the publishing industry."

"We can show that for a lot less money," my mother argues. "Does the manuscript have other offers of which we're not aware?"

Marcus leans across the table as if he's going to lunge at her. "It doesn't appear as if you've ever had an issue with spending a bit too much money to get what you want, Pipes. Why start now?"

My mother removes an invisible piece of lint from her sleeve, a sign she is ready to gut him.

"Who's the agent?" my mother presses. "It's so odd that we haven't spoken with them or had any interaction."

"It's my imprint," Marcus says.

"It's *our* house," my mother says, "and our money."

"VV, if you can believe it," Marcus says with a forced smile. "You can speak with her at any time, right, Emma?"

He turns and narrows his gaze on me.

"Of course," I say. "I know it might be a bit awkward considering your history with her, Mom, and I know she's a shark, but I also know she's beyond thrilled to have her client be our first author."

"We need to make a statement to the world saying we've arrived, and we plan to play with the big dogs," Marcus says, pressing on. "VV is a big dog, and you know she won't let this one go for cheap, especially to you." He laughs. "And I'm a big dog. I promise I will deliver the kibble."

My mother conjures a seemingly real and appreciative laugh.

"Speaking of big, I would love to make a big splash ASAP as we have so much buzz going right now," Marcus continues. "I'd like to leak the first chapter to the trades and influencers and was hoping the art department could jump on this and get us a cover."

"Again, as you know, that's hard to do when none of us have read the full manuscript," my mother says.

"But not impossible, correct, knowing the gist of the novel?"

"No, not impossible," my mother says.

"Wonderful!" Marcus says. "I have been running some numbers and—based on the marketing budgets for my books—I think we should allocate a few hundred thousand dollars for the first book. It will make us or break us, so we need to ante up."

I try not to look at Jess, but I can't help it. Marcus catches me.

"Did you have a thought, Emma?" he asks. "Please, share with the class."

"I think we should go all in," I say with a nod.

"So we're looking at being in the red over a million dollars before we even print a book?" my father asks. "That could kill us. You know that."

Marcus squares his shoulders and stares at my father.

"I'm Marcus Flare," he finally says, "and you hired me to save you. I'm good for it. You know that." He smiles and continues. "And that's a drop in the bucket to me. My publisher spends significantly more on me. If you don't believe you'll make your money back then may I ask why we even signed up to work together? I'm sensing hesitation here. I don't like hesitation."

My father lifts his hands as if he's being robbed.

"No hesitation," he says. "Only an open conversation."

"I understand," Marcus says. "You're such a good father." He looks around the table. "You're such a good family." He looks at Greg. "I did bring my attorney here today because—as part of our contract—you agreed to a certain fiduciary responsibility in our first venture together based on my investment in The Mighty Pages." Marcus turns to his attorney. "Greg?"

"Yes, as a sign of good faith, to draw the best talent and to ensure we do everything possible to make this launch a success, you agreed to invest up to a million and a half dollars in your first book together," he says. "This, I'm sure you remember, is like collateral. Once the first book is officially published, it would then trigger the first of Marcus's investments in The Mighty Pages."

"Twenty million dollars," Marcus adds with a smile.

Greg opens his folder. "I have the contract you signed if you'd like to review again?"

Marcus turns to my parents, beaming. "I think our open conversation has closed, don't you?"

"The contract clearly states 'up to a million and a half dollars,'" my father says. "Our good faith conversations always centered on the fact that we didn't want to spend that much if we didn't have to do so. That's simply good business."

Marcus laughs.

"You don't know a damn thing about running a good business."

"Are you trying to break us before we've even made a penny, Marcus?" my mother asks with a big wink, making it all sound like a joke.

"I think you're already there," Marcus says, his voice cold. "Now, Jess, can you start helping us with the reveal to influencers?"

"Of course," Jess says. "This is going to be huge." She smiles. "But I do have one question. When are we going to be able to meet the author in person, or virtually? The author has such a wonderful backstory from all we've been told, but we don't know if the author is a man or woman, whether they have a social media platform, whether they are a good public speaker..." Jess looks at Marcus. "We don't even know if they use a pen name."

Marcus blinks, once, twice, then smiles and turns to me.

"Emma?" he asks, taking a casual sip of his coffee. "Would you care to illuminate us?"

"I'd love to," I say. "In fact, I've prepared a PowerPoint."

"No wonder I like you, Emma," Marcus says. "You are not only always prepared but you also manage to surprise me at every turn."

He sits back in his chair and folds his arms. I open the laptop before me, and click on a slideshow entitled BOOKS WITH FLARE.

"That has such a nice ring to it," Marcus says.

I click another slide.

A black-and-white prison mug shot appears.

"Who is that?"

"Don't you know your own father?" I ask.

"What is going on?" Marcus asks. "Greg?"

The attorney shifts uncomfortably. "I have no idea."

Another slide.

A newspaper article and photo of little Avery winning the poetry contest.

Another slide.

Emails from GiGi's blackmailer, her offer to help him, the one telling my father to keep it all a secret. This is followed by snapshots of Marcus's spending in the press: homes around the world, his own private plane, jewelry for his wife and lavish parties, as well as financial articles detailing his failed business ventures, including a hotel in the Hamptons, two movies that failed spectacularly that he produced and a line of women's clothing entitled Fashion with Flare.

A FaceTime video of his mother, Jeannette Marcuzzi, pops up next.

"We made so many mistakes, Avery. Let it go. Move on. Hate has consumed our entire lives. Please. I beg of you. You don't have to be your father. I miss you. I'd love to see you again one day."

Marcus slams his fist on the conference table.

"Where did you get all of this?"

"We know everything, Avery," I say. "My sister and I figured out your and GiGi's big secret, the one she was too scared to reveal, and the one secret you've been holding over our heads."

"It's over, Marcus," my mother says.

She doesn't sound angry or vengeful, she simply sounds like a mother disappointed in her child.

"You actually needed this deal more than we did, Marcus," Jess says. "You thought you could get retribution on our family by breaking us, but you're the one who is more extended than an airport runway."

"This is *nothing*," he yells. "I've survived far worse. And who's going to believe you? You signed a contract. I'll say you're wanting to end it because you don't have the funds to go forward, and I'll still take over."

"Then what about this?" I ask.

The video of us at Le Pompeux appears.

"Say goodbye to your reputation as the world's most romantic author, say goodbye to women across the world buying your books, say goodbye to everything," Jess says.

"You little snake," Marcus says, glaring at me.

"There is a price to pay for everything that matters in this world, it just all depends how much you want it," I say, using his words to me at Le Pompeux. "To truly have someone's trust you must own them in some way. They must fear you. They must stay awake at night thinking of how I will hurt them if they do not do as I ask. Family, love, a home, a little money, safety, a feeling of warmth. When those things are threatened, simple creatures will follow basic rules."

"What do you want?" he asks.

"You will rip up the contract," my father says, "null and void starting today, and, Greg, you will write a new one that continues Marcus's financial and public support of our new venture without any say or profit in our decisions."

I click the last slide.

A logo of The Mighty Pages' new imprint appears:

Pauline Page Books
Where Fiction Feels Like Family

Finally, my grandma's real name will be said forever.

"You will fail without me," he seethes. "You don't even have a book to publish."

"Yes, we do," I say. "Mine."

Marcus's eyes bulge.

"VV is representing me, and my manuscript is going to auction," I inform him. "Three of the biggest publishers want it…" I pause for effect. "Including yours. But I'm giving it to my parents for free."

"We will profit off your legacy just as you did off of ours," Jess says.

"Every family is flawed and filled with secrets," my mother says. "The thing that leads us out of the darkness are elders who see the light, those who do not want our children and grandchildren to make the same mistakes that we did. I'm sorry your father damaged you and your family, but know this—should you ever come for my family again, I will burn Marcus Flare alive without an ounce of remorse *and* without smudging my lipstick."

"By the end of today," my father says, "I want the new contract in my hands, and, Marcus, you will help us make a public statement to the press about our new imprint that honors a woman who was harmed by a man her entire life and, thus, could never receive the public and critical attention she so richly deserved. Ironically, you will say, it is her own granddaughter who has followed in her legacy by writing the book of the year, and you couldn't stand in the way of letting a family honor that legacy. In fact, it was all your idea."

"Greg," Marcus says, standing and going into the hallway.

After a few minutes, Greg returns to the conference room, Marcus following, head down like a scolded puppy.

"I'll have the contract by end of the day," Greg says, "and let me know when you would like to schedule a press conference with Marcus."

He gathers his things and leaves.

"Marcus, Emma told us you were a fan of the writer O. Henry," my father says out of the blue. "He of the surprise ending?"

Marcus looks at my father but doesn't reply.

"O. Henry was actually a pen name for William Sidney Porter who chose a pseudonym. He allegedly embezzled money from the bank where he was working to keep his struggling magazine afloat, and when that was discovered, he fled to Honduras leaving his wife and young daughter behind. He returned only when he learned his wife was dying, refused to speak at his trial or acknowledge any guilt and was sentenced to prison."

My father waits until Marcus looks him in the eye.

"That was the secret he spent his entire life trying to hide, even from his own daughter," he continues. "I've lived with a secret much of my life, and I am exhausted. You must be, too. The sad thing is the world will never know the real truth. They will never receive a climactic reveal like in one of his stories. Too many women writers, like my mother, were forced to choose a pseudonym to protect themselves and have their work taken seriously. Men like you and O. Henry hid behind one out of shame."

Greg ushers Marcus out of the conference room.

As he passes by, I can't help myself.

I give him the finger just like all those childish boys in college.

PART FOUR

Third-Person Omniscient

CHAPTER THIRTY

One Year Later

Marcus Flare grabs my hand and squeezes it tightly.

"Emma Page is the real deal," he announces. "To bring her voice to life and to shine a light on the legacy of her grandmother, Pauline Page, aka S. I. Quaeris, a true literary trailblazer, is probably the greatest honor of my career."

He beams at me, and I smile beatifically.

Beyond the camera lights, I see my parents and Jess smiling. VV rolls her eyes.

"I cannot tell you how proud I am that *The Summer of Seagulls* is not only the first book from The Mighty Pages' new imprint, Pauline Page Books, but also the July Read With Jenna selection," Jenna Bush Hager says. "It heralds not only the voice of a new generation but also a voice deserving of widespread recognition. To you and your GiGi!"

"Thank you so much," I say. "I'm humbled and honored."

"What was it like to write this book at such a young age?" Hota Kotb asks. "This book has such an old soul to it, if you will. Were you channeling your grandmother when you wrote this?"

"I could hear GiGi's voice in every word I wrote," I say. "She not only was a great writer, she was a great woman, but a woman who was overlooked like so many of her generation. She sacrificed everything for our family. She gave us our love of books and taught us what was most important in life. Each other."

I continue.

"I want people to say her name forever. That's a reason we are also reissuing her books—whose rights have reverted back to The Mighty Pages—under her own name. When I am long gone, I know that readers will walk into a library or bookstore and say *Pauline Page*. I hope that reconnects them not only to their family history but also the simple things in life. I also want readers to realize that there should be no limits placed on women, there should be no genres placed on books. Women should be who they dream. Women should read what they want. Women should live without having to hide any part of their true selves."

"Do you believe your grandmother was judged for who she was in her life?" Jenna asks.

"Oh, every single day," I answer, "and we continue to be. I'm sure you are judged every day on TV, probably more for the clothes you wear or your hairstyle than the good you do in the world. My sister is judged for the exact same things. My mother is judged for being smart and driven. I am judged for my honesty, optimism and youth. Women are universally judged for the things we say, the things we don't, the volume at which we say them. We are judged for being happily married, we are judged for being gleefully single. We are judged for having children, or not. We are judged for how we raise them. We are judged for having faith, we are judged for questioning. We are judged, day in and day out, for every single thing that we do and don't do. If you have been able to live your life free of the judgment of others, if you can say what is on your mind without fear of judgment, if you can live your life without fear of retribution, then you do not know what it is like to be a woman."

"Go on, Emma," Jenna urges.

"That's why I'm so honored you chose my debut novel, because even the books that women write and women read face judgment. We call novels like mine 'beach reads,' 'rom-coms,' 'chick lit,' 'women's fiction,' which diminishes their value. As a result, people, believe such books are merely fizzy and frivolous."

My eyes suddenly mist.

"Are you okay?" Jenna asks.

I nod and clear my throat.

"I want to say something, but I want to make sure I get it just right because it's important to say."

"Take your time."

I nod, take another breath and continue.

"My grandmother had a safe filled with..." I pause again, this time solely to make Marcus squirm ever so in his seat "... letters from readers around the world, women who had lost parents, husbands or children. Women in the midst of divorce. Women undergoing chemotherapy. And they all reached for her books as a way to escape and to heal. When they needed a friend. When they needed hope. When they needed a reason to go on in this world. They sought out her words as a way to make sense of an often senseless world. If I can do that, even with one reader, then I will have fulfilled my purpose—just as my grandmother did—in this world. That is the power of books, no matter what you may call them."

Jenna's eyes mist, too. She reaches over, grabs my hands and smiles.

"Beautifully said, Emma," Jenna says. "I know your grandmother is looking down at you from heaven and beaming." She turns to Marcus. "And I'm beaming at you, Marcus Flare. You are not only a magnificent writer, Marcus, but also a magnificent human. A role model for publishing."

Inside, I laugh. Before the cameras, I nod.

"Thank you," Marcus says. He turns to me and smiles.

Jenna looks at me. "Well, I could not put your book down, Emma. You heard it here first, *The Summer of Seagulls* is the Read With Jenna selection for July."

The cover of my novel—*my* novel!—flashes on a big screen behind me.

It is beyond beautiful, a watercolor of two girls floating in the lake, holding hands, the perspective from that of a gull soaring high above them. In the distance, a red lighthouse watches like a sentinel.

"That's a stunner, Emma," Hota says. "So pretty."

"There's an old saying you probably know that my grandmother changed to suit Michigan," I say. "She used to tell me, 'Be a lamp, a lighthouse or a ladder.' That is what I hope my books will be for readers."

"Folks, go out and grab a copy or ten, and make sure to read a Pauline Page novel as well this summer," Jenna says. "Marcus Flare. Emma Page. I know we'll be hearing more from you both for years to come."

Jenna and Hota turn toward the camera.

"We'll be right back."

The lights dim.

"And we're clear," a producer calls.

We take countless photos before emerging onto the street.

"It must gall you to know you're making me even richer, *Avery*," VV says to Marcus before he jumps into a waiting car.

I watch his car disappear into city traffic.

"He still came out smelling like a rose," I say to VV, shaking my head as my family joins me on the sidewalk. "People believe he's a saint."

"Men always do, my dear," VV says. "Let him be the hero. He knows deep down that you are. He knows that there's an asterisk by his name, and he must live with that every day. And he's not in charge of your future. You run the show. You own him. You have all the power, and that resides right here."

She places her hand on my heart.

"That's winning, Emma. That's a secret worth keeping. Now go write that next book that will change someone's life like your grandmother's work did."

She hugs me.

"And the next one's not going to be free!" she yells at my parents. "Now let's see if I can go nail down a movie deal for you! Lots of interest! Lots of calls! See you at five at Liber for a celebration! You're buying, Phillip! I can't afford to after all this! Kisses!"

VV begins to blow down the sidewalk like a cyclone. She turns and points.

My face and book cover is streaming across the front of the TODAY Plaza directly before Studio 1A.

"You did it, kid. You're a writer!"

VV lifts her arm into the air, bangles jangling, and punches the blue New York sky.

And then it hits me: I did do it.

All those years of doubt. All those times I told myself I was a fraud and kept going.

"So?" my father asks, taking a photo of me with my book—as big as the city—behind me. "What do you want to do next, Emma?"

I smile at my father.

"I think I just want to go home and work on my next novel."

CHAPTER THIRTY-ONE

My eyes scan Lake Michigan. Children squeal gleefully as they race into the water at sunset.

I am home.

Again.

Funny, isn't it, how—whether you want to or not—you always have to return home either in person or memory in order to move on to the next chapter of your life? I pivot my eyes to the chapter I'm writing in my next novel.

I hear a familiar voice, the squall of a gull. I look up again.

A large gull rushes a smaller one on the shore. Instead of dashing away, the younger gull stands its ground, squawks, extends its wings. The other gull stands down, and the two warily begin to navigate the same turf.

I refocus on my manuscript.

I write. The words flow.

My parents are reading books under umbrellas.

Jess has just docked the new boat she bought—a tritoon named *The Ni-Ko-Nong II*—on the beach before Eyebrow Cottage. She is lying on a towel in the seat, GiGi's hat covering her face.

The gulls squawk, their voices carried on the wind.

"You have to practice and see the real gull, the good in every one of them, and to help them see it in themselves," GiGi used to read from *Jonathan Livingston Seagull.* "That's what I mean by love."

What is love?

No, more importantly, what is unconditional love?

It is love *without* conditions.

I will love you *but...*

I will love you *if* you change for me.

Do *this*, and I will love you.

Some of us are lucky enough to be shown unconditional love in this world. Too few of us ever experience it, and so we go through life expecting conditions on the love we give and receive.

We must have good teachers. We must be good students.

My parents didn't buy that Hamptons house. They realized they had everything they ever needed and wanted right in front of them.

A home with a history and a heart. A family bound by strength.

And we are all writing again. My father is working on his next novel. It's commercial fiction.

My mother is working on a memoir.

"Lord knows you have the voice for it," I tease her.

I am working on my next novel for Pauline Page Books, this one about a recent college grad, a young writer who discovers a hidden manuscript in her grandmother's cottage that upends her parents' elitist literary lives and threatens the devious plans of the world's bestselling romance novelist...

And misogynist.

And you wonder where authors get their inspiration?

Jess has expanded The Swans. She is now doing author interviews and book recommendations as part of the *Today* show and has brought her followers and influence back to The Mighty Pages, where she started.

Marcus is begging to work with her.

Speaking of Marcus, he recently sent me a copy of my own novel. He had re-created the cover by drawing on it with his own illustrations: dollar signs for birds, *Solar Flare* written across the summer sun. He had superimposed a photo of himself as the lighthouse, as if he were still watching over me.

Inside, he had written how working with me had made him even more popular among female readers. His sales were skyrocketing.

Thank you helping the rich get richer! XOXO, Marcus

He had also enclosed the old NDA with a note that read, "Wish to reconsider?"

He continues to send gifts—unannounced—to me in Michigan.

I've received stickers of classic book covers from *Little Women* to *Pride and Prejudice*, and he sent me a Taylor Swift Eras Tour T-shirt on which he had scribbled, *Keep writing, little girl!*

I am no longer angry at him. I am no longer scared or envious either.

I simply feel sorry for him.

And the T-shirt—which I'm wearing right now—fits like a dream.

I type furiously, finishing my chapter.

When I look up, the summer world is a Technicolor dream. The lighthouse shimmers down the shore.

The sun is halfway below the water on the horizon.

The final wink.

I type the final period of my chapter.

I hear profound silence.

And, in that silence, I hear the voice of a strong, young woman.

This is the power of literature. This is the power we must unleash in life.

The only thing that separates writers from one another is voice. The only thing that separates each of us from our intended destiny is using that voice.

Every story is important. Every voice is powerful. It's finding the strength to share it and use it that is the trick.

And when we don't, the deafening silence we hear is simply sadness.

We all nearly drown at one point in our lives, and we too often let that experience serve as a final period in our existence. We stop living. We let the villains of the world silence us.

It's only by listening to that voice within—the one that speaks to us late at night, the one calling to you right now, the one we try so hard to ignore because we just want to fit in and we just want life to be less painful—that we can bring our stories to life.

That *we* come to life.

Because when we do, our words are no longer our words, our stories are no longer our stories, they belong to you, the reader. You make them your own, and, when you do, for a moment the pain eases, the words are no longer jumbled, your heart is superglued back into place once more, it is whole, we are one, and the world actually makes sense again.

If even for a single, mighty page.

An acorn bounces onto the deck beside me.

I reach over, pick it up and place it in my pocket.

★ ★ ★ ★ ★

A PERSONAL LETTER TO READERS

Dear Reader:

The Page Turner is a novel about how books save us, whether we are writers or readers. The novel is also about the judgment we place on one another, and often the books we read, simply by a casual glance at the collective covers.

Growing up, books saved my life. I mean that. As a gay kid growing up in rural America in the 1970s—who liked to write, read and wear ascots—I had a big target on my back. I believed there was *no one* like me in the world, so I turned to books.

My grandma—my pen name, Viola Shipman—and my mother—a floor, ER and ICU nurse and, later, a hospice nurse—sensed I was "different," and they swept me under their wings, loved me unconditionally and made sure I cherished my uniqueness. One of the ways they did this was by pushing books into my hands from the earliest of ages and making it clear that reading and education would not only change my life but quite possibly save it.

My grandma never finished high school and yet she was a voracious reader. She pushed books into my mother's hands from the earliest of ages, saved change in an old crock in her garage that eventually started a college fund for her, and volunteered at the local library.

As a kid, I didn't dream of being an astronaut or baseball player. I dreamed of being a writer.

Books allowed me to see a vast world beyond the small town in which I lived. They allowed me not only to escape from the cruelty I often experienced but also understand the reasons behind the hatred. They allowed me to see—as my mom and grandma instilled in me—that being unique was an incredible gift.

Books aren't just books. Books are family. Authors are friends. The stories we read are time stamps in our memories. They bookmark important chapters in our lives and growth.

Books are a chance to right the wrong in the world, an opportunity to rewrite ourselves. We can reimagine and reinvent, see the world in an entirely new way simply by turning a page. Or, sometimes, we can just escape from our own lives.

As Carl Sagan wrote: "What an astonishing thing a book is. It's a flat object made from a tree with flexible parts on which are imprinted lots of funny dark squiggles. But one glance at it and you're inside the mind of another person, maybe somebody dead for thousands of years. Across the millennia, an author is speaking clearly and silently inside your head, directly to you. Writing is perhaps the greatest of human inventions, binding together people who never knew each other, citizens of distant epochs. Books break the shackles of time. A book is proof that humans are capable of working magic."

That's exactly how I feel when I read and write: magical. Like a literary unicorn.

When I talk to readers at events, many tend to believe that writing *is* a magical endeavor, that a muse lands upon my shoulders each morning and whispers gilded words into my ear. Some days can be like that. Most are just damn hard work.

And many readers tend to view writing as either madness or salvation.

I always tell them it's both.

And on the best days, writing is salvation from the madness.

What does a book mean to a reader?

An escape.

A walk in someone else's shoes.

A trip somewhere we've never been.

A fit of laughter, or tears, often both at the same time.

A rope of hope.

A reason to go on.

What does a book mean to an author?

The same.

Why?

Because every chapter of our lives is a storyline in a novel. It's deeply personal but also wholly universal, which means it's an important storyline in your lives, too.

Our broken heart will never heal.

Our love burns more intensely than any other.

Our grief is unimaginable.

Our secret is unshareable.

Our family is unbearable.

Authors tend to write about the same topics—love, death, hope, loss—and we use the same words, the same linguistic tool belt, but it's how we bring those stories to life that sets us apart.

That is why *The Page Turner* is also about voice. Not only the voice Emma Page uses to bring her novel to life, but the voice she owns that makes her special and that she is unwilling to silence. We *all* have a voice. In fact, I bet yours is talking to you in your head right now. However, there's a good chance that you've forgotten the power of your own voice, the beauty of your own uniqueness.

As I address in this book, we tend to bury that out of fear: fear of being different, as I was; fear of being unpopular; fear that our family or friends will disapprove; fear of, well, everything. And slowly that voice becomes so quiet, so distant, we don't even hear it anymore, and we are no longer the unique souls we once were. We are far from being the people we once dreamed.

This novel is about overcoming fear and rediscovering your voice. As I write: Every voice is important. Every story needs to be heard.

I was once consumed by fear. And then I found my voice again.

In fact, when I first started writing and dreaming of being an author, I truly believed that there was a golden key that was passed around New York City. It was handed out—late at night, in a fancy restaurant under gilded lights and over expensive drinks—to "certain" authors. And I would never be one of them. I now know—and you certainly already do—that such a key does not exist. The only key you need you already own: the one that unlocks the door to overcoming your fear and believing in your dream.

This book also addresses—with a wink and a nod—why I made the conscious decision to choose my grandmother's name as a pen name for my fiction.

That is the biggest question I receive at events.

On the surface, as I write in the novel, I know that it sounds very much like a literary *Victor/Victoria*: a man choosing a woman's name to write fiction for women.

But it goes much deeper than that.

I grew up in the Missouri Ozarks. All of my grandparents were working poor. My grandma Shipman was a seamstress who stitched overalls at a local factory until she couldn't stand straight. My grampa Shipman was an ore miner; when that work dried up, he raked rocks off of farmers' fields so they could plant their crops. The story goes that my grandma and grampa had an old crock in their garage. As I mentioned, whenever they had spare change—a dime here, a quarter there—they would toss it in. Over time, the crock got full, so they put it in the back of their pickup and hauled it to the community bank where they started a college fund for my mother. She would become the first in our family to graduate college. That "change" changed our lives.

I spent an inordinate amount of time with my grandmothers growing up: Sundays in their kitchens watching them bake using family recipes pulled from their recipe boxes; evenings in their sewing rooms watching them take scraps and turn them into beautiful quilts; Saturdays at the beauty parlor watching them get their 'did' and sharing stories with their friends they never told when the menfolk were around; and summers at a log cabin that had an outhouse, no phone or TV, just books, inner tubes, fishing poles and each other. My grandmothers were both volunteers at the local library, and they were always reading and inspired my love of books and writing. "You can go anywhere and be anyone you dream when you read," they told me.

Over time, I got to know my grandmothers not just as my grandmas but as real women, who had loved and lost, dreamed and hoped, been knocked down by life and gotten up with grace, hope and strength to soldier on time and again.

One of my grandma's biggest pleasures was watching the sun set over the creek at our cabin every summer night. She told me more than once, "Life is as short as one blink of God's eye, but in that blink, we forget what matters most."

After my parents passed, I found my grandmothers' heirlooms—their charm bracelets, recipe boxes, hope chests filled with quilts, scrapbooks and family Bibles—boxed up in the attic. I began to cry. I finally realized that my grandmothers—all of my elders—were never poor. In fact, they were the richest people I'd ever known in my life because they understood what mattered most in the world.

I began to write what would become my very first novel that day in the attic on top of a cardboard box.

Every novel I write is meant to serve as a tribute to family and our elders as well as to inspire hope and remind readers of what's most important in life: "The simple things," as my grandma Shipman used to say, the things we take for granted. Each other.

My grandma was overlooked in society because she didn't offer anything of "value." But look at the legacy she left—one that will live forever—simply by being selfless and loving unconditionally (love *without* any conditions).

When a reader walks into a library or bookstore a hundred years from now—long after I'm gone—and picks up one of my novels, says my grandmother's name, understands the person she was and the sacrifices she made and, perhaps, reconnects with their own family history to understand how they came to be, then my work will be done and my "blink" will have mattered.

All of which I honor in *The Page Turner*.

As an author, I write—like Emma does in the novel—what calls to me. It is the only thing we can do as writers and souls: be ourselves. It is also the only thing we should do as readers: read what calls to us.

There is so much judgment in the world. Even down to the books we read. We are told what we should read, what is "hot," "TikTok worthy," "literary," "smart." We often put labels on books just as we do one another. Books for and about women are called "chick lit," "women's fiction," "beach reads," "summer sizzlers," "romance," and the implied meaning is that such books are fizzy and frivolous, less serious than others. Nothing could be further from the truth.

When my first memoir was published, some two decades ago, it was not found in bookstores or libraries under "memoir," "nonfiction" or even "humor." It was classified as "gender studies" because it was judged as being something it wasn't, like so many of us are at first glance on a daily basis.

I am still judged for what I write: it's not deemed "literary" enough, or "highbrow" by some readers and critics. It's "too emotional."

I say, *Good!*

I grew up reading with my grandmas. Often, they would pluck books off the spinning racks in our old grocery story. They were books they could afford. Ones they could put in their pocketbooks. We read them together. We talked about them. I *intentionally* choose to make my books accessible to readers from eight to eighty. I intentionally don't write them to be "admired" by a few. I could choose fancy words and dense plots. I could choose edgier themes and populate my books with awful people.

But I heed the voice that calls to me. And I hear *your* voices.

Publishing is a big, tough business. It's not for the faint of heart.

I hope this book gives you some insights into what it's like to be a writer, agent or publisher today. I hope this story reminds you to read the books you love and that your history—good, bad, beautiful, ugly—should never be hidden or forgotten.

Books save us.

We save each other.

And I will always write about hope—as sappy as many "critics" may deem it—because it's the gift, along with a love of reading, that my grandmothers and mother gave me that has allowed me to survive in this tough world.

I will always write under my grandmother's name—as is celebrated in the novel—because the history of those we love, who raised us and sacrificed for us to have better lives, matters.

I will see you soon with my new novel! Until then, keep reading and believing!

XOXO,
Viola

ACKNOWLEDGMENTS

As I write in this novel, publishing is a big business. In many ways, the author is the dreamer, entrepreneur, solitary figure in the window working by candlelight at dawn. Like Emma, I always dreamed of writing a book that readers would reach for on the brightest—and darkest—of days. Most days, I sit alone and write. It is breathtakingly, simultaneously magical and maddening. Most mornings, I race to my office at dawn to write. I am blessed. But, when that book is done, it takes a team to bring it to life. As I always say, you can write the greatest book in the world, invent a life-changing product, build the biggest shopping center on the globe, but no one would ever know it existed if it weren't for a team that can fine-tune it, perfect it, market and publicize it, build buzz on social media and sell the hell out of it. I am blessed to have the greatest team on earth.

It always starts with my agent, Wendy Sherman, who believes in the dream (and always has). We officially started together way back in 2005. *The Page Turner* marks our twentieth publishing anniversary together. Our journey has covered countless books across many genres, and countless discussions—both celebratory and difficult—about my career and our lives. Wendy isn't just my agent, she's my friend, and I am blessed to have the best of both with her. And I can't wait for our next twenty years together (you heard me! Neither of us has any plans to retire!).

Did she inspire VV? No, she's much younger and more stylish, but her drive and passion did.

I tend to say the same thing each and every time about my editor, Susan Swinwood, but she makes each of my books infinitely better with her keen insights into character and plot, gentle hand and unwavering support. I, too, feel she is not just my trusted editor but also my advocate and friend.

How many readers would know about my books were it not for my publicity, marketing, social media and sales teams? As I note in *The Mighty Pages*, this is the team who—in a world where a select few books get the majority of attention each year—work to ensure my book not only receives exposure in the media and online but also gets in bookstores and the hands of readers. Thank you to Kathleen Carter, Heather Connor, Leah Morse, Diane Lavoie, Ambur Hostyn, Lindsey Reeder, Danielle Noe and so many others who work tirelessly behind the scenes not only for me but countless authors.

My publisher, Graydon House, has shown great faith in me and my work since day one, word one.

The indie booksellers across the US are a gift to us and this world. If you have one in your community, don't just be grateful, support them. The same for our libraries, who need our support—including financially—to fight those who are seeking to ban books. Here's a suggestion: if you don't like a book, don't read it. But you do not have the right to remove it from the shelves simply because you do not like it or it challenges your sensibilities. That's why it was written in the first place. And remember that there is someone out there right now—just like I did when I was a kid—who needs these voices so many are seeking to silence not only to feel as if they have a place in this world but also in order to survive. Our indie bookstores and libraries are the hearts, minds and souls of our communities, and they save lives.

To all the authors who inspired my love of fiction and me to become a writer as well as to all the authors who have supported me over the years, THANK YOU. You will never know what you have meant to me: Emily Giffin, Jane Green, Dorothea Benton Frank, Jen Weiner, Jodi Picoult, Jennifer Egan, Annabel Monaghan, Steven Rowley, Mary Kay Andrews, Nancy Thayer, Susan Mallery, Brenda Novak, RaeAnne Thayne, Nora Ephron, Adriana Trigiani, Zibby Owens, Virginia Woolf, Jane Austen, Toni Morrison, Agatha Christie, Harper Lee, Alice Walker, Kristin Hannah, Jay McInerney, Bret Easton Ellis, Taylor Jenkins Reid, Emily Henry and, of course, Erma Bombeck (plus *countless* others!).

Since this is a book about those who love books, I must give HUGE, heartfelt thanks to all the book bloggers, book clubs and book lovers who support my work. Your reviews on Goodreads, BookBub, Amazon, B&N, your support on social media, your attendance at my events MEANS THE WORLD. Jen Hatmaker! Thank you for your fierce friendship and support. The Friends & Fiction Official Book Club and entourage—Lisa Harrison, Brenda Gardner, Bubba Wilson, Robin Klein, Annissa Joy Armstrong, Francene McDermott Katzen, Lesley Bodemann, Barbara Plishka Wojcik, Clare Plaxton, Debby Cooperman Stone (and do not kill me if I missed a few of my favorite folks!); the female Batman & Robin of books, my Michigan superheroes, Diane Housel and Lesley Hayden-Artis; the northern/southern boy Batman & Robin of books, Cleveland's Taylor Lintz and South Carolina's Dallas Strawn; my Michigan Molly (Molly VanZile); and SO MANY OTHERS!

To my dear friend John Fletcher, who also inspired—in name and spirit—Vivian Vandeventer.

My mutts, the divine Doris, all sunshine, light and love, and the great Gerti, our new rescue, found on the streets and now at home in our hearts. Gerti has survived so much and to watch her live now without fear and with such joy is a great lesson each and every day (despite the fact she wakes me up at 5 a.m. by standing on my larynx and kissing my face).

A large part of this book is about the support we give and receive, especially when it comes to writing. I would never have written my first book—or my seventeenth—without the love and support of Gary and my late mother who told me simply, "Write a book. We believe in you."

On New Year's Eve in 2004, I walked down the street of our St. Louis neighborhood holding fifteen envelopes addressed to literary agents in New York City. I stood in front of the blue collection box at the end of the street, my mother on one side of me, my husband, Gary, on the other.

"Here goes nothing," I said, opening the bin.

My mother and Gary grabbed my arm and stopped me before I dropped the envelopes inside.

"No," they corrected. "Here goes *everything*."

Mostly, this book is an homage to YOU, my readers. Many of those in my publishing sphere call my readers *The Violas*. I do the same now as well. I've come to understand that this is not simply a clever homage to my pen name, it's a tribute to the type of readers I have: souls that embody the themes of my work. You are kind, funny, giving, gracious, smart, the best mothers, daughters, grandmothers, sisters, cousins, aunts, co-workers and friends anyone could ever ask for. And I am forever humbled that you read my books. Books connect us and save us in a chaotic world too often filled with hate and people who focus on what divides us rather than unites us. You, like my books, focus on what connects us. So, thank you…for reading. Thank you…for reading *me*. I am forever grateful by your love and support. The fact that you choose to read my books fills my heart and soul. You will never know how much it means to me. You inspire me every day with your love and support.

DISCUSSION GUIDE

1. A key theme of *The Page Turner* is the way women are represented in literature and film. The syllabus of a lit class I once took had NO books written by women. Looking at the books and movies you read and watch as well as popular entertainment today, how do you think women are portrayed today? Is it better, or worse, than it once was? How would you change this landscape?

2. Another theme in my novel centers on the need to step out of our parents' shadows in order to be seen and make our marks on the world. How did your parents shape you? Did you feel a need to do something totally on your own, be it career, moving away from home or not doing something you were always expected to do? How did that change you? What lessons did you learn? How did your parents react to those decisions?

3. Emma's parents, especially her mother, are not typical parents in terms of the ones I ordinarily write about, or in terms of career or "warmth." While I have known and worked with many parents over the course of my career who have put success, career and money above raising their children, I have also known many who have juggled both

successfully. Do you think you have to choose when it comes to raising children? Do you, or have you, put your children and grandchildren first in your life and career decisions? Discuss.

4. *The Page Turner* is the first novel I've written with sisters as two of the main characters, and sibling rivalry takes center stage. Do you have a sister? What was your relationship like growing up? What is it like as adults? Did you have any sort of sibling rivalry? How did you resolve it, or is it still present?

5. Books written for, by or about women are often categorized as "beach reads" or "chick lit" which can diminish their value in many readers' eyes before they even read the book. In addition, hopeful stories with happy endings are often deemed "less than" by literary critics who tend to prefer books with heavier or darker themes. Do you believe that in order for a book to be of literary value it must be darker in theme and character? Do you pay attention to book reviews? How do they influence you? Do you like reading hopeful books? Why? Why not? Do you care what others think of the books you read?

6. Family secrets play a big role in *The Page Turner*. Did your family have a secret? Do they still? Can you share what is was, how it harmed or ultimately helped or healed you or your family?

7. Marcus Flare is famous, rich, bombastic, narcissistic and a misogynist. Have you ever worked with a man like this, or had to deal with someone like this in life? What happened, and how did you handle it? Do you think things

have changed or not in terms of how men—especially powerful men—treat women?

8. I call publishing BART—business meets art. Yes, it is art, but it's also a big business, which this novel explores. As a result, it is a difficult and ever-changing landscape for both debut and established authors. And, yet, I believe good books find their way to the light and into your hands. What new books or authors have you read lately that have opened your eyes or changed your perspective? Who are your go-to authors? What do their books give you and mean to you? And what is your favorite book and favorite quote from a book?

9. *The Page Turner* is a book about our collective love of books and how reading connects and changes us. What is it about reading that you love most? How many books a year do you read? What is your favorite place to read?

10. This novel is a tribute to grandmothers and family history. I was very close to my grandmothers. Were you close to yours? What are your favorite memories of them? How do you honor your family history?

11. Setting is always as big a character in my novels as my characters themselves. *The Page Turner* is set in South Haven, Michigan, one of my favorite resort towns because of its history and uniqueness, as well as The Hamptons, another beautiful resort area I adore. However, they are very different culturally. I wanted to juxtapose these settings to demonstrate how place changes us. What are your favorite vacation spots? How does being there change you?

12. For better or worse, social media plays a part in our daily lives. Discuss the pros and cons of social media in your

life? In your family's life? Does it influence the books you choose and read? Or in authors (or people) you follow? Why or why not?

13. Without any spoiler alerts, there is a lot of manipulation in this novel, from Emma, Jess, their parents and even their grandmother. Have you ever lied to anyone intentionally, believing that it was for their own good? Why? Why not?

14. The history—and importance—of pen names in literature is discussed in the novel. I chose Viola Shipman as a pen name to honor the working poor Ozarks seamstress whose love, life, lessons and sacrifices changed my life. This was a personal decision I made as I wanted readers to utter her name long after I'm gone. But I also respected the history of pen names in literature and did not want to dupe readers: women often could not get their work seen or taken seriously unless they used a pseudonym (often male). In many ways, so much has changed. In many ways, so much has not. What do you think of pen names? What do you think of me using my grandma's name as a pen name?

15. This is very much a novel about home, especially why we either run toward it or away from it, literally and figuratively. Where is home to you? What does it mean to you?